Ballet for Guys

Ballet for Guys

a novel

Will Kern

CANOPIC
PUBLISHING

Canopic Publishing
389 Lincoln Ave
Woodstock, IL 60098
www.canopicpublishing.com

Cover photo by Lindsey Fisher
Cover design by Lindsey Fisher and Georges Stratan
Book design by Phil Rice

First edition

p. cm.
ISBN-13: 978-0-9971695-0-8 (alk. paper)
ISBN-10: 0-9971695-0-8 (alk. paper)

Printed in the United States of America
5 4 3 2

For Sophie and Wilson
My life. My love. My all.

Some Things before We Get Started

First, this here is a true story. All of the events in it are absolutely 100% biographic, except for the parts what ain't, that being most all of them. Since this is a true story, I had to change the names of some of the folks involved, including my own, and you'll figure out why after a few pages.

Second, if you're interested in learning more about the ballet, go to YouTube. There's a bunch of stuff on there about it. Ought to be more about the history, but I can't help that, I don't run the durn thing. Lot of good books about the ballet, like *Ballet for Cretins* by this Polish fella named Bob Grabowski and *Apollo's Ankles* by this gal Tiffany Talus. You don't got to read them, naturally, it ain't like I could make you, but they's pretty good, just so you know.

Finally, if you're in San Antonio and need some car repairs done, come on down to my garage on West Avenue and Fredericksburg Road across from the HEB. Best service in town, friend, I kid you not. Free coffee (Sanka) while you're waiting.

Billy Jim Hauck

Ballet for Guys

Chapter 1

I was sitting in my armchair watching *Jeopardy* on the TV
when my sixteen-year-old daughter Jill comes in and sits
on the floor next to me. After a minute or so she says,
"You were cleaning a deer the other day."

She'd come out to the backyard while I was cleaning
a buck I'd shot a few days earlier, took one look at what I
was doing and headed back into the house.

"That's right."

"Nasty."

"Ain't so bad really."

"How do you do it?"

I was surprised by the question. I guess my face
showed it.

"I'm just wondering. I never see any blood on the
carport."

"Well, Jill," I says, "that's because there ain't no blood
to speak of, at least not by the time it gets here."

"Okay. So how do you do it? I mean, what's the
process?"

"In cleaning a deer?" It seemed really weird her asking,

but I didn't mind answering her question, just seemed a little odd. My daughter's kind of dainty you know.

"Well, the first step in cleaning is done in the field where the deer falls. After it goes down you got to wait a few minutes to make sure the deer is really dead. I once had one get up and try to run, but it didn't get too far and collapsed. Then you got to gut it so it's lighter and easier to handle."

"Oh," she said. She looked at her smartphone. I wasn't sure if she wanted to hear any more since she was distracted, but she looked back at me and said, "Go on."

"So first you got to gut it. You start with a shallow cut at the top of the windpipe, then go down past the center-bottom of the rib cage and continue to the butt hole. You make the cut through the skin and just into the abdominal cavity, and you got to be careful not to cut into the intestines. Then all the guts is pulled out and left on the ground for the crows and vultures and coyotes to eat. You get rid of windpipe at the same time.

"Then you load the carcass into the back of your pick-up truck and take it to the hanging house, which is on the property you shooting on. The ranch or whatever. Then the carcass spends a couple days and nights in the hang-ing house, suspended from the floor, hung from a beam. That's why there's no blood running anywhere by the time it gets here. It's all drained out in the hanging house. Then it's ready to take home for skinning and processing. At home, the choice pieces that are going to be used for bar-becuing or smoking are cut away and set aside. All the rest of the edible meat goes to the processing plant for sausage and jerky."

"So what did I see you doing out back?"

"So you know that wooden table we got on the back porch with the metal folding legs? That's my butchery shop. First thing I do is remove the skin and hose wash the carcass. Then I hose and scrub the table down, then after it dries I cover it with butcher paper and go to work, removing all the tender pieces for our home cookouts. The skin and bones go into the trash, then I take the paper off the table and hose it down again.

"When I'm finished, I load all the pieces to be processed at the plant into cardboard boxes and take them there. At the plant I pick what percentage of pork will be mixed with the venison for sausage. Dealer's choice is what I like best. I've found that around 40% pork makes a good mix, having enough moisture to keep it from getting too dry during the smoking. Then you can choose to have jerky, or smoked jerky, or whatever else you want."

"Do you ever feel guilty? About killing the deer?"

"Guilty? No. The deer is food, Jill. We eat it. You go to McDonalds, the meat don't fall from heaven. Somebody had to kill it."

"Hmm. Interesting."

"Why are you asking me this? You want to come hunting with me sometime?"

She kind of half-laughed. "Not hardly." She picked up her smart phone and tapped the screen a few times.

I said, "What are you doing?"

"I was recording our conversation. You don't mind do you?"

"No. What's it for?"

"I have to write a paper for my English class. The topic is, 'Something I could never do.'"

And then she got up and bounced into her room, presumably to work on her danged English paper.

It would have been so much simpler if we'd of had a boy. Him and me, we could have done lots together. We could have played sports, I could have taught him how to hunt, how to shoot, we could have gone fishing, camping. When my wife was pregnant, I used to think about the boy we were going to have and I kind of mapped out his life for him, and I used to think about all the good living we'd be doing, like sitting up in a deer blind on a chilly winter morning, drinking coffee from a thermos, eating peanut butter and marshmallow sandwiches. It'd be living, right?

Didn't turn out like that though.

Me and my daughter live here in San Antonio, Texas, in a three-bedroom house on Meredith Drive over by Thomas Jefferson High School. She lives with me even though she don't want to. It turned out to be just the two of us because her mom is going through some kind of crisis. I don't know what it is. My soon-to-be ex-wife Beth and me got married and we were together for a lot of years until she fell in love with some other dude. See, I didn't know this, but she had this kind of thing on the side going on a few years, and then about six months ago she packed up some of her stuff and just walked out of the house.

I said some of her stuff, right? I got, like, clothes in closets and different kinds of shampoo and facial cream still in our bathroom. It sits there looking at me like someday she's going to come back to me, but I know she ain't.

Which is fine. I'm over it, her leaving, and it don't bother me none, really. Onward and upward, right? It's the only way to be.

My wife is in her fifties, but seriously, she is one hot tamale. She's always had the face of an angel, and being fifty years old never really changed any of that. She got a few wrinkles, but none of the saggy jowly saddlebags you see on her friends' faces. She only had the one child, so her body never really went south. She's been eating right, getting her sleep, staying away from tobacco and alcohol, unlike me. We don't look like a couple anymore. Here's this pretty, well-dressed 30-something (she's 53 but looks 38) with wavy shoulder length auburn hair and a cute cleft chin standing next to this George Strait t-shirt wearing fat ass with brown teeth and a scraggly Yosemite Sam mustache and grease under his fingernails and Budweiser running down his chin.

It should have been obvious to me that our marriage was going to break apart. I should have seen it coming when she started changing but that was a while back. She started reading books about ten years after we got married because she said the TV bored her, and she became this huge bookworm, and got really into art and culture and that kind of stuff. She'd try to talk to me about it, but I had no idea what she was saying. She'd show me a picture book and go:

"Billy Jim, look at this painting."

"Uh?"

"It's *Starry Night* by Vincent van Gogh. Isn't it marvelous?"

"Is that the dude what cut off his ear over some hooker? I saw something about that guy on The History Channel."

"He was a great man, one of the greatest artists of all time. Look at these pictures!"

"Yeah, they something." I liked them okay I guess. Not as much as her.

"Well, they speak to me."

You get that? She said the pictures spoke to her. *Spoke* to her. Like they was her friends.

About five years ago she got a job as an administrative assistant for this place called Hope for Children, and she fell in love with her boss, this guy who's in his 60s, this fella named John Lancey. So she and this old John Lancey fella had this red-hot love affair lasting oh about five years, and then John Lancey asks her to move in with him and she says yes. This guy's like swimming in money, which is weird because he runs a charity, right? But they're always going on cruises and taking vacations, doing all the things we never did together. And he buys her diamond rings and gold chains and stuff. Least I spect he does. Maybe they don't go on vacations much, I might got that wrong, but they *do* travel a lot with this charity. Beth is always picking up and going off to some conference back east or in Europe, or going to set up some food bank in Asia or Africa. I know this because she sends me emails with her contact information and dates when she's going to be in and out of town. This ain't for me, of course, she don't give a rat's ass about me. This is on account of Jill. See, the reason Jill lives with me is because Beth ain't never in town hardly, and she wants us to know where she is in case of emergency. She's got a pretty exciting life.

Anyhow, she walked out on us, me and our daughter Jill. She said it was as good a time as any because Jill was going to be graduating soon and she was tired of faking it. So I guess it ain't true that I don't know why she left. She don't live too far away now, and when she ain't on a business trip or a safari in Africa she sees Jill all the time. Well, she sees her when she can. Jill don't ever stay at their place.

My wife started divorce proceedings and she says she don't want any of my stuff, just wants a clean break. She could probably take a piece of my garage if she wanted to, but she don't. I got my own garage — it's called Hauck's Garage, I named it after my dad — and I fix cars for a living. The money's decent, but I ain't saved much of nothing. When Jill graduates in a couple years, she's going to be moving out of the house, and then it'll just be me I reckon.

I was watching something on YouTube the other day that said the life expectancy back in the Middle Ages was twenty-three years old. Can you imagine? You had a long marriage if it lasted until you died, but that was only ten years or so if you got married at puberty. So my wife was with me three times longer than that. I guess she could only take so much. Anyway, she's happy now.

Jill and me, we don't really get along all that well since her mom left. All that bile in her belly comes out of her mouth on occasion. One morning I was sitting at the breakfast table in the kitchen looking over the headlines on my laptop, and I said, "It's supposed to rain today. Which is good. Aquifer needs it." And she said, "I can't believe that you're my father. I want to get a DNA test. There is no way I'm related to you." I should have just left it at that, teenagers being what they is, but I didn't. "What would you do if you found out? Leave? You don't want to live here, you don't have to."

"No, I *do* have to live here. In this miserable city in this miserable state. With you. But I'll be gone soon, I promise you that. First chance I get I'm out of here."

"You're sixteen, Jill. You got one more year a being chained to me, and then you can git. Leave on your birthday if you want to."

"You'd like that, wouldn't you?"

"I'd like to read my headlines and make a comment with being ripped apart for no reason!"

"Oh, no reason?"

"What's the reason?"

"Forget it! Just forget it!"

And out she stomps. Door slams.

The truth is, that's about par for us these days. Words followed by more words that somehow turn angry and then mount up and explode and then door slam.

I know what Jill means when she says there's a reason. I know she's mad about her mom leaving and she didn't take her with, but she don't got to take it out on me. I got this fire-breathing dragon blowing all the hair off my face every time I open my mouth, and that just don't bridge the river. She acts like I'm just supposed to shut up and take it but I can't. I ain't nobody's kick boy.

I support her in the things she wants to do. Wasn't

I the one who encouraged her to get a driver's license when she turned sixteen? And didn't I buy her that beater Toyota Corolla so she'd have something to drive around? She says the only reason I did it was so I wouldn't have to drive her to her ballet classes, which is partly true, but I *did* buy her the dang car, didn't I?

I know she don't want to live here. I know she thinks I'm an idjit. But a fella likes to have a little peace in his castle, that's all I'm saying.

She looks at the things I do and the things I like with disdain. She don't like nothing I like and we don't got nothing in common. Except maybe church.

Jill's been taking ballet lessons since she was about eight. This was one of the things my wife insisted on, part of her new culture thing. She thought Jill would be more refined or something if she took ballet lessons, so Jill started taking lessons and pretty soon her once-a-week class turned into a twice-a-week class and now she has class five days a week.

Brother, I am here to tell you five classes a week is expensive, and there's stuff on top of that. She has classes at a studio over there on Potranco Road that come up to about $600 a month. Then she has private lessons once a week at $100 a pop. And don't get me started on the shoes. Regular ballet slippers cost $30 and a pair of pointe shoes cost a by-god *80 bucks a pair!* And they don't last for nothing, like a couple of days! I wish Nike would develop pointe shoes that were like Air Jordans, you know, tough and durable, then I wouldn't be spending all this money on dang shoes. But they'd put that dang slash all over it and it'd kind of ruin it.

This whole "dance dream" has kind of ruined me financially, actually, but it won't go on forever. The good thing about ballet is if she is going to make it as a dancer, she'll know early. At least that's what Beth tells me, that after a certain point I won't have to pay for the dance lessons because we'll know if Jill's actually going to *be* a dancer. And if she ain't, she'll be disappointed, but then she can get on with her life. I spect that's what will happen.

I don't know nothing about what Jill does. I mean I don't follow it. She competes in dance contests and sometimes she even goes out of state with her teachers, but I never go. I've never seen her dance. No, that's not true. I saw her once. But the whole thing is a mystery to me and I'm not really interested in it. I just write the checks.

Which is fine. Jill don't ask for much from me and it's good to see she's got an interest. Keeps her off drugs. I was passing by her room the other day and I heard her talking to herself. She was doing this mock interview, like she was being interviewed for the TV. "Ballet is the way I express myself," she says. "The moment in my life when I feel that everything is perfect is when I'm on stage. When I'm dancing, I feel comfortable. I feel happy. I feel satisfied. But it's more than that. I feel like all the planets and moons and stars are aligned and I'm in a place where my body and the music and the audience are all one, and we live and we breathe together, and we are magic." I remember standing outside her door listening and being proud of her. I got a friend, David Coates, he was telling me his boy is getting out of college with a degree in communications from Texas Tech and he ain't got no dream, no goal, no plan. Coates's kid wants to move to Hawaii and be a beach bum, and he can't even get off his lazy ass to do that. Aw heck no, that'd mean he'd actually have to get a job to pay for the plane ticket.

Nowadays, Jill's mad all the time, but she wasn't always mad though. We actually got along pretty well, before her mom left. When she was a little girl we used to go to the mall and eat Baskin Robbins every Sunday after church. And she'd cut up and do imitations of our friends or folks

19

in our family. She did an imitation of my Aunt Gladys that really killed us all. My Aunt Gladys had this funny way of talking through her nose, and my daughter could do her voice dead perfect. My wife and me just used to laugh and laugh every time she did that. Those were good times.

Jilly, Jilly, Jilly.

You used to be such a sweet kid. And then that darkness come.

Chapter 2

So Jill tells me one Friday, "I'm going to my ballet lesson, and then I'm going to sleep over at Margie's house." Margie is her friend, she lives just down the block. We've known her forever. And I said yes, of course, not that I was asked. It was more like she was telling me what she was doing, but I didn't mind. We weren't shouting at each other, and I always liked Margie. Margie's a dancer too, but she takes hip hop. Which is much less expensive. So she gets in her car and takes off.

After she left, I went out to check the mailbox, and pulled out some bills, flyers, and other junk. I get stacks and stacks of stuff from the Republican Party asking me for handouts all the time because I made a donation about ten years ago. Now I'm on everybody's mailing list and I get all these pleas for money, which kind of all sound the same: give me some money and help stave off the economic doom/cultural meltdown the Democrat Party is forcing on the American people.

At the bottom of all the begging for money was an envelope from Walgreens, which I was expecting. Guess it was kind of good Jill wasn't home. I say this because what's in this Walgreen's envelope may be a little funny, and I'm glad I could open it in private. It was a picture, a photo I'd ordered online the week before.

See, I'm not sure exactly how this all came about, but I started thinking about the past, and I started thinking about this girl I knew when I was 13, when I was in eighth grade. Yeah, I know it's kind of ridiculous. Her name was Dee Dee Arnold. She had long blonde hair and she was thin as a stripe, which is not my type really but she was cuter than heck. I fell hard for her, like boys do at that age. It was that kind of teenage wild passion, you know what I mean, that crushing, burning love, that hot coal in the chest that young boys get. Being in love with Dee Dee meant not being able to eat or sleep. All I could do was moon about her morning, noon, and night. Ain't that funny?

I used to go to her basketball games and watch her play. She was sexy in her green and gold uniform, or at least I thought so at the time. Let's put it this way: she was as sexy as one thirteen-year-old thinks another thirteen-year-old could be. We went to a few dances at school and used to cling to each other during "Stairway to Heaven." We were boyfriend and girlfriend for a time, as somehow I'd mustered up the courage to ask her to "go steady," but we didn't do much except talk and hold hands. I did kiss her once, which is kind of the thrill of my life, but it was all too quick, and something stolen after I walked her home from this chick movie that we watched called *The Way We Were* (I think I wanted to see one of the *Planet of the Apes* movies, but I lost the coin flip).

I kind of had this thing in my head where I could see dating Dee Dee all the way through high school, and wouldn't that be great, because we could go to dances together and wear each other's rings — but then she moved.

Her dad was in the army, stationed at Ft. Sam Houston, and one day he got his orders to go to Germany of all places and the next day, just like that, Dee Dee Arnold was gone.

So the other night I started thinking about Dee Dee, wondering whatever happened to her. I got online and after about an hour, I came across this gal's website (wasn't sure if it was a blog or what it was), this gal I knew in middle school and high school named Rebecca McCauley. Rebecca had scanned and posted a whole bunch of pictures from when she was younger, and one of those pictures was Dee Dee right at about the age I knew her.

It was really interesting to come across that picture, but there wasn't really much to the shot. She was just sitting on a bed reading a book. Nothing else to it. She wasn't looking at the camera. She wasn't smiling. She was wearing blue jeans and a white t-shirt, and just reading. The caption under the picture said, "Whatever happened to Dee Dee Arnold?"

Now, I don't know why I did this, but I downloaded the picture, went to the Walgreens website, and ordered a print sent to my house. And that's what had come in the mail.

I took the photo out of the envelope, and sure enough, there was Dee Dee. I just looked at the picture for a minute or so. I turned it over in my hands a couple of times and looked at the back of it, almost expecting there to be something on the other side, but there wasn't, of course. Then I got a pair of scissors and cut off the white edges. I looked at it again for a time and then looked at the back again and then stuck it in my wallet.

Weird, huh?

After that, I didn't have much else to do, so I turned on Fox News and watched the pundits for a while. That got old pretty quick, so I decided to do my second favorite pastime, which was writing comments on the internet. I fired up the laptop and signed in to my favorite lefty websites.

Nothing's as fun as pissing off liberals. I like getting on Mother Jones or Huff Post or The Nation and writing in the comments section under their little lefty articles, which are always about how God and America and Freedom are bad but welfare and gun control are good. So I found me this juicy little piece on Mother Jones about food stamps, and after a few minutes the thread ended up going something like this:

> **Libtard:** A person won't get food stamps unless he needs them.
>
> **GoTeXXa$$ (Me):** You're joking. Do you even live in this country?
>
> **Libtard:** Do you want to live in a country where people go hungry? What do you suggest should happen when a guy needs food? Where should he go?
>
> **GoTeXXa$$:** He should go get a job and stop asking the rest of us hard-working taxpayers to support him.
>
> **Libtard:** What if he can't find a job?
>
> **GoTeXXa$$:** That's tough. A man who's hungry and can't find a job needs to pull himself up by his bootstraps and go get him a job.
>
> **Libtard:** But what if there aren't any jobs?
>
> **GoTeXXa$$:** There's always jobs. It's just that lazy people don't want them and they'd rather live off the government.

And so it goes. If an argument gets really heated and you need to shut it down because you're losing or whatnot, all you got to do is compare whatever they like to Hitler. It's a pretty great way of winning every time.

Anyhow, I was writing my comments on the internet and I ran out of beer, so I walked to the 7-11 and bought another six pack of Bud. I polished off about three cans, then closed up my laptop and just relaxed a little. Educating liberals is hard work. They don't listen to a word you say.

I lay back in my armchair and turned on TCM. Chuck Heston was fighting the zombies in *Omega Man*. I watched that for about an hour and fell asleep.

At around three o'clock, my eyes opened up and the lamplight in my mind switched on. This is not unusual for me. It seems like most nights I wake up at three o'clock, something just nudging me awake. And I think about the past, and all the things I regret. See, life is powerful lonesome sometimes. I think about the past, and I think to myself, what am I doing here anyway? The thoughts weaving in and out go something like this:

Beth's in San Francisco tonight.

One of these days she'll—

Come back to your fat ass?

No.

No. She ain't never coming back.

Momma.

It's done, friend.

Liberals.

Probably should have listened to her more.

She's gone.

Shoot myself.

Stop.

I could have stopped him.

Coward.

Yes.

I love Jesus Christ with all of my heart and all of my soul and all of my mind.

So I'm half-awake on the couch with these thoughts running through my head when I hear a car door slam out front. Then voices, sounding like they was coming from across the yard. Teenage voices. High pitched. Couldn't tell if they was boy or girl. Then scurrying feet, another car door slam, and somebody gunning it. I got up and opened the door.

I couldn't see nothing because it was black as your hat, so I turned on the porch light.

Jill's car was out front, and Jill was in the passenger seat looking to be asleep. Or passed out.

I stepped out to the car, opened the door, pulled her out. She smelled a little like beer, but not much. It may be from her breath, or it may be from her clothes. Or maybe it was me.

I carried her to the house. She got this brief moment of consciousness and started hitting me, smacking me in the face and neck and chest. It didn't hurt none, Jill only weighs a little over a 100 pounds. She screamed at me, "Let me GO!" I laid her down on the porch and she was fast asleep again. I stepped back from her and smiled. It was pretty obvious by this point that my daughter was drunk and passed out. That was amusing to me. She went drinking, experimenting with being an adult.

But then I had this feeling that something was just not right.

Jill didn't drive home, which is good. I knew this because she was in the passenger seat. So she took my drunk driving lectures to heart after all. But how did she get here? I heard voices and car doors slam. Somebody dropped her off. Somebody drove her car home, then got out of the car and into another car and drove away. That was obvious. But who did it? And why? Where'd she been?

I started to look at her. The porch light cast a yellow glow all over her and the concrete she was a-laying on. Her clothes was a mess. Stuff spilled on them. The button on her jeans was missing and there was mud on the front part of her cuffs. It suddenly hit me that something bad had happened to my little girl.

"Jill, let's go inside." I put my hand on her shoulder. She was passed out again. I lifted her up and brought her inside. I took her to her room and laid her on her bed. I took off her socks and shoes. I started to cover her with a blanket. Then I stopped.

I got a good look at her. She was wearing makeup (makeup? Jill?), and it was smeared. Her lipstick looked like someone had pressed their fingers against her lips and dragged the red upwards. Eyeliner ran out of her eyes and down the side of her cheeks, following the path of tears. It was dark and dirty, billowy. Then I looked down and saw her shirt.

She had on a tight black t-shirt flecked with gold spangles and the word "Star" written across her chest in red and gold letters. I noticed she was not wearing a bra, but naturally I didn't see if she was wearing one before she left the house. It's not like I look for that kind of stuff. The t-shirt collar was stretched and torn a little on the right side. You could clearly see her shoulder and collarbone. I just stared at it for a second, I guess kind of stupidly, unsure or maybe unbelieving of what I was looking at. And then I knew.

It was a bruise. Pretty obvious a thumb. It had dug into the soft area of her skin, right above the collarbone. There were others on her shoulder. Four of them. Fingers.

Had somebody held her down? Somebody who was on top of her?

I tried to wake her up. I pulled her up, shook her, said

her name. I wanted to slap her in the face very lightly but I just couldn't bring myself to it. Should I call an ambulance? Should I let her sleep it off?

I thought about bundling her in a blanket, picking her up, heading out to my truck and driving her down to Methodist downtown. Then I wondered if I was legally drunk. I'd polished off nine beers earlier. If I got pulled over I might get a DUI. So should I call the ambulance? That's $500 just for a ride to the hospital, and my insurance won't cover it. A cab then? That sounded like a bad idea. She was drunk and she needed to sleep it off. I decided to just wait until she woke up. We could take care of all this in the morning.

The next thing I did probably should have waited until morning too, but I was p.o'd. I got my smartphone and called Margie's dad, Gordie Powell. The phone rang about ten times, then he picked up.

"Hello?" He sounded asleep.

"Hey Gordie. This is Billy Jim Hauck. Is Margie there?"

"What? Billy Jim? Do you know what time it is?"

"Is Margie there? I want to talk to Margie"

"You sound like you're drunk. Are you drunk?"

"Jill said she was going over to your house after her dance lesson."

"She hasn't been over here tonight."

"She said she was going to sleep over at Margie's."

"She hasn't been here."

"Did Margie go out?"

"No, Margie's been here all night. We watched a DVD and she went to bed about 11:30. You ever seen *Titanic*? That's the stupidest movie."

"Is she in bed now?"

"Of course she's in bed. Where else would she be?"

"Could you check?"

I could tell he really didn't want to by the way he sighed and said, "Hang on." But he did.

I heard him get about of bed, mumble something to his wife. The line was quiet for a couple of minutes. Finally he got back on.

"She's sound asleep."

"All right. Thanks for that. I appreciate—" But he'd already clicked off.

I hung up the phone and thought, now what?

Now I had to wait until Jill woke up. I clicked on the TV, not wanting to think about any of this. By a major coincidence, the end of *Titanic* was on TCM. I watched it for a few minutes. Leonard Deciprico was in the water freezing his ass off, and Kate Winslet was floating on top of some door crying her eyes out. I watched it a minute or two and my mind was blank. And then when he slid under the water and disappeared, one word popped into my head: *fake*.

Chapter 3

Jill woke up the next day around five o'clock. She'd been home and asleep for about fourteen hours.

She came out to the kitchen table and sat down. She was really groggy and kind of rumpled. She didn't say nothing. I asked her if she wanted some juice, she just shook her head. We both sat there or a couple of minutes, not saying nothing. Then she spoke.

"How did I get here?"

"I heard voices out front. Teenagers, I think, and car doors slamming. I went outside and you were sitting in the passenger seat of your car. I picked you up and put you in bed."

"Oh."

"This was about three o'clock in the morning."

Another long pause. She looked okay. Really hungover. Maybe I been making too much out of this. Maybe the bruising was just her and some boy horsing around. But she wouldn't look at me.

"You want some soup or something? How do you feel? You want some aspirin?"

"Daddy."

"Yeah?"

"I hurt."

"Where do you hurt?"

"Down there."

"Oh."

Another long pause. Then she said:

"I got invited to a party. It was at Mike Saint's. You know him? His parents are out of town, so there was this big party at his house."

"Uh-huh."

"I don't know. I've been feeling kind of down lately. I feel like I don't have a life, so much goes into my dancing. And I just wanted to have some fun."

"Yeah, sure. I understand."

"Meet a boy. I've never had a boyfriend."

"Right, I know."

"But mainly I just wanted to relax."

"Sure. Sure."

"So I walked in, and there were, like, a lot of people there."

"Uh-huh."

"And somebody gave me a beer. And I was talking to kids. And then somebody gave me another one, like a half hour later. And I drank it."

"Yeah."

"And that's it."

"What?"

"That's all I remember. I don't remember anything else."

I didn't know what to say. So I said, "Why don't you take a shower? And then we'll go eat someplace."

"I don't feel like eating."

"You probably ought to take that shower though. You'll feel better. Get all cleaned up."

"I think somebody spiked my drink." She started to cry.

"Well, not necessarily. It could be a lot of things. Maybe you just can't hold your liquor. And you just passed out."

"No."

"Well, it doesn't mean that—"

"I *hurt*, Daddy."

Jill started to cry. I just sat there. After a minute or two, she stopped, then got up and walked out of the kitchen. I heard her bedroom door open and a couple minutes later she came back into the kitchen with a towel wrapped around her. She stood in front of me. I could see the handprint bruise on her shoulder clear as day. There was also one on her thigh. I looked away.

I said, "We should go to the hospital."

"What good would that do?"

"You should see a doctor."

She went to the bathroom. Door open, door close. Then after a time, I heard the shower running.

There has to be some logical explanation for this. It can't be what I think it is.

But what else could it be?

It's hard to believe something like this could happen. What kind of a person would do that? Even if you could drug a girl and have sex with her, why would you? Why would anybody want to have sex with somebody who's passed out? It'd be like having sex with a dead body. The whole point about sex is it's fun because you're with somebody and you're enjoying the thing together. I suppose something like this *could* happen, but what are the chances?

Is it possible Jill's lying? Maybe she had sex with somebody last night and she just doesn't want to admit it. Maybe she's making all this up because she doesn't like the choices she made. Maybe this is all some kind of elaborate scheme because she knows I'd be red hot.

That don't sound like her.

Kids say all kind of things to keep out of trouble. This whole thing could be a ruse. She's just trying to make me feel sorry for her. She's trying to get out of being punished.

But the bruises...

She don't got experience, I reckon, and it got a little rough.

But... It can't be. Jill would never do something like that. I know we've had our problems but—

This whole thing is her doing. She lied to me last night when she said she was going to Margie's. She's lying to me now about somebody spiking her drink. She had sex with some boy, and it hurt, and she's ashamed, and she doesn't want me to be mad at her because she knows that if she let some kid pop her cherry at a party it'd be the Wrath of God. That's it. That's all it could be.

I sat there stewing. What a dope, getting all worked up about this, when I know *exactly* what happened. When she gets back in here, I know what I'll tell her. "Look. I know you got drunk last night, and I know you lost your virginity. But don't try to make it into something it ain't. Just admit it."

Then she walked in. She had on a sweat suit. She sat across from me and looked down at the kitchen table.

I don't know. Maybe it was the way her shoulders were angled, kind of caved in, pushing her chest inward. Or the way she was staring at the table. Maybe just behind those dark eyes, she could see what happened to her and her brain just couldn't or wouldn't process it. Or her skin. Clean and without makeup, but drained of color. Not so much pale. Just somehow dead in a way. How a body might look at the start of decaying.

And right then I knew, I *knew* she wasn't lying.

"I spect you'll need to get your clothes from last

night," I said. "The police will want them as evidence." I'd seen this on cop shows. I knew the drill.

A few minutes later we were driving down I-10 to Methodist Hospital downtown.

    We got to the ER. I walked Jill to the waiting area then went to the check-in counter, up to a young nurse sitting behind a computer. I cleared my throat and said a string of words I never thought would come out of my mouth: "I think my daughter's been raped."

Chapter 4

The hospital folks, to their credit, immediately went into
disaster mode. They called the police and a rape crisis
center advocate, and we were moved to a separate waiting
area. Police detectives Julia Neary and Paul Dybek from
the San Antonio Special Victims Unit (yeah, we got one
too), and a victims advocate named Amy Landreau were
there within minutes. The police officers asked questions,
and Jill answered them as best she could, but there wasn't
a whole lot to say. She didn't remember nothing. They
kept asking her the same questions over and over, trying
to jog her memory I reckon, but couldn't get nothing. The
victims advocate was very cool, reminding her that none
of this was her fault.

The cops said it was likely Jill was drugged by either
Ketamine, which is a horse tranquilizer; Rohypnol, known
as a "roofie;" or GHB. Most likely it was GHB. The toxicology report would tell us.

Or not. Depending on the drug and when the test is
given, it may or may not show up in the toxicology report.
It may wash out of the system.

The police asked Jill if she smoked pot or did cocaine at the party. She looked at me sideways then back at the cops and said no. They told her toxicology tests for Rohypnol can show if a person snorted coke or smoked marijuana earlier in the evening and this information is something defense attorneys love to use to discredit the victim.

She signed a victim's statement and the cops left. Then she had to talk to the Sexual Assault Nurse Examiner. She and Jill and the advocate Amy Landreau went into a separate exam room, and the nurse collected evidence. It turns out Jill did exactly what she should not have done: she took a shower, washing off all her rapist's DNA. But she still had the clothes. She handed them over, and the nurse said we'd find out later what was on them. Then a doctor came in. He was very gentle and kind, exactly what Jill needed. He said he had to do some tests and it was pretty routine, but he would be doing a pelvic exam so it would be better if I waited outside.

The waiting room was what you'd expect. Grey furniture. Landscape paintings. CNN. People coming in and out, hacking and coughing and bleeding all over the place. I sat out there and I started thinking. I had been pretty calm up to this point, but as the minutes passed, and it began to sink in, I started to feel this burning.

I am going to find the son of a bitch who did this and I am going to get *Game of Thrones* on his ass. I am going to sneak up behind him with a machete and he's going to turn around and see me and scream for his pathetic life and I'm going to plant it right in his face and split his head in half! But not before I make him suffer. I'm going to tie him down and dissect him like a Nazi torturer! I'm going to chain him to the back of my pickup and drag him on a back road until body parts start flying off! I'm going to—

"Sir, are you all right?" The nurse from the front desk was at my shoulder, looking down at me.

"What?"

"You're beet red."

I waved her away.

"Is it okay if I take your blood pressure?"

"No."

She touched my arm... "Sir?"

"I said no!"

...and guided me out of the chair.

My blood was pressure 175 over 100. Borderline heart attack. I had to see the doc for blood pressure meds and a sedative.

Jill's test for HIV was negative, but she'd have to take another one in a few months. The doc gave her some pills for gonorrhea and syphilis and she got a Hepatitis B shot. He gave her a pregnancy test and said she shouldn't take it until "first pee of the day," meaning after midnight or tomorrow morning, or the results would be inconclusive. The advocate gave us her card and took our contact information, saying she wanted to schedule Jill for counseling.

By this time it was Saturday night, about eight o'clock. The ER was starting to really get busy. We got back in the truck and headed home.

Jill put the pregnancy test on the toilet, then went straight into her bedroom and closed the door. I turned on the TV and watched the last half of this movie called *Castaway* with Tom Hanks, and then this show about Napoleon and the battle of Waterloo on the History Channel. I was drinking beer, but I never get drunk, just catch a good buzz. I spect I had about ten.

After the Napoleon thing, I stayed up and watched Fox News. It was late, so it was mainly the pundits. They were all angry about something, but I don't recall what they were so worked up about.

Seeing all this talk of politics and all that had happened today made me think back to a presidential election a couple of light years ago. There was this candidate that I really liked, a staunch conservative and pro-lifer like me. He said that if he was elected president, he would try and overturn *Roe v. Wade* and make abortion illegal even in cases of rape and incest. I saw him being interviewed, and he said that he knew rape was horrible, but rape victims need to accept that God has given them the gift of human life, and they need to make the best out of a bad situation.

I'd thought about it briefly in the past few hours — what if Jilly's pregnant? — but was able to store that into the "not right now" file in my brain. Now it was suddenly in front of me.

What if Jilly is pregnant? What happens then? She wouldn't get an abortion, I know. Would she? No. Jilly's a good Christian, she would never do something like that. So that means bringing this rapist's baby into the world. It means we raise it or give it up for adoption. If we raise it, how will we be able to forget what happened? What if this child looks like his daddy? For the rest of her life, Jill will have to look at the face of her rapist. If she gives it up for adoption, she'll be giving up her first born child. And that child might come knocking on her door one day, wondering why her momma gave him away. And she'll have to tell this kid "I gave you away because your father *raped* me!"

I suddenly did not want to think about this at all.

I changed the channel to the Home Shopping Network but I couldn't watch it long because the gals they got on there are always so dadgum cheerful. So I clicked on a program of supposedly funny home videos hosted by this joker who thought he was God's gift to the by-god comedy universe. I watched this for about half an hour. Guys getting kicked in the balls or children smacking into doors or flying off sleds. I didn't see what was so all-fire funny about none it. Fact is, it kind of made me want to find out who took a video of his kid flying off a sled and slap his mouth off. Maybe then he wouldn't think it was so darn funny. I fell asleep on the couch.

I woke up when I heard Jill walking down the hall to the bathroom. I looked at the clock, and it was 3am, right on schedule for my nightly flogging. I waited for a minute, then got up and stumbled over to the hallway and stood by the door. She came out of the bathroom with the pregnancy test in her hand. She showed it to me.

"Negative," she said. She stepped back into the bathroom and flipped the little plastic cylinder into the trash can. Then she turned out the light.

I moved in to hug her, but she pushed me away. "Get away from me, you old drunk." Then she walked down the hallway into her bedroom and shut the door behind her. I heard the "click" of the bolt lock. Quiet then.

I went to bed and just kind of stared at the ceiling a while, figuring out all what was coming. I slept, but not too good.

The next morning, I went looking for Mike Saint.

Chapter 5

I started online and found a Saint that wasn't too far away, on Olmos Road. I didn't call first because I didn't want to tip my hand. If the kid was there, I needed to talk to him and I didn't want him high-tailing it because he knew I was coming.

I drove up to the Saint house, a large two-story brick structure with painted columns and a porch swing. Looked like any old house. I rang the doorbell and a guy about my age answered. He was all grizzled, looked to be about half asleep, dressed in his bathrobe. It was nine o'clock in the morning at this time.

"Yeah?"

"You got a son named Mike? Mike Saint?"

"Is this about the party?"

"I'm Billy Jim Hauck. I got a daughter named Jill."

Mike's dad kind of clenched his jaw and took a deep breath through his nose. Then he said:

"The police were here last night. A couple of detectives named Neary and Dybek. My son gave a statement. If you want to read the statement, you should contact Detective Neary. She's in charge of the case, from what I gather. My lawyer has advised me not to talk to you or to any other person or persons who might be connected other than the police. Bottom line is this: Mike had a party, there were maybe a couple hundred kids here. He didn't see anything. He didn't hear anything. He doesn't know anything."

"My daughter was dropped off in front of our house at around three. By at least two people because I heard voices talking to each other. Somebody drove her car to our house, and then got in another car and drove away. Your son had to have seen them leaving. Somebody had to have seen two guys dragging a girl out to a car."

"He didn't see anything. He didn't hear anything. He doesn't know anything. Contact Detective Neary, or contact my lawyer."

"I need your lawyer's name."

He went back inside and got me his business card. Then he shut the door.

I got back in my truck and drove around for awhile.

San Antonio on Sunday morning is basically just folks heading to church, so the streets was quiet, though my mind wasn't.

The kid has to know something. Don't he?

He's already lawyered up? How is that possible?

Was it him? Did he do it? How could this happen?

Where was God?

I drove downtown. Saw the highway sign for The Alamo on I-10. San Antonio is famously known as the Alamo City and the Cradle of Texas Liberty because Davy Crockett and Jim Bowie and William Barret Travis and a couple hundred other fellas fought the Mexicans and lost, but that was a rallying call for The War of Texas Independence which we eventually won. I say "we." I didn't have nothing to do with it. Because of all that, now

San Antonio is called The Alamo City, and pretty near everything is named Alamo this or Alamo that. Alamo Concrete, Alamo Hardware, Alamo Stationery. Alamo Pest Control.

Where is God?

What they ought to rename this is town San Fuego, St. Fire, because San Antonio has the distinction of being the hottest city in the US. That's why it's November and I'm driving around in a t-shirt. In summer it's Saudi Arabia hot.

Where *was* God?

Where was I?

I drove back to the house, put on a clean shirt and tie and got ready for church. I knocked on Jill's door.

"Jill? I'm going to church. You want to come with me?"

Nothing.

"I think you should come with me."

Still nothing. I decided to let it be, got in the truck and headed out to Trinity Baptist, where I been going pretty much all my life.

Trinity Baptist is not an apologetic Christian church. We're conservative. We're traditional. We don't change the Word of God to suit the times. These days you see preachers everywhere wringing their hands saying, "Yeah, Jesus said you'd go to hell if you don't believe, but He didn't really mean it." Well sir, we don't cotton to that kind of talk. We believe there is a hell and it's a hot place and you don't want to go there but you will if you don't accept Jesus as your personal savior and become born again. We believe The Bible is the Word of God, and we're not open much to interpretation. I like it like that. Times change. God's Word does not. There is certainty in that, my friend.

Today though, as I was driving to church, I didn't feel like that. I didn't feel like that at all.

In times of trouble — and I've had many — my faith

in God has always pulled me through. But it wasn't today. There was no comfort. Only questions.

I sat in church. We said prayers and sang songs but I just couldn't keep my mind on any of it. Pastor Jeff gave his sermon but it was all blah blah blah and he may as well been speaking Eskimo for all it meant to me.

After the service, I waited for the "thanks for coming" handshake line to peter out, and when he was near by himself I asked him when would be a good time to talk, that I needed to talk to him about something important. He said we could talk right now and we headed up to his office.

I like Pastor Jeff. He's a little younger than me, but he's a good man and he loves God and he's extremely knowledgeable. I've known him for about ten years now, since he first came to our church. He was real helpful and sympathetic when Beth told me she was leaving.

He sat at his desk and I sat across from him. I started out and told him about Jill. The look on Pastor Jeff's face was genuine. Shock. Then sadness.

"Oh, Billy Jim, I'm so sorry."

"Yeah.

"I guess you took her to the hospital?"

"Yeah, we did all that. And she gave a statement to the police. The cops say it was most likely GHB."

"Oh, that is so awful. She must be going through a terrible time."

"I can't really tell. She stayed in her room last night, and I didn't see her this morning."

"We don't have rape counseling here, but we ought to. It's a terrible scourge in our society, so prevalent in our country. And so evil. I'm so sorry this has happened to her."

"I think I'll need you to pray for her."

"I will, of course, Billy Jim. I will include you and Jill

43

in our prayer group, and ask Jesus to give you strength in these dark days."

"Please do, Pastor."

"Her healing process is not going to be short and it's not going to be easy. But we're here for her. And you. You tell Jill to come around anytime she likes. There is always something going on here. It's good to be around friends, people who love you. Your family has been with this church for three generations. We are at your service, whatever you need."

"Thank you."

"How are you doing, Billy Jim?"

"I'm okay, I guess. Well... truthfully... I ain't doing so good, I reckon."

"I expect not."

"I just — how do I say this? I just don't know how this could happen. We're good folk. Jill ain't never hurt nobody in her life."

"I know."

"So how?"

"That's a question that can never be answered. There is evil in the world, Billy Jim. The devil, he's a-roaming this planet looking for lives to ruin and souls to steal. He saw an opportunity and he took it. It's not your daughter's fault. But it happened to her just the same."

"This ain't Jill's fault."

"I know. But we let our guard down for a second, the devil takes advantage."

"Why didn't Jesus protect her?"

Pastor Jeff sighed. "I don't know. And it's not for us to know. It's not for us to question God's mercy or His mystery."

"I been a good Christian all of my life."

"I know."

"He could have protected her, but He didn't."

"And we don't know why."

"He chose not to."

"But there is a reason."

"What is it then?"

"To set her on the path of a new beginning? I don't know. What we do know is, all this will be revealed someday."

We didn't speak for a time. Then I said:

"I got my troubles, pastor, about Jesus. Where was He? Where was God?"

"The world is full of tragedy. One more senseless than the next. 'Where was God?' is a question that has been asked millions of times. And there is no answer. Perhaps it is not for us to know."

"If this happened to Jill and he could have stopped it but he didn't, meaning he chose not to, then I don't believe he loves us. Because if he did, he never would have let it happen. Supposedly he loves us more than what's humanly possible, but if that's so how could this be? No. I don't reckon he could have stopped it. I don't think he got the power. And if that's so, then he's not god. Or at least he's not what he says he is. Or what you says he is. Or what I've always believed."

"You've felt His power. You know the power of Christ's love."

"I have."

"Then you also know it is a healing love."

"You think this rape is part of some eternal plan he has for her?"

"No."

"Or me? Whatever trials he wants to bring to me, he can. And he has. My momma. My marriage. I've suffered through them. But now my little girl? What did she do?"

He looked at me with understanding, and he knew what I was feeling. He reached out his hand to me.

"Let's pray together," he said. He extended his hands and I took them and we bowed our heads. He closed his eyes. "Merciful Father, Your servants Billy Jim and his daughter Jill are suffering. We thank You for Your divine mercy, and ask that You please give them comfort in their time of need. Lead them through this valley of darkness. Give them strength and keep them strong as they tread this rocky path in the weeks to come. Show them Your love and mercy, give them peace of mind, and heal their broken hearts. We ask this in Christ's Name. Amen."

I said, "Amen" too. And we were done.

I pushed back my chair, got up and walked towards the door. He called after me, "Bring Jill by later. We can help her through this." But I didn't know how.

Then my mind did this really tricky thing. It flashed back to the *Titanic* movie I watched a couple of nights earlier. Leonard Dicapra was freezing in the water, and Kate Winslet was crying, and then he slipped under the water and died, and I thought, "fake." And that's what I thought of this. Jesus loves us? *Fake.*

Chapter 6

When I got home Jill was sitting at the kitchen table looking out the window at the pecan tree in our back yard. We have an old pecan tree that yields probably a hundred pounds of pecans every year. Jill and me pick up the pecans every week or they just get piled up. Now she was looking at that great pecan tree, the size of which is probably four times taller than our house. I didn't know what she was thinking. After a moment I said:

"I'll find this fella, Jill. I swear it. And when I do..."

"You think I want vengeance?"

"Justice, Jill. Not vengeance."

She didn't look at me. Just kept staring out the window. This next bit I knew was going to be a little sticky but I had to get it out.

"I want to take you shooting. It's about time you learned how to shoot a pistol."

She didn't say nothing, so I pressed on.

"Lot of kooks in this city, in this country. Got to be able to protect yourself. I can give you one of my guns. We can go down to the firing range on Bandera and I can learn you how."

She said, "I didn't do anything..."

"I know."

"You don't believe that."

"No, I do."

"Because I don't. It *was* my fault."

"Jill..."

Then she turned towards me. "You really think I want to learn how to shoot a pistol?"

"For your own protection..."

"You think having a pistol would have protected me the other night?"

"It might have."

"How?"

"If he'd seen you packing he might have drugged somebody else."

"And if I caught him spiking my drink, I would have shot him?"

"If you was armed he wouldn't have spiked it."

"You really believe that if I'd had a gun on me, none of this would have happened."

"Yeah, I do."

"So let me make sure I understand what you're saying. You want to arm teenagers and then put them in a room full of beer?"

"Of course not. Nobody said anything about mixing teenagers with firearms and alcohol."

"So teenagers, once they get their guns they're not going to want to drink beer?"

"All I'm saying is that if you had a gun, you would've been safe."

"And all I'm saying is you don't know what would have happened. He could have spiked my drink and then raped me and then stolen the gun. Or maybe he would've raped me with the gun. There is no way you could know what would have happened. Speculate all you want to. You don't know."

She turned away from me and looked out the window again. We were both quiet for a spell. Then she said:

"I don't want to live in a society with guns."

"I know you don't like them."

"I don't know how much I really want to live in society. Or live."

"Don't say that, Jill."

"Why not?"

"Because it's wrong. You're young. You have so much to live for."

"It didn't happen to you."

"I know... but..."

"It could actually be pretty easy, you know. I'm not saying I would do it. But I've thought about it."

"Well..."

"Haven't you ever thought about it?"

"No."

"Then you don't know what it's like."

She went into her bedroom and locked the door behind her. I didn't see her for the rest of the night.

It's Sunday, and I usually don't drink on Sunday but I felt like it today, so I went down to the 7-11 and bought a 12-pack of Bud. Then I came back home, turned on the TV, and did one of the things I been dreading: I wrote Jill's mom a detailed email of everything that happened.

I had to go to work the next day so I went to bed. At around 3am, my eyes opened up and I started thinking about Mike Saint. I knew there weren't no getting back to sleep so I went to my laptop and googled "Mike Saint" "San Antonio." I wanted to see what this kid looked like. But it was all middle-aged guys.

I went back to sleep at some time. Don't know when.

I woke up again at six o'clock and made coffee, turned on the news. I was putzing around in the kitchen when my phone rang. It was an international call. Beth.

"Hello," I said.

"What is going on?" She was actually calm. I didn't think it would last.

"Guess you got my email."

"Yeah, I got your email. What happened?"

"Everything... That's all I can tell you. There ain't anymore details, really." The email I wrote was long, and pretty thorough. I didn't leave nothing out.

"We're flying back on Wednesday. I will pick Jill up on Wednesday night on our way home from the airport. She will be spending Thanksgiving with us."

I forgot Thanksgiving was this week. Not that it mattered, I guess.

She went on: "I will be contacting a lawyer next week to see what I can do about getting permanent custody. Without visitation. You've proven to be incapable of taking care of her."

"Bring it on," I said.

"I want you out of her life. I want you out of our lives, forever. Do you understand?"

"Yeah, I got it. Not that it matters."

"Put Jill on."

I took my phone to Jill's door, and knocked. "Jill? It's Beth." I heard a rustling, and she opened it. She was dressed in the same clothes she wore from the night before. She hadn't slept, didn't look like.

"What?"

"It's your mom."

I handed her the phone, she shut the door and locked it.

I heard talking, but I didn't listen. I went out to the kitchen and made oatmeal, and got dressed. Right about 7:30 I knocked on her door again. No answer, so I opened it. She was sitting at her desk, staring blankly at her computer, which wasn't even turned on. My phone was on her bed and I pocketed it.

"You need to get ready for school."

"I'm not going to that school again."

"You got to go to school, Jill. You'll get behind if you don't."

"He's there."

"Yeah. Okay. Well. You don't got to go, I reckon. Will you call that Amy Landreau gal about setting up a time for counseling?"

"Yeah."

And that was that. I drove to work.

The day passed about like any other. Well, I shouldn't say that. I told the guys I was going across the street to the HEB to get some milk because what I'd put in my lunch bag was sour, and this Korean kid who works for me, this real nice fella named Jimmy Song, said to me, "Hey Billy Jim, you mind stopping off at Starbucks and picking up a latte for me?" For whatever reason, that was like getting stung by a wasp.

"A latte?" I said. "What do I look like? Your servant? Get your own damn latte!"

"O-o-kay. I didn't mean anything by it."

"You got a lot of nerve asking me for anything! *A latte!*"

Poodie Watts, my assistant manager, said "You don't got to shout, Billy Jim."

"Was I talking to you?"

"No, but—"

"Then shut your trap! As for you..."

"It's okay, Mr. Hauck," Jimmy said. "I'll get it myself."

"You're darn right you'll get it yourself, and you'll get it when I say you can get it! During your lunch break! Now *get back to work!*"

"Yes sir."

I didn't speak to my crew much after that. They saw I was in a mood so they gave me some space.

It got to be the end of the work day, and I bought some more beer and headed home. Jill was in her room. I called her name but she told me to go away and I did. I made mac and cheese for dinner but she did not come out to eat it. I watched TV and fell asleep.

Woke up at 3 a.m., thinking about all the stupid things I done in my life. Went back to sleep at 5:00, got up at 6:00, went to work at 7:30 and got home at 7:00, and that basically repeated until Wednesday.

Jill didn't eat during this time, or if she did eat, she ate while I wasn't there. And she didn't say nothing to me. I called at her door once or twice to see if she contacted the counselor but she didn't answer.

I knew that come Wednesday night though all of this was going to change because Beth was coming to pick her up. Beth could take care of her so much better than I could.

Wednesday come. I'd only been home a few minutes when I heard a car pull up out front. It was Beth and her boyfriend John Lancey.

Beth and John Lancey walked in without knocking. He looked a little embarrassed, giving me this slight nod, kind of rolling his eyes. Beth went straight to Jill's room without even looking in my direction and knocked on the door.

"Jill, honey, it's mother. Do you have your things packed? We've come to take you home."

No answer. Then Jill came out. She had dark circles under her eyes, and her hair was dirty and matted. Her mother embraced her, and the two of them held each other for a long time. Beth was crying softly. Finally she pulled away.

"Get your suitcase."

But Jill didn't move. Beth turned to me.

"You've said all your life that you were her big protector, this angel of safety and she never had anything to fear. I made the mistake of letting her live here because I thought it would be good to have her father in her life. What a terrible, terrible decision on my part. One which I am going to rectify right now. From this moment on, you will never see her again. If she wishes to make contact with you in the future, she will be able to when she is of legal age. But until that time, you are not to have any contact with her, for any reason. Do you understand?"

"The hell you say."

"Jill. Get your suitcase."

But Jill said, "I'm not coming with you."

There was this little pause, and the curtain of anger on her mom's face kind of parted a little.

"I'm not. I live here."

"Jill..." Nothing. No response. Then, "Don't you want to have Thanksgiving with us?"

"Not if it means I have to move."

Then, of all things, John Lancey spoke.

"Uh... Beth..."

"What?"

"Well, you know I'd love for Jill to move in with us. We get along fine, don't we Jill? But you have to be practical about this. Are you going to quit your job and stay home? Because you and I work together."

"We talked about this."

"We did. And I was hoping with a little time you would see—"

"What are you saying?" Her eyes narrowed.

"I'm saying I don't think you're being practical."

The anger again. Only oddly enough, it wasn't directed at me. Technically, it was at all three of us.

"What the hell are you talking about? You think my work is more important than my daughter?"

"Of course not. But if Jill is going to move in with us you're going to have to stay at home. Which means you're going to have to quit your job. We go on at least two business trips a month, sometimes we're away for weeks at a time. We're supposed to be in New York City for ten days in January. Who's going to look after Jill? You?"

"If that's what it takes to get her to move in with us, yes."

"And I just don't think that's being practical. It's Thanksgiving. You want me to find someone who can take your place by New Year's?"

"So the charity is more important than your stepdaughter?"

"No, I'm not saying that. But you're not being practical. And you're not being fair either. Look, you say you don't want your husband to see Jill again until she's eighteen. Why? You're afraid he's going to — what? What exactly did he do? Jill told him she was going to her friend's house, but she went to a party instead. How could he stop that?"

"He could have said no. He could have checked in on her. He could have set a curfew."

"How is he going to set a curfew when she's at a sleepover?"

"He could have checked on her."

"Jill is sixteen. She knows right from wrong. Now honestly, sir, I know you hate me because you think I broke up your marriage, but honestly, this isn't on you. This isn't your fault. It's a terrible thing, Jill, what happened to you. And all of us wish we could set the clock back to stop it from happening. But you're the one who made the decision to go to the party. What happened to you happened because of a decision you made, and not something your father did."

It's still my fault though. Because it happened on my watch.

Beth said, "She's moving in with us."

"I am not."

John Lancey turned to Jill, brushed the hair from her forehead, and looked in her eyes.

"Jill," he said. "I would love it if you could spend Thanksgiving weekend with us. When the weekend is over, I will be happy to drive you back here. If you only want to have Thanksgiving dinner with us, that's fine too. But we would love to have you come over and spend some time with us." Then after a long pause:

"I'm not moving in with you."

"That's fine. Stay tonight. And see how you feel tomorrow after dinner. We'll bring you home whenever you feel like it."

She stepped back, looked at her mother and me.

"I didn't pack."

Her mother said, "We'll wait."

The three adults sat out in the living room in silence. It seemed like Jill was taking forever to get ready but really it was only a few minutes. She came in with her small camouflage backpack hanging on her shoulder. Beth and John Lancey stood up and the three of them left together.

With Jill gone and nobody in it, the house was quiet as a bone yard, without even the littlest of sounds. No refrigerator hum or crick in the walls. It was pretty much just nothing, like a deaf man's world. Deaf and death. And I thought, is this what death is like? This emptiness?

Who will miss me when I go?

Chapter 7

The night was young, but way too much time had passed without beer. I set about to remedy that situation immediately.

After popping five or six cold ones, I started thinking about what I was going to do about Thanksgiving. I'd bought a turkey weeks ago even though I knew it was just going to be me and Jill, and Jill probably wouldn't eat much of it. Guess I had to let it thaw now. I took it out of the freezer and put it in a sinkful of water. I should have took it out a couple days ago, but too much was going on.

About nine o'clock or so I got a call from my older brother Ed.

"Hey, what's up, bro? Happy Thanksgiving, almost."

"Oh, hey. What are you doing?"

"Nothing. I'm just wondering what you're doing. Are you going out to see Dad tomorrow? I thought we could meet up at The Hill. Me and Gloria are going out there in the morning. Why don't you get up with us out there?"

"Can't. I got to fix the turkey tomorrow."

"Yeah? You got people coming over? Imagine that.

I thought it was going to be a solitary holiday for you, bub. Guess Jill couldn't get out of it. Ha ha!" Ed is kind of a jerk, actually. For some reason, ever since we was kids, he's lived to bait me.

"Yeah, guess not."

"You're going to miss that girl when she goes. You're going to have to hire prostitutes so you can get somebody to hang out with your fat ass."

"I got friends."

"Yeah, and they're all busy. So why don't you meet us for breakfast? Get started on your cooking in the afternoon."

"Can't. I'm up at the crack of dawn. I'm going to barbeque this year."

"Yeah. Well. Just thought I'd ask, you fat bastard."

We said some more pleasantries and hung up. There's a saying that you can't choose your family. Sometimes I'd rather be kin to a pile of day-old watermelon rinds than be related to Ed. But he ain't always bad.

The next day, I waited until the afternoon and then headed out to Independence Hill where my dad lives. My dad's eighty-three, and he's been living at The Hill for about five years. I think he likes it. It's a little hard to tell. He don't seem to like much of nothing. I think that's why Ed called me. He didn't want to go out there just him and his wife.

My dad really ain't been the same since our momma died. I was twenty-five so my dad must have been about the same age I am now. Eyewitnesses said there was a malfunction on the signal light at the railroad crossing at Jones-Maltzburger and 281. She went over the railroad tracks and a freight train plowed right into her Chevy Impala. They said she never knew what hit her though I spect she did. She was on her way to the HEB to buy groceries. She died at 11:02 a.m. We all had our problems after that.

We all kind of went crazy. That was thirty years ago.

As part of the settlement, the City of San Antonio gave my dad $114,000. Taxes and lawyers took about half that. He gave 10K to me and ten thou to my brother Ed, and kept the rest for himself. He got married not long after my mom died and his second wife took what was left when she split. I used my money to open my car repair shop. Smartest thing I ever did. If I hadn't done that I'd be living in a shotgun shack. What Ed did with his I couldn't tell you.

After my dad's second wife left, he was pretty much flat broke, and he didn't want to live in the house where he had so many memories of Momma, so I bought it off him and he moved into a small condo on Perrin Bietel and lived there until he moved to Independence Hill. Now he lives off his railroad pension.

This house we live in now, this house on Meredith Drive, has been in the family for three generations. I grew up in it. It's pretty run down now, nowhere near what it used to be when I was a boy. When I was a kid this place was pretty nice. Now it's weeds growing through the cracks in the sidewalk and the walls tilting and bugs. My grandfather bought it for my grandmother back in 1938 and it was super modern then. At the time, it was the last house on the outskirts of town. Now the outskirts of town is miles from here, and we're considered close to downtown. My grandmother was in the hospital recovering from colon cancer surgery and my grandfather wanted to surprise her, so when she checked into the hospital he found the house and bought it and hired movers to move all their stuff in. When he picked her up from the hospital he took her to this house here on Meredith and said, "Surprise! We live here now!" She was pretty taken aback, but she loved it. I always thought that was a really great gesture.

The house has always had its problems with settling

because of the shift from hot to dry weather, from drought to flood. The house would settle in that old black gumbo, the mud it was built on, and the settling would split the walls, and we'd have to patch them up all the time. The way my dad resolved this problem temporarily, at least until the next flood or drought, we'd get under the house and drive wedges between the floor trusses and the top of the cedar posts the house was sitting on, because the whole house was sitting on cedar posts. And we'd get in there and drive a wedge on top of the posts, tighten them up and close the cracks, then put another coat of paint on them. Got to watch out for the bugs too. How many times have I been under that house sweating those black widow spiders. They're everywhere in San Antonio but it seems like I got a gazillion of them living under my house.

This house has seen more ill than good: my folks was living here the day Momma died; my grandfather had that stroke in the bedroom Jill stays in now and he died there; my wife left me and found a new life with John Lancey; my dad's second wife run off and emptied his savings as a parting gift. And now this thing with Jill. Sometimes I believe this house is cursed.

Thanksgiving late afternoon I headed over to my dad's retirement home. I brought some Chinese food with me but didn't know if he'd eat any of it, seeing as how he ate with Ed and Gloria in the early afternoon. To my surprise, he took it out of the box and started in on it. Kung pao chicken and egg rolls.

He was in a real state. My dad is something of a cyberjunkie. He's got lots of retired friends, folks he knew from his days at Amtrak and people he knew growing up and they don't do much of nothing all day except pass emails back and forth. He got this email earlier that really set him off. When he gets in these moods I just nod or agree or try and change the subject, whichever works.

"Heard this one?" he said. "Damn woman in Beersheba. You know where that is? It's in Israel."

"Wonder what kind of beers they got in Beersheba?"

"This woman, this little Muslim whore, she's messing around on her husband behind his back. And her family gets so mad at her that they set her on fire. *They set her on fire!* You know why? It's because they's barbarians, that's why."

"Ever seen *Conan the Barbarian?* Schwarzenegger was all muscled up back then. Not like today. Now he got them saggy man-titties."

"You ain't so great yourself."

"Hey, I got them."

"So this Muslim whore, she has to go from her home in Gaza to Beersheba to get treatment. To this burn clinic. And they fix her up."

"Yeah."

"For free. She was invited to the clinic for follow-up visits. They *invited* her."

"Yeah."

"*Free, for nothing.* Then one day, they catch her at the Gaza border wearing a suicide vest. She was on her way to the clinic where she got the skin treatments. Her skin grafts. To blow it up. To blow the place up! *She was going to blow up the place that gave her skin treatments for free!*"

"This kung pao's awful tasty."

"And you know why? Because Muslims is a bunch of killers. They's a bunch of killer extremist murdering bastards."

"Seriously."

"Do you know what's going to happen to this world if the scourge of Muslim extremism is not stopped?"

"Seriously tasty. The Chinese, they know how to make some Chinese food."

"Don't even get me started on the Chinese. I never

buy anything from China. They're out to kill us."

"So I heard."

"There is a war a-coming. Muslims versus the West. And only one is going to survive."

The next thing that happened was really, *really* weird. My dad took a bite out of his egg roll, and he stood it up on the Styrofoam takeout pack. I just sat there staring at it. I couldn't help it. The egg roll standing up like that looked like this big erect penis. Well, not so much of a *big* erect penis seeing as how it was an egg roll. But an erect penis just the same. Standing there staring at me. And I kept trying to listen to what my dad was saying, and he kept talking, and I'd try looking at him, but my eyes would drift down to this erect penis sitting on his takeout box.

"Little school children all over the Arab world are being taught to hate the infidel (*erect penis*). That's us. Anybody who's not an Islamisist (*erect penis*). They are being taught to hate us in their schools (*erect penis*). They are being taught to kill us in their mosques (*erect penis*). They are being taught to wait until one day, all of Islam is going to rise up (*erect penis*) as one and kill off all the Christians in one final battle (*erect penis*)."

"Dad!"

"What?"

"Why don't you eat that egg roll?"

"I'm getting to it."

"Why don't you eat it now?"

"I said I'm getting to it."

"Because I want it."

"You got your own egg roll."

"Yours looks tastier than mine. How about if I eat it then?" And I did, I snatched it off the Styrofoam box and popped it in my mouth before he could say no. He looked at me like, "Man, I don't believe you just ate my egg roll!" But he didn't say nothing at all about it.

I sat there listening to him for a half hour more or so and got up to leave.

"Why are you in such a hurry?"

"I'm not in a hurry. I just got to get that turkey started. I'm cooking her outside this year."

I wanted to talk to him about Momma some. I miss her. And I know he does too. But we never talk much about that kind of stuff. We don't talk about the past much. Just about whatever's making him angry that day. That's the way he likes it, I guess. Talking about Momma would make him too sad. And I guess being angry is better than being sad.

"All right. Well. It was good to see you."

"Yeah. It was good to see you too."

Back home, I fired up the grill and set it low, then made the stuffing out of a mix. Took the plastic wrap off of the turkey, took her out of the sink. The dadgum thing was still half-frozen. I washed it in hot water trying to melt the ice some, stuffed her with dressing, and took her outside and set her on the grill. Put a can of water on the cooking grids to keep her moist. It was about seven o'clock. The turkey was going to be done around ten or so. Guess I'd be eating it for breakfast. Or maybe a late dinner.

Not sure why I decided to cook the turkey. I could have left it in the freezer and ate it at Christmas, but I didn't. Sometimes I'm so stupid I even amaze myself.

Anyway, I sat next to the grill, cooking that turkey and drinking a bunch of beer. I'd put potatoes on later, about an hour before the bird was done.

I started thinking about Jill again. Wondering where everything went wrong. Thinking and thinking.

Oh, Jill. Jill. Sweet child.

Beth is right. I swore all of my life to protect you. And I failed you.

When you really needed me, I was not there for

you. When you were unconscious and being raped I was watching TV. I don't know what I could have done, but I could have done something. And I failed you.

I remember when you were a little girl, how you used to do girly things like dress your Disney princesses and brush their hair and serve them tea in thimbles and feed them cookies made of Play-Doh. And now you've been attacked and I was nowhere to be found. I did nothing because I am an impotent bastard and I am powerless. I have no power. And I failed you.

I have always believed that things would work out for you in a big way. Your dancing is like a shining star and I always knew you were destined for great things.

But that's not true. Seriously, how would I know that? You asked me to go to your recitals and competitions all the time and I never did, except that once. Why? It was only an hour of my time but I always found an excuse to do something else.

Truth is, I never understood it. It never had nothing to do with me. It bores me.

I'm a terrible father. I could have been a good father to you, but I wasn't. I paid for your lessons and your food and that's about it. I never took an interest in what you like. I never really took an interest in you. And when I look at you now I see this little child that's been shattered.

What's going to happen to you, Jill?

Everything I have ever worked for. Everything I have ever believed in. Everything I have ever done. It's all nothing. I failed you.

I can't tell you this, but the truth is, when you were talking about not being part of this world, I've thought about that too. A lot.

I'm not sure how serious I am about it, but I have my troubles, and I've thought, I got guns. I could take my Glock and put it in my mouth and blow my head away. Or I could go find a high building and do her, some time when there ain't a lot of folks around, like downtown on a Sunday. The Smith-Young Tower or the Weston Center or the Marriott. I could just go up there and just drop off the thing. It'd be terrifying for about five seconds, but then it'd be done. I've thought about it a great deal, actually. But I could never do it. Or at least I never did. Because of you, Jill.

Yeah. I never did because of you.

Remember Frankie Naylor? He shot himself in the head, shot his brains out of the back of his skull, and his family had to clean up the bone and brains and blood off the walls of his trailer. Can you imagine plucking the bullet that killed your husband out of the wall? Or Gretta Herndale, who shot herself in the head with a .22 long rifle, only she put the barrel of the gun to her temple behind her eye bone, and the bullet went straight through, in one side and out the other, cutting through her eye socket and optic nerves. She died in the hospital two days later.

Jesus.

I checked the turkey. Should have taken her out of the freezer earlier. Not sure what this bird was going to look like. A big fat crispy popsicle.

I got up to take a piss. Why did I go all the way into the bathroom? Not like anybody would see me if I just took a piss in my own back yard. Maybe I was hoping I wouldn't get to this next part.

I went back outside, sat next to the grill. Cracked open another can of Bud. And sure enough, I started thinking about what *I'd* done. How maybe what happened to Jill was because of *me* in some way. In spite of what John Lancey said, maybe this *was* on me. Maybe this was all some kind of payback. The truth is, I've done some things in my life I ain't too altogether proud of. And they could be the reason for what happened to Jill.

Once, not long after my momma died, I drove to

the border with a couple of high school friends and we crossed into Mexico looking to get some tail. A girl I'd been dating a few months broke up with me because I was going crazy, and me and the boys really wanted to get some action, so we went south of the border into Nuevo Laredo. Once we got there we started bar hopping, sucking down beers and tequila shots. We didn't know where to go so we asked this taxi driver to take us to a bordello. He took us to Boys Town, a walled compound of about two or three blocks. We picked a cantina as a meet-up place then split up.

I went just across the street into this short, two-story structure with yellow and blue ceramic suns hanging off the burglar bars. The place was run by this tough-looking dude with a face that looked like five miles of asphalt with a gold tooth sticking out of it. I asked him how much, and he said in broken English it depends on the girl. Some girls are $30, some are $60 for a half hour. I told him I only wanted to spend $30 (this would have been in 1980s money). He motioned me to follow.

I followed him up the stairs. Dirty, sleazy looking place. An old hotel from the looks of it. Worn red carpets, paint peeling off the banister, dingy, aged walls. I was put in a little room with a couple of benches and a picture window that looked out onto the hallway.

Asphalt Face left, then came back a couple minutes later with a small glass of beer. "Here. Drink this." I took it from him and he left. I set it aside. A couple of minutes passed and he came down the hallway with a girl. I stood up.

She was Mexican, of course, real good looking, about twenty-one. Dressed in a strange crinkly plastic skirt with matching top. She was a little bleary, a little wobbly on her feet. Not a good sign. She stumbled when he led her to me. Asphalt Face kind of half-smiled but he did not look too happy about her condition, you could see in his eyes. I wasn't in the mood to start dickering, and had the sudden feeling that I wanted to get this over with as quickly as possible, so I just told the guy "sure" and she took my arm and we headed into a bedroom just off the hallway.

She closed the door and turned on the AC. The room was stifling. Not much in it. A shower stall. A bed. The walls were wood panel. It took me about ten seconds to realize there was something seriously wrong with this gal.

Besides being wobbly on her feet, her speech was slurred. I started glancing up and down her body. There was a small brown bruise about the size of a quarter on her left backhand, and inside the brown bruise were these little black bruises, what looked to be pinpricks.

Junkie. She was a junkie.

In the room next to ours, I could hear a couple laughing and talking in the shower, the water running. They were speaking Spanish. I looked at this girl's face. She had on a ton of makeup on but was really quite pretty. She had bad acne scars. Another sign of heroin addiction, I come to find out later.

She didn't look at me, just went over to the bed and laid down on her back and motioned me to come over. I took off my shirt, put it on the bedpost. By the time I got on the bed she was passed out cold. Dead to the world.

I looked her over, noticed a long, lip shaped bruise across the crook of her arm. This girl was really just a person waiting to die.

I should have just left the bordello right then and there, but I went back downstairs and told Asphalt Face what happened, with sign language because he didn't speak English real well. He suddenly got really pissed and motioned me to follow him again. I thought we were going to get a different girl but we went into the same room and — I didn't mean for him to do this — he pulled the girl up

in bed and started screaming at her and slapped her hard
in the face with his open fist. *Whack!* Then he grabbed her
by the top and shook her and then hit her again. *Whack!*
And again. *Whack! Whack!* She was awake now and her
head was bobbing every time he hit her. Then he started
punching her. He smashed her in the nose and it split
open. It was bloody, there was blood flying everywhere.
I backed out the door while he was clocking her and
screaming at her and I just left.

I went out to the designated cantina across the street.
A waitress was outside, trying to wave in passersby. I went
in. The place was deafening, loud mariachi music blasted
out of two cracked and rattling speakers. I ordered a beer.
The bartender poured up my cerveza and then went back to
smoking his cigarette and looking at the wall. I took a seat
outside on the front patio to get away from the noise. I looked
at the waitress but she ignored me, just continued waving
in folks on the street. My table was directly across from the
bordello I'd just left. I thought about what just happened.

If Asphalt Face had struck her one more time, I would
have kicked his ass. You can't treat folks like that in front
of me, no sir. I'll take you to town. It's one thing to beat
on a girl. Let's see how you like dealing with me.

Then the screaming. A woman screaming, my woman
screaming coming from the old hotel. I knew it was her.
But I couldn't see nothing, just hear it. Wailing. Agony.
Coming from someplace inside. What was he doing to her?

It ain't my business. It's just some junkie whore.

It went on and on. Like slow murder. I sat there,
wanting to do something, but I couldn't move. I was too
scared. I watched the wind kick up the dust on the road,
wishing my friends would finish their business so we could
head back to SA.

And just like that it stopped.

They got to the bar about a half hour later, both really

happy, talking it up like whoring in Mexico was the greatest thing. And I went right along with them. Yeah man, getting Mexican pussy is *fun!*

Then the next morning I was taking a shower and the whole thing came back to me and I just got sick. I could have stopped him but I didn't. I've broke up ass-kickings before and I don't back down from fights, but I didn't do nothing. When I closed my eyes I saw him punching her and her nose all blood and laid open.

And now, all these year later, as I sat in my backyard, I had to wonder: is Jill suffering because some pimp in Mexico beat his prostitute nearly to death while I did nothing? Because I had to think the answer to that question was yes.

Who cares about her? She was just some junkie whore. Just another insect in the world.

Did I think that at the time? No! Do I believe it now, sitting here sucking down these beers? No. But... yeah. Part of me, yeah.

And right then I knew, I was *certain* that somebody had seen something the night Jill was raped, and they did nothing. They could have stopped it and they didn't. They chose not to. Like I did.

And as I sat there watching the smoke come out of the top of the grill, hearing the soft voice of George Jones singing from somebody's radio somewhere down the block, I knew. Things are never going to get better for you, Jill. You are never going to get better. You are in a night where the stars are disappearing and soon you'll be surrounded by blackness and empty space, where everyone who has ever loved you and everything you have ever loved has faded away.

I could have stopped it. But I didn't. And I failed you.

Chapter 8

Cooking a turkey that's half-frozen is just about the stupidest thing a body can do. The outside was cooked, so I ate a little of the outside, but the inside was bloody. What a mess. I put it in the fridge but I knew I was going to have to chuck it.

Ate the potatoes and dressing — it was a little pathetic, eating dinner alone and so late — and talked to myself the whole time. I do that, for some reason, get in these long conversations with myself. I think the night of my great Thanksgiving feast I was going on about liberals, how much I hate them, and why they're responsible for all our problems. I can't remember specifically what they'd done that I was so bent out of shape about, but it was something. Right near the end a voice came into my head saying, *"You know, liberals didn't create your problems. They didn't fail your daughter, and you didn't fail your daughter because of them. You failed your daughter because of you. Nice try though."*

I went to bed and woke up the next morning and went to work. Wasn't much reason not to.

We had a little business, not much to speak of. Some guy in a Hyundai Grandeur came in needing a new alternator, and some soccer mom came in wanting to replace a burned out headlight on her BMW. Sometime around mid-afternoon I decided I'd had enough, and told Poodie Watts I was going home and I'd see him on Saturday.

I got to home and wondered why I just didn't stay at work. The place was empty, and all there was to do was watch TV. No, that's not all. I had to pay bills. That'll give me something to do, I thought.

So I pulled open the drawer where I keep all my bills. I don't do my bill-paying over the internet because I'm afraid the utility companies will get hacked and somebody will clean out my checking account. I shouldn't really worry about it, it's perfectly safe I reckon, but I never signed up for it and I'm not going to now.

So I look at what I got. Gas, water, electric, cable. Then I pull out something I didn't even know was there, an envelope with Jill's name on it from the San Antonio Ballet. I open her up and it's a couple of tickets to *The Nutcracker* at the Convention Center downtown. Yeah, I remember now. Jill's mom had ordered the tickets and had them sent here as one of Jill's Christmas presents. They was expensive too, $115 each. The date on the tickets was November 25th. Today.

I sent Jill a text message. "found your nutcracker tix. what u want me to do with them?"

An hour passed, it was getting on about 5 p.m. I texted her again, got no response.

Two tickets at $115 a pop was $230, and that's a lot of dinero to just drop on something you ain't going to use. So I decided to go down to the Convention Center and see if I could get a refund on them. If I could, I'd give Beth her money back. Or maybe I'd just keep it. Sure, it crossed my mind. Since I'm taking the trouble to do all this.

I got in my truck and drove downtown, parked, and went to the ticket window and got my refund. I was going to head back to my truck but I stopped.

Didn't see no reason for going back home. Wasn't going to be nobody there except me. I could watch TV but that weren't nothing new and there probably wasn't nothing on. I knew I was going to be slamming down some beers later but didn't see the point of rushing it. I'd never been to the ballet. Maybe if I saw it, I'd get to know a little more about Jill. Maybe watching the ballet would give me an idea of what she cares about, and who she really is, and maybe I could help her.

At least I told myself that. Probably the main thing was I just didn't want to face myself alone again. Going to the ballet was going to postpone it for a time and I kind of liked that idea. And if it was boring I'd just sleep.

I went back to the box office and bought a single "Heart of the House" ticket on the aisle. I always sit on the aisle because a football injury from high school makes it where I got to stretch out my right leg and I can't sit cramped too long. I was feeling a little underdressed because everybody was in ties and coats and I was just wearing what I always wear, but it didn't bother me too much.

I sat in my seat and waited for the show to start. I could just imagine what some of the guys I work with would say if they could see me now, or my brother Ed. Ed would go "You're gay!" I know it.

A couple minutes later a guy sat down next to me, and from what I could tell, he weren't too happy about being there. He was kind of slumped down in his chair, and he sighed a lot. He looked through his program and went "tsk tsk" a lot and shook his head.

Then the lights went down and the show started.

I wasn't really prepared for what I saw that night. And I don't really understand it. But it kind of went like this.

The curtain came up, and it was snowing, and all these kids were around. And then this guy comes on, and he's got this long cape and big old top hat, and everybody's making a big deal out of him. And he's got this nutcracker, see, that he gives to this girl. She looks to be about twelve. And she's really happy to get it. But her jerk brother breaks it, so she gets all sad. And at this moment I think I kind of snorted or something, and I might have said, "Yeah, that's just like my brother." Because the guy sitting next to me looked at me, and he nodded.

Then the girl went to bed, and she woke up and there was a bunch of toy soldiers fighting a bunch of mice, and then the Nutcracker from earlier shows up, only he's a dude now, and he starts sword fighting with this mouse who must be the king or something because he's wearing a crown on his head. And this Nutcracker hombre is just about to get killed but the little girl rescues him by throwing her shoe at the mouse king guy and dinging him on the head and the Nutcracker kills him and everything's cool.

Then the kid and the Nutcracker go over to the guy with the long cape and the lights flash like lightening and presto-chango suddenly they're all grown up and the girl who is supposed to be twelve is now this extremely hot twenty-something and the Nutcracker fella is this real handsome dude. And then about something like fifty gals dressed like snowflakes come out and the Nutcracker guy is lifting up this woman who's supposed to be twelve and throwing her all around and it starts snowing for real and everything is blue. Then the guy in the cape comes back out and escorts the Nutcracker and the hot babe to this sled and the two of them go floating off into the ceiling and he throws the cape over himself and flies out the other way.

The lights came up, and I was a little stunned. I really spected I was going to be bored out of my skull, but I wasn't. Just the opposite, really.

The guy next to me wasn't too impressed. He said, "Ghastly!" under his breath and scrunched down in his seat more. I probably shouldn't have said nothing, but I did.

"You didn't like it?"

"Dreadful. Did you?" He had an accent.

"Yeah, kind of."

"Well, to each his own. I shouldn't be surprised after all. This *is* Texas. Maybe the second act will have dancing oil wells." It was a British accent.

"There's a second act?"

"Yes, my dear man, there is a second act."

I decided to just keep my trap shut. To heck with him if he didn't like it.

A few moments later, a gray-haired gentleman came over to the man sitting next to me.

"Sir David!" he said. "They just told me you'd come." Sir David? So this guy is some kind of royalty. Well, whoop-de-do.

"Yes. You have an airport, so I flew in. You'll be getting schools soon, I hear."

"Enjoying it so far?"

"We'll talk."

That ended the conversation. The gray-haired man looked like he wanted to say more, but didn't. He nodded to the British guy, who did not acknowledge him, and after an awkward second, went back up the aisle.

I went to the bathroom, and while I was washing my hands, this really weird thing happened. The lights started flickering on and off. I thought we might be about to have a power outage so I was going to go home, but when I stepped into the lobby I noticed that everybody was going back into the theater and nobody seemed to be concerned about it, so I just followed everybody else.

The second act started. The girl and the Nutcracker guy were kind of sidelined for the first part. Out comes this gal in this white tutu and everybody's all impressed with her. Then the girl and the Nutcracker just watch this show that's being done for them, and it's got this Spanish couple dancing in bullfighting clothes, then a whole slew of characters out of *Arabian Nights* (wonder if my dad would think they're Islamisists?), then some Chinese folks, and lastly some Russians kicking up their heels. I remember seeing something like the Russian thingy in a Bugs Bunny cartoon once. After that, the gal in the white tutu came out again, and she was surrounded by gals in different colored dresses and stuff. And they were all standing on their toes and jumping around and all.

Then the stage cleared except for this guy with really tight pants and the girl in the white tutu and they danced together for a while. The music got to be slow and really sad. And he was turning her around, and she was holding these perfect poses, and he would pick her up and toss her in the air like I couldn't believe. He was flipping her, she'd go up and up and around and around and come down and he'd catch her in mid-air, and then dip her to the floor.

The sad music really got to me. It was so beautiful, and it reminded me of Jill, and I thought about how beautiful she is and how much she would have liked this.

The funny thing is, seeing this ballet, I understood her for the first time why she wanted to be a ballet dancer. It's because she wanted to bring beauty into this world.

That's weird to say as a parent, to say that I just discovered it. But there it is.

The girl in the white tutu came out again and danced by herself. She looked so much like a toy, like something that should be on a music box. The music actually sounded like a music box, like one of those xylophones or something. And I remembered back to the music box my momma had when she was a child. I used to take it out and look at it when I went over to our gram's house.

And seeing this here ballet dancer made me feel Jill was also a like toy, and how fragile she is, and how easily she can break. How broken she is.

God I miss my momma.

Everything in my life started going wrong the day she died. And here is this ballerina dancing like her music box. And I adore her.

There was some more dancing, but it was mainly the same people we'd seen before. Then the girl and the Nutcracker got crowns, so I guess they was the new king and queen of the rodeo.

Then everybody came out onstage and surrounded the twelve-year-old girl in her bed, and then they all went away and she woke up with her nutcracker and realized it was all a dream.

And the music at the end was really big, and I felt like it was hitting me in the chest. And the man sitting next to me, Sir David, he was looking at me and he leaned in and he said, "Are you all right?" but I didn't say nothing. People started applauding, me too. The lights came up and I just got up and walked out.

I sat out in the lobby and watched the crowd thin out. Stalling. I really did not want to go home again. So I just sat there and tried not to think about stuff. I was trying to make my mind as blank as I could. It wasn't working. I kept thinking about that dancer in the white tutu, and how beautiful and innocent she was. Wouldn't it be great, I thought, if Jill could dance like that in front of people some day? I guess that's never going to happen now.

A minute or so later the guy who sat next to me during the show came out into the lobby. He was searching for somebody, probably the guy he was talking to earlier. His eyes fell on me and he smiled, then he came over.

"What does your shirt say?"

I didn't know. I had to look.

"Lynyrd Skynyrd."

"Oh, it's a person's name. I thought it was indiscriminate letters thrown on a shirt. Is he a singer?"

"Lynyrd Skynyrd ain't a singer, friend. Lynyrd Skynyrd was a country rock band. They died in a plane crash back in the 70s."

"And you have them immortalized on your chest. You should be buried in that shirt. Then archeologists will know what mattered 100,000 years from now when they dig up your remains."

"Won't that just be dandy for them."

"What's one of their songs?"

"'Free Bird,' 'Sweet Home Alabama.' You never heard of Lynyrd Skynyrd? How is that possible?"

"I didn't listen to much rock music when I was growing up. I listened to *Phantom, Pippin, Superstar,* that kind of thing."

"Never heard of Phantom Pippin Superstar. Is he a singer?"

"Well played, sir. Well played." I had no idea why he said that. I *hadn't* ever heard of the guy.

Then he asked me, "Did you like the show?"

"Yeah. A lot."

"I noticed you were crying at the end."

"I wasn't crying."

"Oh, I'm sorry. That was your clone."

"It wasn't my clone and I wasn't crying."

"It's all well, you know. I understand, really. I'm not a complete git." He looked at me a moment and then said, "A git. That's Britspeak for a silly person, a fool. As in 'I thought San Antonio could possibly have a good ballet company. What a stupid git.'"

"We don't say 'git' in these here parts. We say 'idjit.'"

"As in?"

"As in, 'You didn't like the ballet? What an idjit!'"

He laughed. "You got me again! Truthfully, sir, I *have* heard the expression previously. The Irish use it. And I must say, it describes them perfectly."

"Why didn't you like the show?"

"It was fine, if you like seeing gorillas stomping around in tutus."

"Then why go?"

"I'm directing their next show in the spring. *Romeo and Juliet*. I wanted to see their work."

"Ya'll should do a ballet of country music."

"Yes, when all the artistic directors are dead. Mr. Skynyrd, what brought you out tonight?"

"I had a ticket."

"Really? That's it? A free ticket brings you to the ballet on a Friday night? Maybe we should be giving away more tickets to single men."

"I didn't say it was free. Cost me $115."

He seemed astonished. "You paid $115 and came by yourself? In jeans and a t-shirt. Somebody in marketing needs to meet you."

Just then, the gray-haired man from earlier stepped towards us. He was accompanied by a slender woman in her mid-50s in a slinky black dress and pearl necklace. The gray-haired man was smiling. The woman was not.

"Ah, Sir David," said the gray-haired man. "We've been looking for you."

"Yes, I've been avoiding you."

I stood up and shook the British guy's hand and said, "It was nice meeting you..."

"David. David Derrick."

"Billy Jim Hauck. It was nice meeting you, David."

"And you, Lynyrd Skynyrd, and you."

I turned to leave, and heard a bit of their conversation floating in my ear.

David: "Your ballet was quite painful."

The woman: "Honestly. I don't care if you liked the show or not."

Chapter 9

I woke up at 3 a.m. rolling in fire. The fire inside my head.

I got the Glock. I could go out in the back yard.

No.

I could put my head against the pecan tree.

No.

The bullet would lodge in the tree. Nobody would need to dig it out. The tree is huge, it won't kill the tree.

Jill.

Jill will understand. You're a burden to her. She hates you.

She needs me.

You're an old drunk. You're a joke to her.

No.

Go out to the refrigerator and drink the rest of that beer.

This

Go on, you deserve it.

It can't

Then go out to the backyard

***

Sit down in the grass
It
Lean up against the tree
No
Put an end to this once and for all.
It's
Do it.
This
Do it!
This has got to stop.
This has got to stop.

****

This has got to stop.
I know. But what am I supposed to do?
I don't know. But I know that this ain't working.
What do I do?
I don't know. But what I do know is I am sick to death
of this.
Things have got to change. I don't know how. But they
do.

Around six o'clock I got up and started to work on that
pile of bills. Got out my checkbook and wrote out checks
for the electric, gas, water, and cable. Put stamps on them
and took them out to the mailbox. Wasn't sure when the
postman would come, and I didn't want to leave them in
the box because they'd get stolen, so I decided to drop
them by the post office on my way to work. I brought one
extra check with me.
Saturday morning. It felt good to get out of the house
again. But I only stayed at work until noon. Business
was slow. I knew work would pick up once Thanksgiving

passed, and anyway, I got three mechanics besides me to cover any business we got coming in. I had something to do. I had to take care of Jill's ballet class.

I pay for her ballet lessons once a month, and I was supposed to give her school a check the next week. But I wasn't even sure Jill was going to continue her lessons. I didn't know what she was going to do. So I stopped by the studio to talk to her teacher about it.

It was the first time I'd ever been there. Usually I give Jill a check and she just takes it in with her. There was a young girl working the front desk. Wasn't sure to who to ask for. Didn't even know her teacher's name.

"Excuse me, I need to talk to my daughter's teacher."

"Who's your daughter's teacher?"

"Uh..."

"What's your daughter's name?"

"Jill Hauck."

She looked it up on the computer.

"Her teacher is Inez Garza. She's in class now, but she'll be out in a few minutes. Do you want to wait?"

I said I did, and the receptionist went in the back to tell her I was there. I sat in the waiting area and watched TV. It was the end of an *Andy Griffith* show, and Andy was giving Opie some fatherly advice about bullies. Then a talk show came on and folks was throwing chairs at each other.

After about ten minutes of waiting, Inez Garza came out. I expected her to be dressed in a leotard since she was teaching, but she wasn't. Jeans and a hoodie. She was about thirty-five, maybe. Mexican-American. Long black silky hair. Quite stunning. She looked like a model. They's some hot mama's in ballet, it turns out.

"Are you Jill's dad?"

"Yep. Billy Jim Hauck."

"Inez Garza. Where's Jill been? She's missed two weeks of classes, and she doesn't respond to my texts."

"Can we talk someplace private?"

"Is anything wrong?"

"I saw a Jim's across the street. Can we talk there?"
Jim's is a coffee shop chain in San Antonio. They're all over the place.

She said she had some things to take care of but could meet me in fifteen. I went to the Jim's and sat in the corner away from the rest of the customers and ordered coffee. About ten minutes later she came in. She sat down across from me and the look on her face said she knew this was not going to be good. I explained why Jill had been absent and did not mince words.

"Oh, god," she said. I felt sorry for Inez Garza. It's terrible to hear, and I knew they were close. Or at least I figured they were.

"How is she doing?"

"Not too good. She's with her mom now. But she's not going to school and she stays in her room all the time."

"I'm so sorry. Poor Jill. Such a lovely girl."

I didn't really know how to say this next part. I didn't know what I wanted to say.

"So..." I said, "What do I do?"

"Did you report the crime?"

"We did all that. I mean, what do we do about her now?"

"Meaning?"

"Meaning I don't know what to do."

"She'll need to see a therapist. A counselor."

"She's got a counselor's number. Who knows if she's called her or not. She won't talk to me about it."

The waitress came by and Inez ordered coffee. Then we both sat there in silence. The coffee came. She didn't drink any. Then she said:

"Why don't you have her call me?"

"I'll try, but if you sent her text messages and she

didn't get back to you, then she probably won't."

"So what should we do?"

"She's at her mom's until tomorrow night. When she gets home, I'll send you a text message and then you can come over and talk to her."

"Okay," she said. "But... Well, she's in a very vulnerable state right now. I don't know how I feel about me just showing up at your door. She probably doesn't want anybody to know what happened to her, and that's the reason why she hasn't reached out. If I just come over barging into your house she might be relieved or she might feel like her privacy is being violated. I'm not sure that's such a good idea."

"Okay."

"When you see her tomorrow night, tell her you think I'd like to speak to her. Don't tell her you and I talked. But tell her that she knows I care about her and I care about what happens to her, and if she needs an ear she knows I'll listen. It's important to know she's not alone. It's easy to feel lost in all this."

"Yeah." My eyes wandered down to the paper placemat. A smiling cartoon cowboy looked back at me, saying "Howdy!"

I took the check out of my shirt pocket, slid it across the table to her. "So... I got this here check. It's $600 for lessons and $400 for privates. Who teaches her privates? I always just make it out to the school. You'll need to let them know."

"Gail Godfrey."

"This is for December but I don't know if she's coming back."

"Keep it. We would never charge you for services we don't render." She slid the check back to me.

She closed her eyes and put two fingers on her forehead. "Jill is like family to me."

"I know." I really didn't.

"YAGP regionals are in Chicago next month. She's supposed to be getting on a plane in three weeks."

"Excuse my ignorance, but what's YAGP regionals? Is that one of her contests?"

"YAGP stands for Youth American Grand Prix. It's the biggest ballet competition in the world. There are regional competitions — you know this, right, because you've paid for these — and every year about 200 dancers are selected out of these regionals to perform solos at the YAGP Finals in New York City."

"Sounds like a big deal."

"It's a very big deal. Dancers who do well can get scholarships to prestigious dance academies like the School of American Ballet, or offers to join professional ballet companies. It's a potential ticket to a career. Jill has been to YAGP regionals three years in a row."

"She has?" Some father. I can't believe I didn't know that.

"Yes, but never went to the big show. This is supposed to be her year. She's been working all of her life for this. She's actually a shot at going to New York in January."

"Huh..."

"Or at least she did." She looked despondent. "The thing I can't wrap my head around is 'why?' Jill has been training so hard for so many years. She's sacrificed so much. She has been on a strict diet since she was in eighth grade. She's worked and worked and worked perfecting her craft, and everything she's ever done has been leading up to this competition. Why would she go out drinking? It's just not like her. She's so focused. This is supposed to be her year!"

I didn't know none of this about Jill. I never really took it very serious. This was supposed to be "her year"? I never thought of it like that. I never knew her work was leading up to anything. It's just dreaming and dreams really don't come true. Maybe I just expected her to fail. Like me.

Then Inez said: "How are you holding up?"

I didn't really want to get into it, but I found myself saying, "Not so well."

"I imagine."

"Yeah."

"You need to keep your mind occupied. Who have you reached out to?"

"You."

"That's it? Just me?" She didn't say it in a surprised way, just matter-of-fact.

"Yeah."

"You poor man."

"Not hardly."

"What are you doing to keep yourself busy?"

"Well. There's drinking. And then there's work. And that's about it. I went to the ballet last night. I saw *The Nutcracker* down at the Convention Center."

"You did? We're going next Thursday. Did you like it?"

I thought about the woman, the ballerina on the music box.

"I was kind of shocked, actually."

"Why?"

"By how much I liked it. I was really moved by it. I, uh, cried, so they tell me."

"Did you go with friends?"

"Friends? No. My friends wouldn't be caught dead at a ballet. No, the guy who was sitting next to me told me that." Friends. Where were my friends? Who were my friends?

"I understand," she said. "I'm sure this has been a very emotional time for you as well."

"Tickets are a kind of expensive."

"Have you ever thought of taking ballet?"

I laughed out loud at that one. A fifty-five-year-old fat dude taking the ballet. What a thing to say.

"Me? No. Can you imagine me in a tutu?"

"A tutu is what women wear. Men wear tights."

"And look silly in them."

"Did the dancers look silly last night?"

"If I thought about it, probably."

"What about NFL football players? And wrestlers. They wear tights."

"That's different."

"It's not different. They're all athletes. They wear tights so we can see the human form."

"Ain't nobody interested in seeing *this* human form."

"You wouldn't have to wear tights. You could wear sweat clothes. We have an adult beginner's class that starts after the holidays. It's for absolute beginners. You'd fit right in."

"I don't think so."

"The age range in our class is from early twenties to seventy. The people who study with us are not doing it because they want a career in ballet, obviously; they're too old for that. They do it for a lot of reasons. For exercise, or to meet other people. To get out of the house. Are you single?"

"Yeah."

"The class is like 90% women."

"Yeah, I imagine it would be. Your kids' classes are 90% women too. Not women, but you know what I mean. Girls. Female."

"It's higher. It's 95%. We never get boys. Too much stigma attached, especially in Texas. Boys take ballet, then they go to school and get called gay and then drop out. But you don't have to worry about that. In your case, you'd join for your own reasons. To meet people. Or get your mind off your troubles, think about something else."

"Well. That would just never happen in a million years."

"Okay. Just thought I'd throw it out there."

"I'll tell Jill to call you. Thanks for meeting me."

And that was that. I picked up the check, got into my truck and drove away.

Then I got to thinking, they must be really desperate at that ballet school to start a class for adults. I wonder if they're any good. Maybe Jill ought to find a new place to study.

Saturday night. Not going anywhere, not doing nothing, nothing going on.

I'm on my third beer, half-watching Fox News and half-defending the Second Amendment against internet libtards. I say half because I wasn't doing neither one of them very good. The folks on Fox was going on about the same stuff they always go on about, so it was the usual thing, and I was getting tired of making the same arguments to the same people.

Nothing ever changes. It kind of fungles me how often I repeat myself. How often I say the same thing over and over. How often I have the same thoughts. Nothing ever changes. And it hasn't in as long as I can remember.

Last night I woke up at 3 a.m. thinking about shooting myself and thinking "things have got to change" but as I sit here watching the TV I got to wonder, will they ever? I reckon this is what I got to look forward to for the rest of my days.

I been considering drastic action. Toying with an idea. But I wasn't sure if it was the right thing. This drastic action would keep Jill safe, I reckon. Maybe even me. But would it really? Maybe not.

Having one part of my brain trying to talk me into shooting myself is messed up, but it ain't the worst of the thunderclouds what come into my mind sometimes. I got stuff like, "I could buy an AK, go to Washington, casually walk the halls of Congress and shoot every stupid politician in there." Or this one: "If I shot one or two liberal Supreme Court justices, then the scales would tip forever. The liberals would never be able to pass any legislation because it'd always be blocked by our guys."

I can't tell you how much I hate that. Don't know why these dark thoughts twist inside my brain or where they come from. But I wish to god they'd stop.

I sometimes wonder if what goes through my head is normal. It don't seem normal, but who knows? It's hard to know because who would ever admit to thinking it? Can you imagine some famous actor getting on the TV and saying, "Sure, I've fantasized about killing a congressman. Who hasn't? Now go see my movie." So maybe folks have thoughts all the time but they just don't say nothing about them because it's one thought among a million others and it all gets jammed together and it don't seem like such a big deal. "We need to wash the truck. This beer sure is tasty. I could kill the president. What time is the game on?"

Thankfully, I wasn't having the dark thoughts when I was sitting on my couch that Saturday night. I was actually thinking about change, and the lack of it. And this other possibility. Wishing something different would come along so I wouldn't have to take action. I don't want to do nothing. I just want things to happen. Then there was a knock on my door.

Maybe this here is change, I thought. Maybe change is on the other side of my front door.

But it weren't. It was only my brother Ed and his wife Gloria.

"Hey fat ass, happy Thanksgiving!"

"Shut up, Ed," said Gloria.

"Oh, hey y'all."

I'm not sure how Gloria has managed to stay with Ed all these years. She has way more patience than anybody I know. Maybe she takes medication. Anyway, she don't like Ed's jokes any more than I do.

"You going to invite us in?"

"Sorry, come in, come in."

So they ended up on my living room couch.

"Ya'll want a beer?"

Ed said, "Sure. We was just passing by this way, thought we'd see how you're doing."

"Where's Jill?" asked Gloria.

"She's still at her mom's."

Ed said, "I thought you said she was going to be with you on Thanksgiving."

"She was. Then she went over to her mom's."

Why did I lie? At this point, I needed to start telling some truth, even if it meant taking Ed's insults.

The crazy thing about Ed is, I really kind of hate him, but he's family, and he's one of the only people who really cares about us. Us being me and Jill.

"No, actually, no. She didn't spend Thanksgiving here. She spent it at her mom's."

"Huh. How about that?"

"So, um, I'll get those beers."

I went out into the kitchen and grabbed some beers and pretzels. Ed and Gloria were both watching Fox News when I got back.

"So what really brings you over this way?"

Ed turned the volume down. "We need to have a talk. About Dad."

"What about Dad?"

"You need to pick up the slack when it comes to taking care of Dad. You been letting me do it all, and I don't think it's fair. You could have met us on Thanksgiving but you didn't, so I had to go over there just me and Gloria."

"Where's Ron and George?" Ron and George are Ed's children. He named them after Ronald Reagan and George H.W. Bush.

"They busy. They too busy these days to help out much."

"Or inclined to," said Gloria. It really didn't surprise me that Ron and George was busy. It's kind of a mystery what they do that makes them so busy, but they *always* busy. I never see them. They could be in prison for all I know.

"Look, Ed. I didn't meet you and Gloria over there on Thanksgiving, but I went over to Independence Hill."

"You did?"

"Sure. Later in the afternoon."

"I talked to Dad and he didn't say nothing about it."

"We had Chinese."

"He ate too? Well. He didn't say nothing about that. Seems like he would have."

"So you think I'm lying?"

"No. I just thought he would have."

I could see Gloria's eyes drift over to the TV. She'd kind of looked at me, and then her eyes would drift back over to the TV.

"You want to watch TV, Gloria?"

"Me? No. What else is on?"

I handed her the remote and Gloria flipped to the home channel. I motioned Ed to follow me and we headed into the kitchen.

Ed cracked his beer and we sat down at the table. I told him all about Jill from start to finish. He was sympathetic throughout, and didn't make his usual jokes at my expense. Ed's pretty classless, but even he wouldn't go there.

Then I got down to telling him about me, and I hate to say this, but I had a real hard time looking him in the eye. I weren't ashamed, really. I just don't speak like this ever.

"The thing is," I said, "something has got to change."

"Like what?"

"Like... I don't know. But it's got to. Something's got to. This really ain't no way to live."

"You're life really isn't all that bad, man. You're doing okay," he said. "Stuff happens, that's all. You'll be all right."

"Doing okay? How? How am I doing okay? Look at me now." I felt like my insides was a slow boil.

"It ain't your fault, Billy Jim. It's not like you could have done nothing. Blame the rapist. It's the rapist's fault."

"It is, but it isn't. Because, you know, that's only part of it. Who do I blame for the way I felt before this happened? There is nobody to blame, not one single person, for what's eating me. Because it's everything in my life, not just one thing. You get it? Is it Jill's fault? Am I supposed to blame god? Because I do. But how do I say this? It ain't about finding fault, man. I can do that easy. I can blame the rapist. But then nothing changes. I'm still me. And honestly speaking, bro, I'm sick and tired of living in this condition where every time I turn around I got to point a finger, I got to say it's somebody else's fault. It's expected. But it don't do no good. There's nobody to blame for what's going on inside me. Nobody. Except me."

"All right, all right, I didn't mean nothing by it."

"No, you *did* mean something by it. Because I been doing that all of my life. I feel like I'm a robot what's been programmed to blame. It's the Democrats. It's the gun control crowd. It's the Washington Redskins. You know what I mean? It's got to stop."

"You sound like you need to go to the doctor."

"You mean the head doctor?"

"Maybe."

"Can a doctor prescribe a pill that'll take away anger? Because I'm tired of being angry. I'm angry at everything and everybody. I'm angry at Beth. John Lancey. The guys I work with. My customers. My friends, who have disappeared in middle age. I'm angry at Jill."

"Are you angry at me?"

"Are you kidding me? How could I not be angry at you? You're the worst person I know. If you weren't my brother I'd never speak to you and cut off all ties with you. You think I like the way you talk to me?"

"Well, you ain't lost your sense of humor."

"I'm tired of being angry. I'm tired of being sad. I'm tired of being lonely. I'm tired of drinking. I'm tired of this life. In case you haven't figured this out, things ain't right with me. Something's got to change."

"Like what?"

"I don't know!"

Before Ed and Gloria came over, I'd been thinking about doing this one thing. This drastic action, as I saw it. But who knows if it will —and then I thought, aw, the hell with it. You want change? Here she comes.

"Stay here a minute. I got to get something."

I went under the kitchen sink and got a paper bag, then into the living room where Gloria was watching TV. I had to get something under the couch but her feet were in my way, so I said "Excuse me," and she moved them and I reached under the couch and pulled out my .357 Magnum and unloaded it and put it in the bag. Gloria never even looked at me, she had no idea what I was doing.

Then I went into my bedroom and into my nightstand. I took out my Glock, pulled out the clip and emptied the chamber, and put it in the paper bag. I went to my closet and brought out my two hunting rifles, my .30-06 and my .270. I knew they were empty but I checked anyway. I had boxes of shells but didn't see the need to pack them.

I walked back into the kitchen carrying the two rifles and the two handguns in the paper sack. My brother cocked his head sideways like a dog'll sometimes do when he don't understand something, but he weren't scared or anything like that. Which was fine. It wasn't like I was going to shoot him.

I said, "These here are my rifles. My Glock and my .357 is in this here bag. I want you to keep them for me." I put the sack on the table.

"Why?"

"I just don't want them in the house right now. "

"Is it because of Jill? Because if she wants to commit suicide, not having a gun won't stop her. All the evidence points to it."

"I got a daughter who's going through a rough patch now and I don't know what she's feeling and I don't know what she's capable of. Screw the evidence."

"You going to give me all your knives too? You going to give me her car? She could run herself over with her car."

"When this happens in your family you can judge me."

"She ain't going to kill herself with a hunting rifle. I bet she don't even know how to load it, let alone fire it."

"You think it takes a rocket scientist to figure it out?"

"Why don't you just lock them up? You say she's going through a rough patch, but that don't mean she's going to suddenly become a master safe cracker. And what does that even mean anyway, a 'rough patch'? She's depressed, or...?"

"A rough patch. She's depressed. She ain't eating. I don't think she's sleeping."

"Well, that's terrible, Billy Jim. But, well, what are you going to do? You can't coddle her. As harsh as this is probably going to sound, she needs to pick herself up by her bootstraps and dust herself off and get back to the real world."

"It... it ain't like that!"

"Well, sure it is. When folks got troubles in life, things

knocking them down, they got to get back up again. I know what happened to her was terrible and everything, but she needs to get over it."

"You going to take the guns or not?"

A few minutes later, he was packing my guns into his car. He had a wide grin on his face, like he done won a bag full of prizes at the county fair.

"Don't look so happy," I said. "I'm just getting rid of them for now. I'm going to get them back eventually."

At least that's what I told myself. Truth is, I got rid of those guns for Jill, but as you probably know by now, I got rid of those guns on account of me too. That's why I couldn't just lock them up. Because the way I been feeling these past few days, I felt like those guns was a-calling me, like they was waving me over to them. They was offering me permanent solution for all the misery I'd been feeling, and I really didn't know how much longer I could say no.

Jill came back home on Sunday night. Beth dropped her off at the curb then drove away once she was inside. I closed my laptop as she walked in, but she didn't seem to notice. She mumbled a few words as she passed me and went into her room and locked the door. I didn't see her the rest of the night.

Chapter 10

So right around the end of the Thanksgiving holiday, I
started reading up on the ballet and watching a bunch of
stuff on the internet. That's what I was doing when Jill
walked in. I couldn't tell you why I suddenly got interested, but I was. This is kind of tough because I don't really
understand it but let me try and explain.

I been doing the same things all of my life and I come
to realize that I'm sick to death of everything. My life has
come down to a pattern of Work TV Work TV Work TV
with the occasional hunting and fishing trip thrown in to
break up the monotony. And I'm just sick of it. There's
never nothing new. I been hunting and fishing hundreds
of times and there ain't nothing exciting about it no more.
It all just bores hell out of me. *Life* bores hell out of me.
I am honestly by-god tired of all of it and I don't care
nothing about none of it. Following politics is a waste of
time. Politicians are professional liars that are only in it for
themselves. Getting all worked up about what those knuck-
leheads in Washington do is bad for my blood pressure, and
I can't change what they do. Sports used to be interesting
when I was a cub, but that was when athletes was part of

the community they played in. Now they just a bunch of millionaires crashing into each other, hopping from one paycheck to the next. They don't care about the sport, they care about the money. Up until the time the ballplayers cancelled the World Series I was a big Texas Rangers fan. And then I thought, to heck with them. If they don't care about the game, why should I?

Yeah. All that.

So I started looking up stuff on the internet about ballet. When I started, I told myself I was doing it so's I could get to know something about Jill, but is that really it? Maybe it was because I liked *The Nutcracker* and I was curious about it. The way I been feeling lately, it's nice to be curious about anything to get my mind off stuff. Whatever the reason, I started reading about the ballet and what I found out was pretty interesting.

It don't seem like it much, but ballet is really a melancholy sport. It's really beautiful, but it's really dark and sad too. A lot of the most famous ballet dancers had these really sad and tragic lives.

Take Nijinsky for instance. This fella is one of the most famous ballet dancers in history. It was said his leaps and pirouettes and suchlike was so unbelievable that folks rioted at his shows (by the way, guys, just so you know, a "pirouette" is when you spin around on one foot; it's really hard, and it'll make you real dizzy). This dude was probably the best of all time, but then right around the time he hit twenty-eight he started acting all weird, and the docs said he'd developed schizophrenia, and he spent the next thirty years going in and out of asylums. Then he died.

Then there's this fella Tchaikovsky. This guy wrote the music to the ballets that folks do every year, namely *The Nutcracker* and *Swan Lake*. In his time he was famous as all get-out, one of the most famous composers of his day, but he couldn't make a living at what he was doing. He had to rely on patronage from the Tzar, that's what they used to call the head honcho in Russia before they turned commie, and this gal named Nadia van Meck, a widow whose husband left her a couple of railroads and a pile of money so wide you couldn't throw a cow chip across it. But can you imagine writing something like *The Nutcracker* and having to live on money somebody else gifted you? It'd be like Willie Nelson getting chump change from some Rockefeller, and liking it, or else having to head back to Luckenbach and live in a trailer. Tchaikovsky died of cholera, which is a miserable death, and some folks think it might have been suicide because he was depressed all the time.

Another one's this French gal named Emma Livry. She started dancing professionally in 1858 when she was just 16, Jill's age. She was another gifted dancer, famous for her ballon. No, not balloon, though ballon comes from the word balloon. A "ballon" is when you jump and it looks like you're suspended in mid-air, like a balloon, and it looks like you're breaking the laws of physics. Emma Livry was all kind of famous for this. Folks said she moved like a hummingbird skimming over flowers, and when she fell to the earth it was soft and slow, like a snowflake. This poor kid was in a rehearsal for this show called *The Mute Girl of Portici,* and she shook out her skirt too close to a gaslight and it caught on fire. Then her dress went up in flame, and near her whole body was burnt, except for her face and breasts. Her mentor, this gal named Marie Taglioni, who is one of most famous ballet dancers of all time, saw the whole thing, and she rubbed greasepaint on her wounds thinking that this would act as some kind of sav, but it didn't, it only made things worse. Emma Livry died of sepsis eight months later.

The list goes on and on. I'm sure you heard about this dude Sergei Filin, he was all in the news not too long ago. He's the big cheese of this place called the Bolshoi, which from what I can tell is full of crazy people, though he seems like a pretty likeable fella. So one of his dancers out there, this nut job named Pavel something-or-other, didn't like Filin's casting choice so he hired this Moscow thug to beat him up, only the guy threw acid in his face instead and now this Filin dude is pretty near blind! Can you imagine? Getting acid thrown in your face and losing most of your eyesight because you didn't cast some psycho dancer's girlfriend? Guy works hard all his life to be the best she can be and some scumbag come along and takes it all away from him. It's just wrong is what it is, and a damn shame.

Now you might know the name Margot Fonteyn. She was one of most famous ballerinas of the twentieth century, but did you know she was arrested for running guns to Panama? She was married to this Panamanian playboy who was trying to stage a military coup, and old Margot was in on the plot, but she got arrested and the plot kind of petered out. Well, guess what happened to her? When she was old and couldn't dance no more, she was diagnosed with cancer and spent three painful years struggling with it, and then she died broke and alone and ended up being buried in a potter's field. Her dance partner was this dude named Rudolph Nureyev, this Russian fella, this Russkie, and let me tell you what, he was famous, like the most famous dancer of his time. Well sir, he died of AIDS. And I didn't know much about the AIDS until I read about it. It just ain't no way to go. It's worse than the cholera. Extremely cruel is what it is.

There are a lot of tragic stories about ballet folks. Depression, suicide, insanity, early death, anorexia, mutilation, decay. I don't know if there's more sadness and tragedy in that profession than the rest of the population, but it sure seems so.

Then you look at all these young kids, and they all got stars in their eyes, and these hopes and dreams, and you think, well, what's the use being a kid if you can't dream a little? Like I used to dream of Dee Dee.

Lots of dancers have their own internet TV channels, and they post videos of themselves talking about their lives and what they want to accomplish. You can see them on YouTube interviewing themselves, like Jill was doing in her bedroom that time. The thing I realized about these young mostly gals is that the reason they do it is because they want to perform. These gals live to perform. They work so hard, sometimes hours and hours a week, like Jill used to. And the payoff to it all is doing it in front of people. They don't do it for health or exercise or because they can. They do it because they're good at it and they want the world to know it too. They want to be appreciated. They want folks to look at them and say, "Wow, I can't believe you just did that."

There's also the storytelling part of it too, though I can't really say I understand it much. These young kids want to tell stories with their bodies, and I really can't tell you much how it's done. I watch the ballets on the internet and I have to look up a synopsis to know what's really going on. But the more I watch them the clearer they get. I can understand why a girl or woman or a man for that matter would want to tell a story, can't you? These folks just do it with their muscles and bones.

Watching these kids on the net, it's funny and a little bit sad too to hear them talk. Lot of them see ballet as a career they plan on doing "for the rest of their lives," but from what you read most dancers have to retire in their thirties. Some gals can last into their forties, but most don't. The thing is, these young folks don't realize that being a dancer is something that only takes up half a lifetime. If you retire when you're thirty-five, you still got half a life to live. And what are they going to do with the second half? Look through a scrapbook? I suppose you could teach, but does ballet really need that many teachers?

So I started getting interested in ballet but don't really know why, even now. Maybe it's because of the sadness. Or maybe it's because I identify with the work ethic.

In ballet you can't be successful without the work. If you don't work, you don't succeed. Period. Nobody is going to give you a job in ballet because of your looks. You have to have the ability. And the ability comes from years of hard work and struggle. There are no handouts in ballet. A girl might be so beautiful she might look like an archangel's better-looking sister, but if she can't point her foot the right way then she can't be a ballerina. I heard somebody talking about it on the net, I think it was this old gal named Martha Graham, and it made a lot of sense to me. Ballet dancers are realists. Either the foot is pointed or it ain't. Wishing don't make it so. And that appeals to my conservative values.

These days kids roll out of bed and expect to be famous. A guy who sings in the shower expects to sell out the Alamodome. Or a gal who acts in her high school play expects to go to Hollywood and star in movies after a week of being there. Or these kids who think they're so great that camera crews ought to follow them around and show every part of their lives even though they don't got nothing that makes them interesting. They got no talent and they got no ability but they demand attention and they expect success.

Ballet ain't like that. Ballet is training. It's work. It's competition. And even after years and years of perfection, and being the best you can be, you can still fail. And that's like life.

I did not tell Jill I went to the ballet because I knew she would ridicule me, so I kept it to myself. I had to be sneaky about this whole thing. I'd be setting out on the couch watching these videos or reading about ballet on the net, and Jill would walk in and I'd close my laptop because I didn't want her to see what I was doing, and she'd kind of look at me all suspicious-like but she didn't say nothing. Then when she went into the next room I'd open her up again and keep reading.

I went out fishing with Ed the Sunday after Christmas and Jill stayed with her mom. I sat in the boat and listened to Ed go on and on about the government and how much he hated it and how the liberal politicians was all trying to take our freedom away, how the government was coming for our guns and if they take our guns away how can he protect his wife when some dude breaks a window and comes into his house. I sat in the boat and listened to him and I thought, "He sounds like one of those homeless guys you see on the street talking to himself." Crazy. But mostly scared, which is something I understand completely. What I wanted to say was, "You sound like a child who's afraid of monsters under the bed. Yeah, there are bad guys out there but having a gun don't necessarily mean you're going to stop them. The bad guy could even be you. Or could be in you," as I knew it could be because the bad guy is in me sometimes. But I didn't say nothing.

I used to love the outdoors, going fishing and hunting, or just being outside in the trees and the clean air. But there wasn't no joy in it now. Things got so bad that day with Ed, listening to his talk and feeling all ground down, that I couldn't remember what year it was. I tried and tried, but it just wouldn't come to me. Something so simple.

And so it was on that first Saturday after New Year's that I found myself standing outside Jill's door.

I been going back and forth on this all morning and I'm not sure this is a real good idea. I can understand reading stuff on the internet and buying a ticket and going to a thing. Sort of. But that's different from something that puts you in front of people, and makes you actually have to show up some place at a certain time to do whatnot in front of a group of people. It's much easier to sit on the couch and just drink beer and look stuff up on the internet. This other thing, you run the risk of folks laughing at you and all.

Yeah, but there'll be lots of women.

Yeah, but none of them's going to be interested in you. True. So don't kid yourself. Right...

What'll my buddies say? What are they going to think of me?

Who? What buddies? I got internet friends. I'm in touch with people but I ain't close to none. Who would possibly care?

Who would know? Right...

Okay. I'm doing it. For the love of Pete, something's got to give. Getting rid of the guns didn't do it. I may as well have been getting rid of vacuum cleaner attachments. Maybe I'll go this one time and if it's stupid or whatever I'll do something else, but I've got to try something.

But will it even work?

It could... This thing though...

Okay, the only thing that will keep me from going is if Jill'll leave the house. Jill's the coin toss. Heads, she agrees to go out and do something like, I don't know, get ice cream or go to a movie or something; and tails, she don't, she stays in her room.

So I knocked on her door and she opened up a crack and poked her face out but she wouldn't look at me. She never seemed to look me in the eye anymore.

"You want to take a drive with me? Get some ice cream, or..."

"No."

"What are you going to do all day?"

"I've got a physics test on Monday."

Jill is really good at science. When she was younger I hoped she would get into science more than ballet, but she didn't. Now she ain't really into neither.

"Why don't you come with me?"

"No."

"Come on. We never get a chance to do much."

"I'm busy. I got to study for my test."

"Well, okay. I'm going to work later. I'll be home around 7:00."

And that was that. She shut the door. I put on my sweat clothes and left.

I was hoping she'd come out with me so I wouldn't have to go through with this. I got in my truck and headed to Jill's school, the City Ballet Institute. At times it was like I was having an out of my body experience, watching myself from above. This is just wrong, and I knew it. But it's also desperate times, being what they is.

I just wish I knew what this was actually supposed to accomplish, what it was actually supposed to do.

I pulled into the parking lot and sat there for a minute. It was 9:55, almost time to start. I got out of my truck and walked to the front door, feeling more than a bit foolish.

This is a mistake! Clearly! This is wrong! Stop right now and get back in your truck and go to work. You have to work today! Go!

I *do* have to work today, but Poodie has keys and he'll open the shop. I'll be at work before lunch.

This is wrong this is wrong this is *wrong!* Everybody is going to laugh at you!

I stepped into the building and up to the reception desk. It was a different girl behind the counter now.

"Can I help you?"

"I'm here to sign up for the ballet for old folks class."

"We have an adult beginners class."

"Yeah, that's the one."

I filled out some papers and gave them my debit card and the whole thing was done in a minute.

"The adult beginners class is in studio A, down the hall on the left."

"Okay."

As I was walking down the hall, Inez Garza stepped out of another studio.

"Hey, look who's here."

"Yeah, I'm here to try out your old folks class."

"It's not an old folks class, it's an adult beginners class. Glad you could make it. How's Jill?"

"About the same."

"She never called me."

"I know. I've been trying to get her to, but she won't."

"What can we do?"

"I haven't asked her in a while. I'll mention again you want to talk to her. That be all right?"

"Please do."

I motioned to the studio. "You going in?"

"I don't teach that class. Ricardo Rodriguez does."

"Oh. Okay."

Well, that's a fine thing. I sign up for a ballet class and don't get the teacher I want. Ain't that just great. We said our goodbyes and I headed in.

I noticed that everyone had on dance shoes and I was wearing work boots, so I took them off and left them by the door. The class was in this really huge room with mirrors all over the place and little exercise bars what look like handrails set up all over. This handrail thing is called a "barre," I come to find out. Everybody was standing at one, so I did too. They all looked at me when I came in, then turned away. They was all warming up, stretching and such like. I looked at myself in the mirror, at that durn mustache hanging off my lip like a mutant caterpillar. Wish I could shave it off. One of these days, maybe, one of these days.

I was the only non-female in class, except for the teacher. Ricardo Rodriguez was just a kid, and looked to be still in high school. Turns out he was, but he was also a student at the academy full time, taking advanced classes. He told us all about what he'd been up to, that he'd competed at YAGP in New York the week before but was not offered a scholarship. He said he was hoping to try again next year, that it would be his last time. He was also applying to UT Austin and a couple other universities for the fall semester just in case it didn't work out. I spect this kid's just a couple years older than Jill.

He had us introduce ourselves and then told us about the class. The class was actually two hours, which I found really hard to believe. How am I going to do this? I'm not even sure I can stand up for two hours!

He said the goal was to get to performance level, and that we were shooting to do six to eight performances this year at nursing homes and schools. Performances? He's got to be kidding. I'm not doing any performances. That's Jill's thing, not mine.

Since this was a class for beginners, and this was our first class, we went over feet positions, first through fifth. Then we went through arms positions, one through five. Then the demi plié and the grande plié ("grande" is pronounced GRON, not like the Mexicans do it, which is GRAN-de, and "plié" is pronounced PLEE-yay, not PLY).

It wasn't too hard, but I was a little freaked out about trying. The demi plié just means you bend your knees and keep your heels on the floor, so you go down about halfway, but the grande plié goes a lot lower, and your heels come up off the floor.

First time I did this, I just knew folks was going to be looking at me and laughing. But that didn't happen because on our first demi plié, everybody's knees went crack!, which caused some folks to chuckle, and then when we did our grande plié, all the knees and ankles in the room went *snap! crackle! pop!* and the room sounded like a big bowl of Rice

Krispies, which was really pretty funny. So yeah, nobody in class paid much mind to me. They was all too busy looking at themselves and working on what they were doing to care about the fat guy.

Ricardo corrected folks, and when he did he was really nice about it. He wasn't sarcastic at all, just kind of cheerful. "Marie, a little lower." "April, turn out your feet a little more. Good!" Then he came to me and watched me grande plié, and I thought he was going to say something but he patted me on the shoulder and smiled and said, "Good, Billy Jim." It was impressive to me that he remembered everybody's name.

As the class continued, and folks got a little less self-conscious, there was smiles and nods and encouragement all around, but I didn't say nothing to nobody, I just looked at the floor mostly. In that first class, we also learned a "releve" (which is pronounced ruh-luh-VAY, dang Frenchies) and the "saute," which sounds like SO-tay and doesn't have anything to do with sauce, but is actually jumping and landing on your two feet.

They had some guy playing piano throughout, and he was pretty funny because he would go into a boogie-woogie at times just for laughs.

We took breaks, and a couple of students came up to talk to me. I'm sure I looked like a real dunderhead because I had absolutely nothing to say. But it was nice. Folks was actually talking to me. Women folk especially.

Don't get the wrong idea. They was just being nice, they wasn't looking at me like I was potential husband material. This dance class is the last place you'd go to try and impress people with your looks. Everybody is dressed in sweat clothes or tights and sweating like pigs. And not just me. Everybody, except for Ricardo.

Class ended, and there was a few people going to lunch, but I had to go to work. As I was putting my boots on, Ricardo came up and gave me an address and phone number of a place called Dorothy's Dance Shop on Huebner Road, said I needed to pick up a pair of men's dance shoes before the next class.

On Monday I headed out to Dorothy's during lunch. The place wasn't very big, and it seemed to be crammed to the ceiling with pink and glitter. I asked the clerk, this woman in her 30s, for a size-12 men's ballet shoe and she didn't look at me like I was crazy. They didn't have much of a selection, which is no surprise, but I found a pair of black Capezios, and they looked all right, so I bought them.

Then as I was heading out the door, I noticed there was a stand-alone wooden barre, the handrail thing, like the kind we used in class. I made a mental note. Maybe I should buy one for Jill. Maybe if I did, and brought it home, she'd start her ballet again. Wasn't sure though. But I knew I had to do something.

New Year's came and went. Jill did not go to the YAGP regionals in Chicago. She would not be going to YAGP at all this year. That dream was now officially dead, at least for the time being. She could possibly go next year, but it was looking less and less likely. When she got back home that Thanksgiving weekend I asked her if she wanted to go to *The Nutcracker* but she said no. As the weeks passed, it became pretty clear that she wasn't much interested in dance, or anything else that makes up living and breathing.

I called the cop assigned to Jill's case for any news or updates but she never had nothing and she told me she would call me when she did. She told me she needed a break in the case, most likely a witness coming forward. I called her once a week, but in January I started calling her less and in February I think I called her once. Then stopped.

Me and Jill's mom talked about the education situation and decided it would be best for her to change schools. Jill was all for it, so she transferred to Providence High School, a Catholic school for girls, and started classes at the beginning of January.

Poor Jilly. She weren't really happy about nothing. There was a sorrow in her pretty face that she had even when she was smiling. Which was close to never.

I told her — again — that Inez Garza wanted to talk to her, but Jill wouldn't call her. I asked her what the kids were like at her new school, but she didn't know. Nobody spoke to her much, and she didn't speak to nobody. I asked her how her day went. "Fine," was the answer I got. Always "fine." Then silence.

One Sunday in February I went out to The Hill to see my dad. I'd seen him a few times since Christmas but he was in fine form this day, angry as a vegetarian hoot owl. One of his retired friends had sent him an email and he couldn't stop talking about it.

"It's the biggest scam in the *history of the world* and the scientists are in on it because there is a ton of money to be made. How is it possible that climate scientists make more money than Wall Street bankers? It's because the Democrat Party is *stuffing the bank accounts* of these liars with *our tax dollars.*"

"Dad..."

"The Democrat Party gets political contributions from *anti-business environmentalists* and then they give out billions to these rich fat cats in the form of research grants. *Research grants!* Get that? Our tax dollars is being spent on *research* to support *lies* that hurt *American business!* And if that ain't bad enough, they funding *foreign* scientists! Our tax dollars is being shipped off to *Iceland* and *Sweden!* It's all part of the Democrat plan to make us a *socialist nanny state!*"

"Dad..."

"You mark my words, boy, there's going to be a

revolution soon. There is going to be blood in the streets! The Democrat Party is—"

"Dad!"

"What!?"

"Dad."

"What?"

"I understand why you follow politics. I do. I do too. Or at least I used to. And I understand how following what goes on in Washington is like following a soap opera, one that changes every day, and it's got heroes and villains, the black hats and the white hats. I understand it. Really, I do. But you got to stop getting so worked up about it. You can't do nothing about it anyway, except vote. So why dwell on it?"

"But the Democrat—"

"I want to talk about something else."

"But they—"

"Dad!"

"What?"

"I said I want to talk about something else. Talking politics bores me. And it's bad for my heart. Talking politics too much clogs your arteries, in case you ain't up on the latest medical reports."

"Okay. Well. Hmm... All right."

"Good."

"Well... What do you want talk about?"

"I don't know. I don't actually have a subject. What do you want to talk about?"

"I *was* talking."

"Let's talk about something else. Like fishing."

"Fishing?"

"Sure. You used to love to go fishing."

"Me and you and Ed used to go to Medina Lake."

"I remember."

"Those were some good times."

"You must got lots of stories about fishing in Medina Lake."

"Stories? I don't know. Maybe. Yeah?" He started thinking about it, and after a time I saw him getting that dreamy look in his eye and I saw his mind go back there. Which is what I was hoping.

"One time," he said, "we were coming back from that place we always stayed at. We'd been up the lake, and we fished, and we'd caught a couple bass, nothing to brag about. And I was just trolling along. You know, you don't go very fast with a five-horsepower motor, and I was running about half speed. And I was trolling, laying bait out behind the motor. When all of the sudden up ahead I saw one laying on its side, floating. So I went over by that fish, and it was a big old bass. And I picked it up, and it had a perch, it had grabbed a big sun fish about four inches long, and he couldn't swallow it, the old sun perch had raised his dorsal fin up, he stuck it in the top of the fish's mouth, and his tail was caught one way and his head the other in the gill work and the bass couldn't get rid of it. And he rushed through the water so fast trying to shake it off that he drownded himself. And when I picked him up the perch was still alive but the old bass was dead. But he wasn't stiff yet, so into the ice box he went." Then he laughed, hahaha, the first time I'd heard him laugh in a long time.

"Oh yeah, take the perch along with it," I said.

"I'd like to go up to Medina Lake and go fishing again. That was a good lake. I liked it. Had a lot of cover for bass. Had some huge catfish in it."

"When did you start going to Medina Lake?"

"When I was a boy. My dad took me."

"You don't talk about him much. Were ya'll close?"

"My dad was a hard man to get to know."

"Apple don't fall far from the tree."

"Maybe. Your grandfather was a complex man. He was

married before he met my mother. Did you know that?"

"No." This was news. I'd never heard this. My father never talked about family. Ever.

"Well, he was."

"You never told me that."

"Never came up in conversation."

"Who was she?"

"Yeah. My father had been married previously. But the marriage didn't last, and she run off on him. And he never saw here again. As I recall, they were on the way to Montana and they pulled into a train stop and she got off the train, and the train pulled out and she wasn't on it. That was the last he ever saw of her. Of course, he didn't get off the train and look for her. He was heading to Montana."

"So Grandpa got a divorce."

"Don't know if he ever did. Things was different back then. I spect he did."

"She must have been real desperate to get off a train in the middle of nowhere with none of her possessions."

"You can take that couple of ways. Either she couldn't take living with him, because of the way he was. Or maybe she loved another man somewhere. Who knows why? I don't. But after he died, I found some love letters he'd written to my mother. Your grandmother. He loved her so deeply. That's one thing I know for certain."

"Why didn't you tell me he was divorced?"

"What? Uh... Well, it never came up."

"All this time I thought I was the first one to get divorced in the family, and it turns out I'm not."

"What about me? I got divorced."

"Your second wife don't count."

"What's it matter anyway? Divorce is bad, but it ain't the worst. Not even close."

"Bad enough."

"You really ought to be writing all this stuff I'm saying

down. You was always good with telling stories."

"What?"

"Sure. Then you can tell it to folks later."

"So if divorce ain't the worst, what is?"

"Well. My dad worked for the government. He worked at Swift and Company in Fort Worth. I think that was his first connection to the government job. He ended up being in the Bureau of Animal Industries, I guess you would call it. He worked with the Blackfoot up north. The Indian. The Blackfoot Indian. The Sioux. The Crow. And the Navaho. He worked with all four of those tribes on a program that the government was trying to enforce. The dipping of the cattle to get rid of the spotted tick fever. If you got bit by a tick you was lucky if you didn't get tick fever. And so they was dipping these Indians' cattle, and they had built dipping vats, and they would run those cattle through there, and Dad would make a count on them, and keep books on them so to speak. And he'd go to another tribe and he'd do it again somewhere else, you know, all across Montana.

"When Dad came back off the range to where he and his new wife, our mother, was living, and I don't know how old she was at that time, but they ended up at a cabin somewhere during a blizzard in Montana and they was snowed in. And she had a miscarriage. And it was pretty darned cold there in Montana. They didn't have any heating facilities that you have today. Oil heaters and that kind of stuff. But anyway, she told him she'd had a miscarriage. And he said, 'What happened to the baby?' And she said 'It's out on the back porch.' And he went out and saw it... it was a-laying on the box out there. Frozen solid as a rock. She didn't even have a chance to take care of it. And it sat out there for I don't know how long. And they couldn't leave the cabin because they was trapped. So they sat in that cabin, with the baby frozen on the back porch, for days and days and days.

"So divorce ain't the worst thing, son. No sir."

Chapter 11

A couple of months passed and it got into March. Jill still wasn't talking to me except for the odd "yes" or "no," whenever she answered my questions. "You hungry?" "No." You want to eat?" "No." "You finish your homework?" "Yes."

I continued with the old folks class. It turns out Ricardo was teaching classes on Tuesday and Thursday nights too, adult classes not strictly for beginners, so I decided to take class on both nights. I didn't have nothing else to do, really, and some of the students were in our Saturday class too. I was getting along really well with these folks, and started to get to know them pretty well.

So one Saturday after class, I had a thought. You know, I could go back to Dorothy's Dance Shop and pick up that barre. Jill would use it. She'd start her lessons again. I just know she would. Yeah. I'll get it for her. I'd also been watching all kinds of videos on YouTube by then, and they got lots of exercise and ballet class videos so maybe I could use it from time to time when she wasn't home. Wouldn't hurt to see how much it cost anyway.

I drove to Dorothy's and the same gal was working as

last time I was there. I pointed to what I wanted and asked her, "How much for the barre?" She looked it up, and a 12-foot barre was $385 for the oak and $173 for the poplar. I didn't need the Cadillac, so I took the Chevy. I helped them load the box into my truck and put it together in my study when I got home.

The thing about the barre is, I was going to put it together in the living room, but when I thought about it, I wasn't sure what Jill would say. I hadn't actually told her about my hobby yet. And I didn't want to just put it in her room because that'd be too obvious. So I hauled it into my study and set it up in there. My plan was to cover it up with a sheet and keep the door locked. This was going to be my little secret until I got ready to tell her.

I got the internet going, this really hot teacher going through the paces with some Carter Burwell. In case you don't know it, Carter Burwell is the dude what wrote all the music for those teenage werewolf movies. And I was in my sweats. So I decided to try it out.

We started out doing warm-ups, and I was counting along, five, six, seven, eight. Then she went into the arabesque. "Put your left hand on the barre. And plié. Chasse. Transfer to attitude. Keep both thighs pulled up. And lift. Stretch the legs. And digasche. And close. It has to roll forward in the socket, forward in the socket, like that. Again, and plié. Transfer to attitude. Keep both thighs pulled up. And lift. Stretch the legs. And digasche. And close. Good."

Then Jill walked in.

I couldn't believe it. This was supposed to be my secret and she found out five minutes after I started practicing!

The look on her face started at confusion, then went directly to bewilderment and ended up at anger. I closed my laptop and the music and the hottie stopped. I reached down and picked up the bedsheet...

"What are you doing?"

... and threw it over the barre.

"What are you doing?"

I didn't answer her. I couldn't even look at her.

"Where did you get that?"

"Dorothy's Dance Shop."

"Why?"

"Why do you think?" I suddenly got really flustered. I hate being questioned.

She was mad now. "I don't know what to think. What is this?"

"What?"

"You heard me. What is this?"

"I don't understand the question."

"Every time I walk into the living room, and you're on your laptop and you close it."

"That's right."

"Why?"

"I'm looking at something I don't want you to see."

"What?"

"If I wanted you to see it—"

"Pervert!"

"What?"

"You into little girls? You into 15-year-olds?"

"What? No!"

"Is that it? You want to fuck my friends?"

"Jill! Don't talk that way!"

"Don't shout at me!"

"Don't use that kind of language!"

"You're an old pervert and you're telling me not to use bad language? I'm calling mom. I have to get out of here. You're a... You're a..."

"You're scared."

"I'm not scared. I'm a little sad."

"You really want to know what all this is about?"

"No."

"I'm stepping back. I'm holding up my hands."

"I'm not afraid of you!"

"Now I want you to pick up my computer, and I want you to take it into your bedroom and I want you to lock the door and I want you to look at my internet history. I want you to take a look at what your father's been watching."

"No."

"I want you to. Because I think you'll find it really shocking."

"I just want to be normal."

"Did you go to the counselor?"

"No."

"Then how do you spect to get right? How do you spect to be normal again?"

"Don't give me advice."

"Take the computer."

"No way."

"Take the computer. And if you find something incriminating or illegal or perverted, call the law."

"I'm not touching your computer."

"Go ahead."

"No."

But then she did. She walked to the laptop and opened it. The hot dance instructor's voice came up, and she clicked off the webpage. She looked up at me, like she wasn't sure she should take her eyes off me, and I took another step back. She looked back down at the computer, and hit the history toolbar. Her eyes focused. She scrolled through my browsing history. And after about a minute, she stopped.

"What is this?"

"You asked me that already. What you want me to say?"

"Just tell me what it is."

What the hell. How do you explain it?

"When you were over at John Lancey's on Thanksgiving, I sent you a text message and I asked you what you wanted me to do with *The Nutcracker* tickets your mom bought you for Christmas."

"Yeah..."

"And you never got back to me. So I went down to the Convention Center to exchange them. But I didn't exchange them. I went. I watched it, *The Nutcracker*. And I thought it was really... okay.... So... You know... I started learning a little bit more about it. You know, reading about it. Watching videos."

"Uh-huh."

"And so I started... taking... ballet class."

There was a long pause while this sunk in. And then she did the thing that I'd been dreading. I knew she was going to do this, and I was hoping that maybe with her liberal ways she'd be nice to me or be understanding but she wasn't. She did just what I expected her to do. She laughed. No, I take that back. She didn't laugh. She bellowed, and her whooping guffaw boomed around my study. I felt my cheeks flush. And as ridiculous as you can imagine.

"You what?" she said, a grin jumping around on her lips.

"At your dance studio. I'm studying with this fella named Ricardo Rodriguez."

"You're taking ballet class with Ricardo?"

"Yes."

"You. You're taking ballet?"

"Yes. They got a class for old folks. It's an adult beginners class. Um, yeah, I like it. Everybody's real nice. Ricardo's teaching it."

She suddenly got very serious. "I hope you're not taking that class because of me."

"I'm not."

"Good. Because I'm not doing ballet anymore."

"So what are you going to do then? If not ballet?"

"I don't know. I don't care."

"So you're just going to throw it away? All the studying? All the hard work and effort you done put in to the thing?"

"Why do you like ballet?"

"I, uh... I didn't say I like it... I..."

"Do you like it because it's beautiful?

"I don't know, I—"

"It's not beautiful. Nothing is beautiful."

"Look, it—"

"It's ugly. Everything is ugly. And you're a freak."

"Are you ashamed of me?"

"Yes."

"You're ashamed of your father."

"Yes. Look at you."

"I'm ashamed too. I should take this barre out in back and split it with my axe and burn it. Because you've seen it. You've seen me."

She gave her head a little shake and then turned and walked out. I heard her go back to her room and close the door.

She thinks I'm a freak. I figured that. She confirmed it. She's ashamed of me. I knew she would be. She confirmed that too. There wasn't any reason to hide anything now.

I opened my laptop, found the website with the hot dance instructor and continued what I was doing. To hell with her.

On Thursday I went to my class. It was pretty rough. I didn't really feel like going, but I went anyway. I couldn't concentrate. Couldn't follow very well.

During a break one of the other students came up to me. Her name is Larisa Lakewood. Larisa is about fifty,

I'd say. Very fit. Very pretty. Why she decided to come talk to me was a big mystery.

"Hey, you burn a lot of calories in ballet class? You keep exercising like that and you're going to lose that gut."

"I wish."

"You'll do her, I'm sure. When pigs fly."

"You know what I like about you, Larisa?"

"Nothing?"

"You're a real nice gal."

"Why thank you, Billy Jim."

"You're going to make somebody a great second or third wife."

"And you'll make a great husband. All you got to do is find somebody who likes a guy with a diving board for a stomach."

"And all you got to do is find somebody who likes a gal with a really large head."

The smile went out of her face right quick after that. Larisa looked like I'd slapped her. You could see the tears starting to well up in her eyes. I regretted hell out of saying it but felt no need to apologize. You know the old saying: if you can't take getting hit in the face, don't box.

"That was a mean thing to say."

"You was the one who started with the fat jokes. I was just minding my own business."

"I was joking."

"So was I."

This was not going the way I wanted it to. I really didn't mean to knock this woman down. Larisa didn't really have a large head. Well, it was a little large, but not so's you'd notice much. I thought I'd make another joke, just to see if we could somehow put the steamroller to this road and smooth things over.

"You know who else liked fat jokes? Hitler."

But that didn't work. She had no idea what I was

saying at all. Explaining just messed it up more.

"That's what I say to the libtards on the internet when I'm trying to win an argument. Or end a conversation."

"Libtards?"

"You know. Liberals."

"Libtards? Oh my." She was angry now. "Do you know how insulting that is?"

"I imagine it's insulting if you're a libtard."

"Libtard is a combination of the words 'liberal' and 'retarded.'"

"You figured that out, so I guess you're not retarded."

"Have you ever known anybody with a mentally handicapped family member?"

"Oh, here we go."

"How do you think it makes them feel when they hear folks using the word 'retarded'?"

"Well, using the word 'libmentally-challenged' just ain't as catchy as 'libtard.' Or as easy to say."

I noticed that Ricardo was looking at us. He clapped his hands and headed to the front and we started class again.

Afterwards, Ricardo asked if I wanted to go for a bite, which I didn't but I went anyway. We went to the Jim's across the street. I ordered a cheeseburger; he ordered the salad.

Ricardo's the dude. He told me some stuff about himself as we was waiting on our food, and I got to know him a little better over the next few weeks. He's from the west side, and not the Ingram Park Mall west side out by 1604, he's from the inner city west side, just off downtown. His family lives in a two-bedroom house on Nueces, about three blocks from Guadalupe Street. His folks sleep in one bedroom and his grandmother and older sister in the other, so he and his younger brother sleep in the living room on the couch and a rollaway cot. That's what's

normal for everybody he knows, pretty much. His dad is a
working class stiff, like me. He used to work at Kelly Field
and reupholstered planes and did whatever odd stuff his
supes asked him to do, and when the base closed down he
got a job as a doorman at the Saint Anthony Hotel where
he still works today.

Ricardo started taking dance lessons at the community center on Guadalupe and Brazos when he was a boy.
The community center is a long building, just one bare
room with a wooden floor and a water fountain, right
in the heart of the ghetto. Guadalupe Street is a rough
area known for its cantinas, and the prostitutes and drug
addicts and alcoholics that roam around the place. Getting
to his lessons was sometimes a challenge, depending on
where he was at the time. He had to walk everywhere he
went, naturally, but it's different in the barrio. Every third
or fourth block there is a new group of amigos, or chukos,
so if he wanted to get from point A to point B, and he had
to walk through them, he either had to run, throw down
and go chingasos, or hopefully he knew enough people
where he could just say "hi, how's it going?" and just shoot
the breeze a few seconds and be on his way. Because if
they didn't know him and he couldn't outrun them he was
getting an ass whupping. That was it.

His dance teacher at the community center was this
old Mexican lady everybody called Dinky. She taught folk-
lorico mostly, but some tap and ballet here and there, and
she taught for free. She was in her 70s by the time Ricardo
started taking classes with her. The dance classes were
mostly girls, so of course all the chukos would make fun
of the boy dancers and bully them. Dinky would always
have to walk them out of the community center and down
the street so they could get a running start before the chukos started whacking on their asses.

She saw talent in Ricardo, something that set him

apart from her other students, and after about a year of taking lessons, she made some calls to her friends and found a ballet school — City Ballet, where he teaches now — that would give him a scholarship. He was lucky, he said, because all he had to do for his scholarship was sweep and mop the floors and windex the mirrors. He moved in with a family, a white family, the first white people he'd ever seen other than teachers, and enrolled in ninth grade at North East School of the Arts and began ballet training five days a week. He couldn't sleep at first, he told me, being away from home. He missed the night train that used to pass near his window, its clickety-clackety echoing off the concrete overpass. It was soothing and helped him sleep, but he got used to being without it. And anyway, he heard it when he went home on weekends.

The waitress brought our grub. After a couple bites of salad, he leaned in, kind of nodded his head a little like he had something he wanted to say but didn't know how to start.

"You having a bad day?"

"Most of my days are bad days for some reason."

"Trouble at work?"

"Home."

"Oh." He signaled the waitress for more water. "What did you say to Larisa?"

"I said she had a big head. I probably shouldn't have. But she was going on and on about how fat I am."

"She likes you. Or at least she did. She was teasing you because she likes you."

"How do you know that?"

"I hear things."

"That's like grade school."

"That's why she was making jokes at your expense. Because she likes you."

"Well. I guess I blew that one. But she's one of these

121

politically correct folks, so it wouldn't have worked out. And anyway, I'm married."

"You're not wearing a ring."

"We're getting a divorce."

A boy I reckoned to be about three years old appeared at Ricardo's elbow. "Hospital is really boring," he said. Across the room, his mother called his name and he scampered back to their table.

Ricardo said, "We don't see a lot of guys like you."

"Yeah, I know."

"Wish we did."

"Freaks."

"You a freak?"

"Sure am."

"Are you Jill's dad?"

"Yeah."

"Your last name is Hauck. I figured you were her dad. She's been taking classes at City longer than me. We've had a bunch together."

"Oh, really."

"Her mom would always drop her off and pick her up till she got her car. I never saw you."

"I was pretty absent."

"And now you're here and she's not."

"Freaky."

"Not freaky, but..."

"Let me ask you a question," I said.

"Okay."

"Am I having a breakdown?"

"I — you don't look like it."

"Mid-life crisis then?"

"I don't know."

"But you think it's strange me being here."

"I didn't say it was strange. I think it's great. Like I said, I wish we could get more guys. Especially guys like you."

"Yeah, well..."

"Are you interested in ballet now because of Jill?"

"No."

"Have you ever been interested in the performing arts?"

"No."

"Then I'd say that's pretty special. It takes guts to put on your sweat clothes and come out here and jump around with the ladies. Just because you suddenly like it."

"Do you think it's gay?"

"Am I gay? I do it."

"I don't know. Are you?"

"What do you think?"

"I don't think you are."

"I'm not. And neither are you. And neither is ballet. It's just not something you see very often. A middle-aged man in a ballet class."

"I guess."

"My advice? Lay off the political talk."

"I don't like talking politics no more."

"And right or wrong, calling somebody 'retarded' is going to get some folks upset. You could make a lot of friends here. Maybe even find the next Mrs. Hauck. But you have to be sensitive to how people feel. Think about it. How would you like it if some guy called Jill a whore, but he didn't see anything wrong with it because that's what he calls all women?"

"I wouldn't like it. But sometimes folks is too sensitive."

We were quiet for a time. I went back and forth on this next bit because I didn't want rumors to start. But I was at the end of my rope.

"I'm having trouble... because... Jill went to a party back around Thanksgiving and somebody put a mickey in her drink and raped her while she was passed out."

"No... *no!*"

"That's why she's not here these days," I said. "That's why she's not studying."

"I get it... Damn..."

"She's going down some kind of spiral and I can't do nothing about it. She took ballet for five years, and she got to the point where she can go to the next level. Possibly even go pro."

"I know, she's really good."

"But she won't do it now. She quit. She's quit everything. Ballet. School. Her life. This thing has destroyed her. I've tried to get her to go to counseling. She won't go. She hardly leaves her bedroom, except to go to school. She won't talk to me. She won't talk to her mom. I don't know what is going to happen with her."

"What do you want her to do?"

"I want her to talk to somebody. I want her to get some counseling. I want her to start her life over again."

"I'll talk to her."

"You?"

"Sure. We go back a long way. Jill and I go back a long way. It might not do any good. But then again it might."

"When could you do it?"

"When do you want me to do it?"

"How about now?"

He got in his car and followed me home.

Jill wasn't home, strangely, and I didn't know where she was. We sat in the living room talking. Ricardo did one of those things that I always find funny, mainly because I do it myself. When you don't know what to say to a person, you make comments about the stuff in the room hanging on the walls. That's what he was doing, looking around at stuff and commenting. "Hey, this looks like Jill when she was ten. She was cute." "Hey, who's this? Is that you?" "Wow, that's a big deer. Those are some antlers."

About ten minutes later Jill came in through the front door. Ricardo stood up when she came in.

I said, "Where have you been?"

"I was getting chocolate."

"I thought you didn't go out at night."

"Am I your prisoner?"

"No."

Jill turned to Ricardo, he smiled at her.

"Hey Jill."

"Ricardo."

"What's going on? Haven't seen you in a while."

"Yeah..."

"I see your dad all the time. He's a student now."

"That's what he said."

"He's really good. Very diligent."

"Huh..."

"Where have you been? Everybody misses you."

"Yeah... I've just been, like, really busy."

There was this awkward silence. Jill looked away, then said:

"Listen, I've still got homework to finish. It was good to see you, Ricardo."

She started to walk back to her room. Ricardo followed her.

"I went to YAGP in Chicago."

"How'd it go?"

"I got a 95, and I went to New York but I didn't get any scholarships."

"You went to New York City? Cool."

"Yeah, but I was terrible. I fell, if you can believe it."

And just like that, they disappeared into her room.

The house was quiet for about a half hour. Then Jill and Ricardo came out of her room and went into the kitchen. I heard banging around in there, like somebody was getting a drink, then the back door opened and they went outside. They closed the door, and again, everything was quiet.

Being in San Antonio in March, you can do that. The temperature outside was about 80 degrees. Ain't really such a thing as spring.

So they was outside. Thirty minutes. Forty minutes. An hour.

After about an hour and a half, I went into the kitchen to get a drink. I looked out in the back yard, and Jill and Ricardo were sitting on a bench by the grill, facing towards the garage. Ricardo had his arm around her, and she was crying into his shoulder. I could see her whole body shaking, going up and down. I couldn't hear anything, and I didn't want to. I backed out of the kitchen and went back into the living room.

About an hour later, Jill and Ricardo came back in. She was smiling, but you could tell she'd been crying and she was still kind of sniffing. I stood up, they walked past me out to the front porch. They said goodnight to each other, and hugged each other, and then she came back in and went to her room and he headed out to his car. I went outside and met him just as he was getting behind the wheel.

"She's going to go to counseling," he said.

"Really?"

"Yeah. And she's going to start ballet again. But she's going to take adult ballet, so she's going to be in our class."

"But she's too young. She'll be in there with all the old geezers."

"I think it's just something she wants to do to get her feet wet. Maybe because I'm teaching it. I think that's probably the reason."

"How did you do it?"

"How did I do what?"

"How did you get her to agree to do all that? I've been trying to get her to do it for months. You come over here and talk to her for a couple of hours and now she's fixing to get counseling and start ballet class. How did you do it? What did you tell her?"

"Jill and I have a lot in common."

"Because of the ballet."

"We have a lot in common."

"Because you're both dancers."

"Because I was raped too."

I couldn't say nothing after that. I think I probably nodded and tapped the top of his car. Then he started the engine and drove away.

Chapter 12

Ballet originally came from France, you know. It all started with this Italian gal named Catherine de Medici, who was queen of France and the power behind the throne for twenty-some-odd years in the 1500s. Catherine decided she needed to calm down her Catholic and Protestant subjects, who was fighting each other in a religious war, so she started organizing these ballets at the court, and these ballets had messages of peace and all that, but that didn't stop her folks from killing each other because, you know, they was in a religious war. But she's the one what got the old ballet ball a-rolling and when then Louis the 14th come to power it really took off.

Louis, now, he was quite a dancer himself. He was called The Sun King, not sure why. Maybe he had a sunny disposition? Anyway, he would stage these elaborate dance shows, and I mean elaborate, cast of thousands with diamond studded costumes and the whole nine yards, and he was the star. Of course, everybody, meaning the peasants and the noble folks, they all loved his shows. I spect they had to, else they might be feeling a little drafty above the neck on account of French people liking to chop each other's heads off ever so often. But he also was probably really good at dancing too, old Louis. He come along about a hundred years after Catherine.

Anywho, in Louis's day, ballet was an activity for the upper crust, for the aristocrats, and was mostly done by the fellas. The women was only there to make googly eyes at them, to make sure folks knew how talented these upper-crusty guy dancers was. But then the French Revolution happened and folks stormed the Bastille, and suddenly the guy dancers was having tomatoes thrown at them because they was part of the aristocracy. Some years pass, the techniques change, and afore you know it, the women folk are the center of it all and the men are getting booed off stage. The women took over. Which is as it should be.

Here's why: ballet makes women look good. I never saw a ballet in the 17th Century, of course, but if I did, and it was all about the guys, I'm sorry, but it couldn't have been all that interesting. Because ballet is about what a woman can do physically. It's about flexing torsos and sweaty backs. It's about holding these unimaginably twisted positions and spinning like a top and sailing through the air. Men can do it too, but it's nowhere near as interesting.

Guys, if you're a hetero, and you love women, and you think the female form is beautiful, man you have got to get to the ballet. Call it sexist if you want to, I don't care. Ballet is beautiful because women are beautiful. Period.

So Jill and me went to her first class back on a Saturday morning. She did warm ups in the house so she was ready to go by the time we got in the truck. I warmed up by drinking some coffee.

As we drove in, I tuned in KKYX, the classic country station. Hank Jr. was lamenting that all his rowdy friends had settled down. Jill didn't seem like she was going to say nothing, so I was figuring on silence. But for some reason I said:

"I'm happy you're taking class again. Try not to show me up too much."

"Don't worry," she said, "I'm not even sure I can do it, honestly. What has it been, three months?"

"Something like that."

"I'm so out of shape. When you're doing ballet every day, and you're really focused on it, your body is like an instrument. It's finely tuned. You commit to the life, and it takes more than desire, or just wanting it. It means working on it. I haven't been working on it at all."

"You'll get her back."

"I'm not that optimistic."

"You got time, anyway. And you got the opportunity. Think about them serfs in Russia."

"Them serfs in Russia?"

"Yeah. Back before the Russkies were commies, they were under this fella named the Tsar. Well, this Tsar fella was a big fan of the ballet. He started his own company and it got really big. And his friends, who were like barons and princes and dukes and such like, they started their own companies too. You know how folks is, something catches on, and then suddenly everybody wants to do it. Monkey see, monkey do. And before you know it, there's ballet all over the place. The ballet dancers, though, they wasn't part of the money class. They was serfs. They worked on their master's land for their clothes and food, basically. So these serfs, these guys and gals, these peasant farmers, they would learn how to dance, and they would rehearse and perform, but when they had down time they just couldn't drink tea and eat crumpets or whatever the upper crust did. When they wasn't dancing, they had to go back to work the fields."

"Guess I'm glad I'm not a serf."

"Right. You ain't got to work the fields. All you got to do is get back in shape."

"You think about ballet differently than I do."

130

"I don't know that much about it, really."

"I think of it as technique that has to be honed. You think of it as history."

"Do I?" I hadn't thought of that. "I'm just doing a little reading. You're the dancer, Jill, not me."

"Okay," she said, her face suddenly a scowl. "I know you told Ricardo about me. Who else did you tell?"

I was really not prepared for this sudden change of subject. Especially since I had this bad feeling that the hammer was about to come down.

"Uh..."

"You didn't tell anybody else. Did you?"

"No." I said. "Well. Yeah. I did."

"Oh no... Who?"

"Well... I told Pastor Jeff."

"Pastor Jeff..."

"Yeah. He told me he wanted you to come to church."

"You didn't tell me that. And how come you're not going to church these days? You never miss church."

"I'm... I'm a little busy."

"Who else?"

"That's it."

"Really? You're lying. I can always tell."

"You know, I been having trouble with this. I didn't know who to turn to. I was trying to find somebody who could help you."

"Who did you tell?"

"Now don't get mad..."

"Who did you tell?"

"Well, I told your mom, of course."

"Uh-huh..."

"And I told Inez Garza."

"You told my ballet teacher?"

"I didn't know what to do! You know, you're sitting in your room and you won't come out—"

"So you just thought you'd just blab to everybody—"

"No! I didn't go telling a whole bunch of folks."

"Who did you tell then?"

"Just your mom. And Pastor Jeff. And Inez. And Ricardo. And your Uncle Ed."

"You told Uncle Ed!?"

"I had to tell Ed." I didn't tell her it was because I was getting rid of the guns. "He kind of guessed it."

"Do you know how personal this is, Daddy? You know about the shame I've been dealing with about all this, and you go and tell all these people?"

"I didn't—"

"You didn't what? You didn't think about it, did you? Because it's not about you!"

"I did think about it."

"But you did it anyway."

"I just wanted to help."

"If you want to help me, then help me keep my private things private!"

"Okay."

"Don't tell anybody else."

"All right."

"That's how rumors start. How do I know that when I walk into City Ballet and everybody in there is going to know about me?"

"You think Ricardo would tell? Or Inez?"

"You did."

"Okay. I'll shut up. I didn't know."

"You always say 'I didn't know' is no excuse."

"Okay. You're right. I shouldn't have done it and I did. There. More feeling terrible. I'd like to get to point where I don't feel terrible about everything."

"How do you think I feel? God, Daddy..." The rest of the drive was Jill quietly fuming.

So my daughter took me to the woodshed. I did feel

kind of like a big mouth for telling all those folks, but Jill was mad at me and that seemed kind of normal so it wasn't all bad.

Despite the dust up, the class went really well. I didn't watch her much during the first hour, she seemed to be doing fine. When we first came in she was getting a lot of strange looks because she's so young. What's a kid doing in the fogies' class? But folks was nice to her. When it got to the second hour, and we got to jumping, it was pretty obvious Jill had it over everybody in class, except for maybe Ricardo. Her jumps were high, and her form looked to be near perfect. She looked great, especially since she hadn't seen the inside of a studio in three months. But this was just my thinking. Who knows how she felt?

On the ride home, she told me she had a conversation with Ricardo and she was changing classes. No offense to him, but she wanted to get back with the students she knew. She wanted to study with him, not be taught by him.

When we got home, I moved the barre into her room.

So I get this call from Larisa Lakewood. She says she wants to talk to me after class, so on Thursday night we sit down for a powwow at Jim's. She has coffee, I have curly fries. Meeting was her idea, and she starts things off.

"I'm sorry I called you fat. That was insensitive."

"It's all right."

"I was just kidding around. I didn't think you would be offended by it."

"It's okay. Apology accepted. And I shouldn't have said you have a big head. That was kind of bad. And it's not true anyway."

"But I *do* have a big head. I was born like this. I had a big head when I was a baby. You should see the pictures of me when I was young."

"Well, okay. You have a big head. But you have a really

nice face. Gorgeous, in fact. So having a big head just means you have a wider area to put that gorgeous face of yours. I think a lot of women would be envious."

"They're not."

"Well, they should be. You're really pretty, you know that. Beautiful even. Who cares about the size of your head?"

And she is too. Larisa Lakewood is a beautiful woman, maybe even movie star good looking. Fill in your own details here about what that might be, I'm not much good with all that. All I can tell you is she's got creamy skin and long blonde hair and she's muscular, like a fist full of gold coins. It's pretty obvious she takes good care of herself. She's a dancer, you know, and not an adult beginner like me, she's in the Thursday night class with the folks what actually been doing it awhile. The fact that she's beautiful may be one of the reasons I said she got a big head. I felt a little intimidated.

Anyway, she said, "Apology accepted. Now on to other things."

"Sounds good to me."

"So you're conservative."

"You could say that."

"I'm a liberal."

"Shocking."

"On that line..."

"Yeah?"

"Just out of curiosity, what kind of a conservative are you?"

"I don't know what you mean."

"I mean are you a talk-radio conservative, or are you a Dwight Eisenhower conservative?"

"I'm a right-wing conservative."

"Oh." She looked disappointed.

"Or at least I was. I ain't sure what I am these days.

Not sure of nothing at all, really. I'm proud to be an American but that don't seem to make no difference no more. Pride in stuff. Folks wave a flag and say they is patriots, and I do too. Makes you feel like you part of something. But when things change, and everything goes to hell, excuse my language, your love of country can't fix nothing. It ain't a balm to suffering. It don't got no meaning. Life clips you time and again and waving a flag, it don't do no good. Politicians take love of country and use it to keep themselves in power. They take what we believe, what I believe, and use it for themselves. Wrap up in Old Glory and go rah-rah and blame the other guy and collect the checks. They got no interest in making nothing work. If it's broke, don't fix it. Because the system works for them. Does that sound like Ike or talk radio?"

"It sounds disillusioned." She smiled sympathetic, and that was all right. "Which I think I understand."

"I don't like talking politics and I can't get away from it. My dad's conservative and he goes on and on about it. Always mad about something and his anger makes him miserable."

"My mom is liberal and she's the same way. You should hear her talk. So negative. Well. Let's not talk politics then."

"Okay."

"I have something I want to ask you."

"If it's about cars I can probably answer you. If it's not, I probably can't."

"It's not actually a question. You heard Ricardo talking about the recital in a couple months we're doing at Blue Skies."

"I heard him mention it a few times but I don't know nothing about it."

"Blue Skies of Texas is a retirement community that's south of 1604, about nine miles north of Castroville. It's a good group of folks, mainly air force retirees. The school is putting on a recital, and Ricardo has asked me to choreograph one of the pieces."

"All right."

"And I'd like you to be in the piece I'm working on."

I smiled. "It's nice to be thought of in that way. And I appreciate you asking me, I really do. But there's just no way I can do that. I'm too shy. I have a hard enough time doing it in front of class. I can't imagine doing a dance in front of people."

"It wouldn't be all that difficult, I promise you. Just a few steps. We need some testosterone to balance out all the estrogen."

"You should ask Ricardo."

"Ricardo can't do it. He said he's going to be really busy through March and April. That's why he asked me to choreograph."

"I'm sorry. There's just no way."

"Okay."

"Dancing is something I do for a hobby. I don't want to perform in front of people. That's my daughter's enchilada, not mine."

"Okay. I understand. And speaking of enchiladas..."

"Yeah?"

"What are you doing on Saturday? Why don't you come over to my house for some Tex-Mex. I'm a helluva cook."

You know, I'm learning a lot of things about folks these days. I couldn't believe that a liberal was asking me out for dinner. We probably have more in common than not. We're both around the same age. She's most likely got an ex-husband and some kids. It's the natural thing, right? We live in SA. Our politics aren't the same, but opposites attract, yeah? She's so pretty it's hard for me to take my eyes off her, and when I do, I want to look at her again.

What a wonderful evening it would be, just the two of us.
I'd come over with some flowers, we'd drink a bottle of
wine and tell each other our troubles. She'd tell me about
her ex and her kids, I'd tell her about Beth, how she left
me for John Lancey, and how she is happy with her new
life. And I'd tell her about Jill, about what happened to her
and how she fell in a hole and kept falling until she was
rescued by some poor boy who had been raped and that
boy just happened to be our teacher.

But I can't tell her that. And I can't tell her how
sometimes I feel like an invisible hand is pulling into the
ground, and a lot of the time I think about how good it
would be to end it once and for all.

And Larisa Lakewood is so beautiful. And it would
be so great to get involved with someone, and fall in love
again, to *really* love someone again.

"No," I said. "But I appreciate you asking."

A week passed. I was at work, Thursday afternoon lunch,
looking at my smartphone. I saved her number. I should
just erase it, right? No, I'll keep it. That way, if she ever
calls me again, I'll know not to pick up.

Really? Is that really what you want to do?

I'll be seeing her tonight in class. That going to be
weird?

I got to stop this nonsense, I feel stupid. I decided
to drag myself across the street to pick up some bananas
from the HEB.

I was just about to leave when Detective Neary walked
in. She stood there in the doorframe looking serious as
the Big D. I knew exactly what that meant: They got him.
They got the bastard!

Chapter 13

"Detective," I said.

"Mr. Hauck."

"Well, shoot, Julia, you don't got to call me Mr. Hauck."

"I need to talk to Jill about her case."

"Is there news?"

"Why don't you pick Jill up after school and bring her downtown."

"Okay. Did you get the guy? Who is he?"

"There's no hurry, but I'd like to see the two of you about four. Come to the station on West Nueva. You know where that is?"

"I do, but —"

"I don't want to say too much right now. The wheels are still in spin, as the saying goes. Tell the desk sergeant to call me when you get there."

Then she left. I met Jill after school and we drove downtown to the police station.

Neary sat us down in a small meeting room, a manila file in front of her. The other detective from the hospital, Paul Dybek, sat next to her, but all he did was watch, he didn't say nothing. Neary proceeded to lay out what she had.

"Okay. So this kid. Mike Saint. You know him."

"I knew it was him," I said. "I knew it."

"No, it wasn't him. Saint was the one who actually came forward with the information we have. But let me start at the beginning."

She pulled a picture of a white teenager out of the manila file. Good looking kid. Fresh faced. Jill looked at the photo.

"Do you know this boy?" she said to Jill.

Her shoulders kind of sagged and her eyes got kind of bloodshot.

"Yes."

"His name is Peter Vanderburg. This is what we think happened. Vanderburg gets invited to this party along with a couple hundred other high school students. He sees you, he puts GHB in your drink, he takes you to one of the bedrooms, locks the door and rapes you."

Neary pulled out a couple of color 8X10s out of the file. "And he takes pictures."

She splayed the photographs out on the table. In the pictures Jill was naked from the waist down, her pants were bunched up at her thighs. She was wearing her black t-shirt with the word "Star" on it. In one of the shots her eyes were open. In the other they were closed. Jill put her fists over her mouth and turned away.

I said, "Where did you get these pictures?"

"Mike Saint brought them to our attention."

"Where did he get them?"

"He heard you talking to his father, and I think he felt bad about what happened and he wanted to make it right. I guess he felt guilty. He's not a bad kid, really. He's kind of the hero in this."

"The hero..."

"He heard rumors it was Vanderburg. There was talk going around Jefferson but there was no proof."

"People at my high school were talking about me?"

"I'm afraid so."

"Who was talking about it?"

"Apparently a lot of people."

"How would they know?" I said.

"Rumor."

"But how would a rumor like that get started?" I said. "Somebody saw him leaving. Somebody saw Vanderburg leaving with Jill. He dropped her off in front of our house. They had to have seen her leave."

"It wasn't Vanderburg that dropped Jill off in front of your house. That was Mike Saint. He and a friend named Jeffrey Place."

"Then why ain't Mike Saint a suspect?"

"Saint was the one who found Jill in the bedroom after everyone had gone. She still had her pants down to her knees. This friend Jeffery Place was still at the party helping him clean up, and they didn't know what to do, so they got her address from her driver's license and dropped her off."

"How did he get the pictures?"

"He stole them."

"He stole them?"

"Saint has a gym class with Vanderburg, and during P.E. he broke into his locker and looked through the pictures on his smartphone. Then he forwarded the pictures to himself. Then he came down here with his father and his father's lawyer."

"But this happened months ago."

"I know. It took him a long time to get around to it. We don't think that he had the opportunity before then. Or he didn't know what to do."

"Who else has seen the pictures?"

"We're still going through the phone."

"So what happens now?"

"Vanderburg could be charged with Aggravated Sexual Assault, which carries a minimum penalty of twenty-five years. Plus possible distribution of child pornography."

"Good."

I looked at Jill. Grim. Ashen.

Neary continued, "But as you can probably imagine, we're having some complications."

"What complications?"

Neary tapped the two pictures. "We have two pictures. In one picture, Jill, your eyes are closed. In the other, your eyes are open. In the second picture, your eyes don't necessarily look cognizant, but it's really hard to tell."

"What does that mean?" I said.

"It means this photograph could be used against her."

"How?"

"Vanderburg is claiming through his attorney that the sex was consensual."

"He what?"

"And he says this picture proves it."

"Because he's saying Jill was awake?"

"That's correct."

The room seemed to breathe. I was seeing little firecrackers go off in my brain. After a time I said:

"How do we prove otherwise?"

"This is where it gets tricky."

"Okay."

"He claims the sex was consensual. He has a picture of your daughter with her eyes open. The toxicology reports all came back negative, most likely because too much time transpired between the incident and the blood test for date rape drugs. We don't have any solid evidence. It's unlikely our case will get past the grand jury. So the only way we can get him is if Jill agrees to press charges and testify in court."

141

I looked at Jill. I knew full well she was going to say yes. She was mad as hell, just like I was. She was—

"No."

Detective Neary smacked her lips, but otherwise remained expressionless.

"Jill..." I said.

"You want to put him in jail for twenty-five years?"

Neary said, "Because the crime was committed with a date rape drug, it's a minimum sentence of twenty-five years."

"That's a long time."

"It's the way we keep society safe," I said. "We lock up the bad guys."

"It's too long. How old is he? Seventeen?"

"Yes," said Neary. "He would be tried as an adult."

"Isn't there a lesser charge you could give him? He's just a kid. I know what he did was evil, and what he did to me was horrible, but if you put him in jail for that long, if you give him that kind of a sentence, it means he can't change. That he'll never change. That he is incapable of changing."

"Jill, you're a good Christian girl with a good heart," I said, "and I know how hard this must be for you because it goes against your nature. I know you believe in Jesus's love and mercy. But honey, this ain't no time to be a good Christian. He has to pay for what he did."

"But there has to be some other way. How about ten years? How about five?"

"In the State of Texas you can't plea bargain a crime committed with a date rape drug."

"So what can we get him on? Can't you charge him with anything else?" I said.

"Possible distribution of child pornography, if it turns out he actually uploaded the photos online or sent them to someone else."

"And that's it?"

"I'm afraid so." Then she turned to my daughter and she said, gently, "Jill. Did you like this boy?"

Jill burst into tears. Then finally said:

"I liked him, yes. I went to the party because I knew he was going to be there. But I didn't know it was him. I didn't see him do it. I can't believe it was him. I'm so stupid."

I turned to Neary. "Where's the justice? Where's the justice in this? It can't just end this way."

"Without pressing charges, without testifying against Vanderburg, there's not any other way it can end."

"I can't do it," she said.

Neary nodded her head like she understood. She put the pictures back in the file and me and Jill left.

Silence. On the way home. Silence. In the evening. Jill in her bedroom. Doing who knows what. Crying?

The TV on, noise coming out of it. I can't hear none of it.

This high-pitched ringing.

Silence.

Peter Vanderburg. Peter Vanderburg. Oh, you are going to die, son. I am going to chop off your head and mount it on the wall. I am going to—

You're going to do what?

I'm going to get justice.

You ain't going to do nothing. You never do.

This time is different.

Yeah?

Yeah.

How?

How?

How?

How? How? How?

drinking... getting drunk... getting blasted... never drink whiskey... look at the label tonight i do... whiskey and beer.. peel off the label... i am fucked up man... did you ever see somebody so sad... i am going to butcher that boy... why would he do this... i don't care why... why jill?... when would he ever even see her? he will do this again... he fucked my daughter... he fucked her... she was a virgin... right? he fucked her he fucked he fucked her... she had to be a virgin... and he took that away from her... and she can never get it back... he is one dead motherfucker... the rest of her life she will have this over her head... he fucking took a picture of her pussy and he kept it on his smartphone... he probably bragged about it and showed it to his friends... he took a picture of her pussy... of her pussy! he jerked off to it... he opened her eyes... he fucking came all over her... he came inside her... he stuck his big fat dick into her little hole... he used her like a fucking kleenex... like a whore... and he just walks away... hiding behind a fucking lawyer... no... no... that son of a bitch has got to die... i am going to murder that cockroach... as painful as possible... only... only...

oh, fuck... i don't have my guns....

I passed out some time last night. Don't know when. The next morning I woke up angry. Hungover and angry.

I ain't been hungover in a long time. I stopped drinking liquor and quit smoking cigarettes years ago and after I did that I never had another hangover. But I have one today. A massive one. Like somebody is trying to push two fuzzy tennis balls out of my eye sockets. Like the veins and the arteries in my brain are leaking out of my skull. I'm still drunk, I think, legally, anyway. I keep bumping into stuff. I chew up some Tylenols and wash it down with a Bud.

I heard Jill stirring in her room. It was way past time for her to be in school. She was back in her old pattern again, depressed and checking out. I knocked on the door. No answer.

And I just let her be.

Now I got to think about the inevitable. I got to think about how I can get justice for Jill.

Off my rocker last night, but it was necessary. Don't know what I'm going to do now though. I got to get my guns back. And then go hunting. My head hurts.

I'll show her. I'll make this right. That boy will not win. You mess with my family and there are consequences. You mess with my people and you will pay!

Plan. Got to make a plan.

First off, what's it worth? Do I kill the cockroach and then kill myself? That's stupid. This is Texas. I kill the insect who raped my daughter and the governor will give me a medal. Least I'll get is a short prison sentence. Probably suspended. Guys like me are heroes. We take matters into our own hands when the law fails us, as it is doing now.

Where though? At his home? Yeah. I'll find out where he is and I'll dust him out in his driveway. But what if he sees me coming? What if he sees me coming and calls the police? Or God forbid he grabs a gun and kills me first? Could happen, couldn't it? He'd have to think I might be coming. Wouldn't that be a kick in the balls? Rapes Jill and then kills me. No. Won't happen.

First I find out where he lives and get a good look at him and make sure it's him.

Then I'll follow him to school. And when he steps out of the bus or his car or his momma's car I will put my .357 in his stomach and blow his guts out. And then I'll watch him die slow, trying to hold his guts in when they sliding out between his fingers. And laugh. It'll be the last thing he fucking sees.

School's perfect. And it'll serve as a warning to any other little insects out there that this is what happens to you when you rape somebody's daughter. You get a bullet coming out of your back that blows a hole the size of a baseball.

I looked up a Vanderburg on the net that lived in our

district and wrote down the address. Then I did a google search and found his picture. I wanted to get another look at this insect. It was the same one we saw in the police station. He was all smiling in the picture, posing with some friends and six-packs of beer in front of a Shell station. You keep smiling pretty, son. Be thankful for every breath you take. It's fixing to all come to a bad end.

Okay. Plan. I was a fool to give those guns to my brother. I got to get those guns back.

I called Ed's phone but he didn't answer, so I called his house. Gloria picked up.

"Hello?"

"Hey Gloria. Is Ed there?"

"No, he went to work. What's up?"

"I need to pick up those guns I give him. Can I come by in, say, twenty minutes?"

"I'm actually leaving now. I have a meeting at Trinity Baptist. We're having a spring bake sale and we need to coordinate ovens."

"Yeah, that's fine. How about you put them in a bag and leave them on the back porch."

"I don't know if I can do that, Billy Jim."

"Why?"

"I don't think Ed wants to give those guns back."

"They're not Ed's guns!"

"Well, he said something like 'possession is nine-tenths of the law.' I think he aims to keep them guns. Sorry."

"I really need them guns."

"You'll have to take that up with him. Sorry."

"I'll call you back."

I hung up and called Ed again. He answered on the first ring.

"Hey ass face."

"I need to fetch my handguns from your house. Call your wife and tell her to leave them on the back porch."

"Sorry, buddy, but those guns are mine now."

"I got a situation here and I really need those guns."

"What situation?"

"I don't got to tell you."

"Tell me what's going on. Is Jill in trouble?"

"No."

"Then I don't got to give you your guns back. If you want a gun, I suggest you go to the shop on San Pedro over by you. It opens at ten, I spect. Or Wal-Mart. They'd be open now."

"Ed..."

"They're mine now, buddy. But I tell you what. Next year, you don't got to get me no Christmas present. Birthday present neither."

"Dadgum it, I want my guns back!"

"I'm hanging up."

And he did.

Now, the next thing I did was either the stupidest thing or the luckiest thing I ever done, depending on how you're eyeing it. I decided I was going to go over to Ed's house and get my guns. He was not going to win this.

I could have just bought a handgun because there's no waiting period in Texas. Or I could have gone on the net and found a dealer in about five minutes. But you know, I didn't want Ed to have my guns. I give him the guns not because I was being nice, but because I was being cautious — maybe too cautious — about Jill. His little smug "Hey ass face" didn't help much since I was already pissed. But the fact is, them guns is mine, not his. Mine! I'm sick of people taking everything from me! It's happened all my life!

I got in my truck and drove to Ed's house. I knocked on the front door, but Gloria'd had already left so I went around back and broke the window on the back door, reached through and unlocked it and stepped in. I heard the alarm going off, so I found the alarm box, opened the glass case, jerked out one of the wires, and it quit. My head was throbbing, could feel the blood in my ears. I had to find those guns, and quick.

The first thing I thought is, if I was Ed, where would I put them? I checked under his bed, not there, in his nightstand and his chest of drawers, no go. I checked under the couch, not there. I kept looking.

Then I remembered Ed had a gun cabinet in his computer room. I went in there and Bingo! Staring right at me in matchbook formation with Ed's guns was my .30-06 and my .270. Only behind the glass, and the cabinet was locked.

I wasn't looking for the rifles though. There was a drawer at the bottom of the cabinet and I was sure the handguns was in there.

I looked through his desk drawers to find keys but didn't find none. Then I went out into the kitchen and looked for something I could jimmy the lock with. As I was looking around, my smartphone rang. Who the heck was calling me now? It was Ricardo. I like that boy.

"Hello?"

"Mr. Hauck?"

"Hey Ricardo. How are you, son?" Since I was on the phone, I decided to see what Ed had in his icebox. Mmm. Beer! I popped open a beer and finished it in a couple of gulps. It tasted like liquid Jesus — and you know how much I love Jesus.

"I'm good, Mr. Hauck. Listen, I just wanted to tell you, I'm not going to be teaching the adult ballet class for about eight weeks."

"Oh? Why is that?"

"I'm going to be in the San Antonio Ballet's production of *Romeo and Juliet*. We start rehearsals in two days."

"Well, that's fantastic, Ricardo."

"It's six weeks of rehearsal and two weeks of

performance at the end of April. I just wanted to let you know. I asked the casting director if Jill could audition, and she said yes, but she has to contact her today. Auditions are tomorrow, from nine to five."

"I'll let her know."

"I sent her some text messages but she never got back to me. So could you tell her?"

"You bet. I'm out now, but I'll be home in about an hour. I'll tell her then."

Rummaging through the drawers, I found an icepick. Perfect.

He said, "Yeah, she's a special girl and a great dancer. I think doing a show would be good for her. It's something she really needs."

"You're right, you're right. Listen, I'm kind of in the middle of something. Let me call you back."

"Sure. I'll be free after six."

I said that was fine, we said our goodbyes and hung up. Then I went back into the computer room.

I tried picking the lock for several minutes but no dice, so I went out to his workroom, looking for something I could break open the drawer with.

And what do you think I found? My dad's tools! Now I'm really pissed.

See, when my dad went into Independence Hill, he told me and my brother it was up to us to go through his stuff and decide what to keep and what to throw away. Well, he's got this toolbox full of Stahlwille tools, and I know, I know, I own a garage and I got tons of tools, but these have sentimental value. First of all, they's old as cuss because I was using them when I was just a kid, and second of all, they's good tools. Great tools. Excellent steel, and very precise in measurements — to a gnat's eyelash. And I wanted them. And Ed knew I wanted them, but when we started going through dad's stuff they suddenly couldn't be found and Ed said he was dang absolutely mystified as to what could have happened to them because they'd always been here and maybe somebody stole them, it's what happens when you don't lock stuff up and here they was, right in his dang workroom! I made a mental note to myself to take them with me when I left.

I found an axe and came back in and proceeded to open the bottom drawer of the gun case. It was pretty easy. I knocked the lock a couple of times and it split the wood and popped right open. I pulled open the drawer and behold, there was the sack with my guns. I opened her up and looked inside, and sure enough, there they was, just like I last saw them. My dear, sweet friends.

Now on to business.

I went into the workroom and grabbed the Stahlwille tool box, then went out the back way, heading to my truck in the front yard. Now that I got my stuff, I'm thinking, what do I do next? I'll go back home and try and find out what the license plate is on his car, if he's got one, and then I'll find it in the Jeff parking lot and wait till school lets out. The cockroach has got a couple more hours of enjoying the sunshine. Or maybe I won't. Maybe I'll just—

"POLICE!"

"FREEZE!"

I looked up. Three patrol cars, six police officers. Guns drawn. Shouting all at once:

"DROP THE BAG!"

"GET DOWN NOW! SLOWLY!"

"GET DOWN!"

"DON'T MOVE!"

"HANDS IN THE AIR! SLOWLY!"

"DON'T MOVE!"

"Wait a minute! How can I get down and not move?"

"WHAT'S IN THE BAG?"

"DON'T MOVE!"

"It's just a couple of handguns, officers, I—"

"HE'S GOT A GUN!"

The next thing I see is a cop whip out a taser gun and the two dart-like electrodes shoot out of it and suddenly I'm on the ground shaking like a shivering pig. Then they put handcuffs on me, read me my rights, stuff me in a squad car, and take me downtown.

There was two cops in the squad car, an older fella in the passenger seat and a young fella driving. I tried explaining it to them. "Officers, this is a big mistake. That's my brother's house. I'm just getting some of my property out of it. Those handguns is mine."

The cop in the passenger seat says, "And the tools?"

"Well, technically..."

"You're being booked on suspicion of burglary. I wouldn't say anything else until you have a lawyer."

Then he turned to the young cop driving and said, "Did you tell him not to move?"

The young cop said, "You know, about that..."

"Look, you got to get him on the ground first. You can't say 'don't move' when everybody else is telling him to get down."

"Yeah, but...."

"How many times did you practice that at the academy?"

"But first we get him to drop what he's carrying, then we get him to slowly drop to the ground."

"That's right."

"So I told him to drop his bag, but everybody else was telling him to get down."

"That's because he already dropped his bag!"

"He did?"

"Yeah, you idiot, he did."

"Man. I almost shot him."

"Oh lord!"

"I guess I got to quit smoking that dope."

"Don't wink at me."

"Sorry."

They took me down to the county jail on North Comal. The intake guys, the guards, made me take all the stuff out of my pockets — wallet, keys, and phone — and they put it in an envelope and checked it into the property room, along with my belt and my work boots, and then give me some sandals. I saw a couple of prisoners in orange jump suits pushing broom, but the guards didn't make me change, just let me keep my civvies on. Then I was searched, and they took a mugshot and fingerprints.

Just as they was finishing rolling my fingerprints, out of the corner of my eye I noticed somebody looking at me. It's Detective Neary. A friendly face! Only she wasn't looking at me so friendly. She was looking pretty skeptical, honest.

"Mr. Hauck?"

"Thank god, somebody who can help me. There has been a huge misunderstanding."

"What are you doing here?"

"I was at my brother's house getting my guns. I left some handguns with him, and he wasn't home, so I wanted to get my guns back."

"So you broke into his house?"

"Well, it wasn't exactly like breaking in."

"But you broke the glass on the back door."

"Well, that's because I didn't have the key."

"Why do you need your guns, all of a sudden?"

"What do you mean, why? For protection, of course."

"Protection from who?"

"From thieves."

"From Peter Vanderburg?"

"Maybe. You never know."

"Are you drunk? You reek of alcohol."

"A little, I reckon. Maybe. Can you help me get out of here?"

She was looking at me real suspicious-like, but she said, "Well, we'll see what we can do."

"Thank goodness."

"You're allowed one phone call. Why don't you make it now?"

I wasn't sure who to call. Ed was the one who had to vouch for me, so I had to call him. I dialed his smartphone but it just rang and went into voice mail. Detective Neary was standing at my elbow listening to my message.

"Ed, this is Billy Jim. Listen, I'm down here at the police station. Uh. the county jail on North Comal. I kind of went into your house just now to get my guns back and I tripped the alarm and the cops showed up and arrested me. Can you believe it? Anyway, I need you to come down here and let them know I'm your brother and not a thief and you're not going to press charges. And hurry up!"

I hung up the phone and they put me in a holding cell. It smelled like piss and was full of derelicts. They had a sink and a toilet and both of them was real nasty as you can imagine, but I was powerful thirsty and must have drunk at least two gallons of water out of the tap. There was a young white kid in there, about seventeen. Him and me sat next to each other for about twenty minutes without saying a word. Finally he goes, "What are you in for?" I said "Burglary." And then he got this really scared look on his face and moved away.

After about two hours, they transferred me to the sixth floor. They put me in a cell with about five other guys. The cell wasn't bars, but industrial strength cyclone fence that looked like it'd been dipped in beige paint. The fence was solid as prison bars, but you couldn't reach out of it or stick your hands out of it, like you could prison bars. The guys in the cell, three black guys and two Mexicans, was all in for either burglary or petty theft. I was pretty much petrified, honestly. The time passed.

One hour. Two. Three. Where the hell was Ed? What was taking so long? Four. Five. Six.

In the evening they opened up the cell and we walked down to a small lunch room and we ate dinner, tamales and beans. Then back to the cell.

I was scared at first, thoroughly convinced I was going to get the crap kicked out of me by the guys I was sharing the cell with, but they didn't look at me much or pay attention to me. They was off in their own worlds, dreaming about getting out, I reckon. They'd make conversation with each other a bit here and there, but it was mainly just small talk.

After a few hours, the fear went away and I went into something like thinking. The alcohol had evaporated out of my system. All that was left was me. Lying on the top bunk. Staring at the ceiling.

You could get years in jail for killing Vanderburg. Years. You'd have years of this. Staring at the ceiling. Years.

How in God's name did I end up here?

How do you think, fool? You're as dumb as that cop that almost shot you.

Where's Jill? She going to kill herself when I'm not there?

Good question.

What if Peter Vanderburg comes over while I'm gone?

Nice time to think about that.

He won't. He don't know I'm here.

She's still unprotected.

What was I thinking? Was I really going to shoot his guts out?

He deserves it.

You're going to be a school shooter? Is that it? That's

what you want? You really want to forever be known as the guy who went into the school and shot a kid?

No.

You really think you could kill a teenage boy at a high school and the State of Texas would just let you walk?

No.

The kid who raped my daughter.

You been out of your daughter's life even when you were in it. You want to go to prison for the rest of your life? You think that's what she wants?

No.

She wants a father. I know you're not close. But that's all she's ever wanted from you. To be a father. And you just couldn't do it, could you?

I want justice for Jill.

You don't want justice for Jill. You want justice for you. Jill's got nothing to do with it.

No. I want to help her. I want to help her be normal again.

Yet here you are in jail.

Yes.

None of this is about Jill. It was never about Jill. It was always you. About your honor. About your pride. About your fear.

Then how can I help her?

You can't.

No, there's got to be a way!

What way?

Oh, Christ...

What?

The *Romeo and Juliet* audition! It's tomorrow!

And here you are.

I was supposed to tell her!

Way to go...

No... Ricardo would have called her... Right? No...

Ricardo called you. You were supposed to tell her.

I've got to tell her! I got to get out of here! I got to get out of here right now!

Maybe if you tell the guard he'll — oh, wait... That means he would actually give a damn about some guy who broke into some other guy's house.

But there's got to be a way! There's got to!

I got up and called out to the guard:

"Guard! I have to make a phone call! It's an emergency! Guard!"

I saw a couple of guards sitting in their station, talking to each other. They heard me. There wasn't any barrier between us, except the cyclone fence and they were thirty feet off. But they didn't even look my way. They didn't even acknowledge me. I kept calling, and they just kept talking about whatever they was talking about. One of them started laughing, and they high-fived each other. After a few minutes I gave up.

At around noon on Sunday, two days after I was arrested, I walked out of jail. I was sure Jill never read her text message from Ricardo. She didn't know about the *Romeo and Juliet* audition because nobody told her. That was my responsibility, what I was supposed to do, but the window that had opened briefly to lead Jilly to some freedom from her craziness had had been shuttered and nailed shut. The auditions were now closed. Because of my foolishness, she missed them. This could have been a golden opportunity to turn her life around but it had been made into fool's gold by me, the king ass who believed that shooting a kid on a schoolyard playground was going to somehow redeem us all, in some magical and biblical way.

The guards brought me down to the holding cell again while the jail cops finished up the last of the paperwork. As I sat there waiting, I found myself praying to Jesus for the first time since before Thanksgiving: "Please, Lord, if you can find it in your heart, make my life short. Let me get hit by a bus or a train. Let me suffer electrocution. Let my death be quick, but not something folks would think is suicide. I'm tired, Lord, and I'm tired of failing and I want to come home. Please, Lord, please make me die."

Chapter 14

When I walked out of jail, my brother Ed was waiting to meet me. He looked disgusted. And so superior.

We got in his truck and headed to the impound lot to pick up my truck, which had been towed off his front lawn where I left it. The first thing he said to me was, "You owe me big."

"Where were you? I been sitting in jail for three days!"

"I think what you meant to say was 'Thank you.' As in, 'Thank you, brother, for not pressing charges after I broke into your house and tore up your alarm and split open your gun cabinet.'"

"To get *my* guns."

"If I was a less forgiving man you'd be looking at doing five to ten for felony burglary. Be grateful."

"I broke into your house to get my guns because you wouldn't give them back to me. *My* guns. *My* property."

"*My* burglar alarm. *My* gun cabinet."

"And what are you doing with Dad's Stahlwille tools? You said somebody must have stole them and you had them the whole time!"

"Ancient history."

"Those are my tools. Dad wanted me to have them."

"Did he ever tell you that?"

"Yes."

"Well, we'll talk about it when next we see him. Fact is, you're a jail bird, and the only reason you got your freedom is on account of my good graces and my Christian faith. So don't act all uppity and mad. You owe me."

"And what do you think I owe you? For coming to bail me out of jail three days after I called you?"

"Them guns, for a start."

"I knew it. I knew you were going to say that."

"And technically it wasn't three days, it was like two days, odd-near forty-eight hours, give or take an hour."

"What?"

"And the guns is only for a start. You got to pay for my gun cabinet too. And the alarm."

"What took you so long?"

"What do you mean?"

"What took you so long to bail me out?"

"You called my smart phone."

"So?"

"So you know I don't listen to the voice mail messages on my smart phone. And you called from the jail phone, so I didn't recognize the number. I almost deleted it without listening to it at all. You're lucky. If I'd done that you'd still be in jail."

"I'm lucky..."

"You should have left the message on my home phone."

"I don't even believe that."

"Oh, you going to accuse me of lying now."

"When you came home and you saw the burglar alarm was torn up, and you saw the gun cabinet was broke into, who did you think done it?"

"I wasn't sure. I really didn't know..."

"You talked to Gloria about it. I know you did."

"Yeah, so?"

"I talked to Gloria earlier. I talked to Gloria right before I called you."

"That's right."

"So you knew it was me. You knew I broke into your house."

"Yeah."

"So you knew *that morning* that I was in jail."

"Well..."

"So you let me sit there. You let me sit there for three days!"

"I figured you probably needed to cool down a little bit."

Something short-circuited in my head. I heard a little "bzzz." I screamed and slammed the dashboard with my fist. It hurt like hell. My hand turned into a claw and I'd knocked a little crescent of skin off my knuckle.

"Looks like I was right."

We drove along in silence and it all became very clear.

"You didn't care if I was cooled down. You was just being Ed."

"I am what I am."

"I know why you let me sit in jail. It's because you wanted to. I can see you sitting there two nights ago, watching TV and having a beer, thinking, "Ha ha, that idiot's cooling it in jail. Maybe I'll get him out tomorrow. Or maybe I won't." You sitting there with your little smile on your face, just lording over me. In your mind. Thinking about all you're going to say to me when you finally bail me out, like I should be grateful and I owe you. You with the power, me with the problem. You know, there's all kinds of violent things that happen in a jail. You don't think it would've been a good idea to get me out of that situation as quick as possible?"

"Don't be dramatic."

"But the main reason you did it is because you wanted to stick it in me. Stick that knife in me and twist it around a little bit, right?"

"I dropped the charges. I'm picking you up and taking you to your truck. You broke into my house and broke my alarm and my gun cabinet. This whole thing started with you. If you hadn't done that, we wouldn't be having this conversation."

I didn't have nothing else to say after that. As much as I hated Ed at that moment, he was right. It *had* started with me. After a few minutes, he pulled up to the police pound off of Growdon Road, over there where Kelly Air Force Base used to be. I got out, shut the door behind me. Ed called after me as I walked to the gate.

"You're welcome," he said.

I got my truck out of pound after showing the title and proof of insurance, which was in the glove box, and my driver's license. With the impound fee, storage fee, notification fee, and towing charges, the cost came to something like $250. What a clod. I thought maybe I should get a special bank card set up where every time I do something stupid I can automatically have money sucked out of my bank account. Save me a lot of trouble.

I pulled into an ice house and bought a 12-pack before heading home. I probably shouldn't have, being that it was Sunday night, but I did.

I got home, put the 12-pack in the fridge, and was about to crack me a fresh one when Jill walked in the kitchen.

"Where have you been?"

This was really the last thing I wanted to do, have a conversation with Jill about where I was and what I'd been doing. I felt bad enough. Do I have to keep piling it on?

I put the beer back in the fridge. I was certain I was going to be drinking it in a minute or two, I just didn't want Jill staring at me while I did.

"Did you do something? Where have you been?"

The thing I needed to do was lie. I had to think of a lie, one that she could believe, and I had to do it quick.

Only it didn't seem to matter. I felt like I'd been lying my whole life. Telling the truth was not going to wreck everything. True or false, it didn't matter. Jill was going to be the same no matter what I said. Damaged. Lying was not going to protect her. There didn't seem to be no more reason to lie.

"I was in jail."

"Excuse me?"

"I was in the county jail over there on North Comal."

"What did you do?"

"It doesn't matter. The charges were dropped."

"What were the charges?"

"Felony burglary. I broke into your Uncle Ed's house to get some property I had stored over there and the police thought I was a burglar. It was a big misunderstanding. Ed came by the police station and told them who I was and they dropped the charges."

"You've been gone since Friday!"

"Yeah, I know. Didn't you call Uncle Ed?"

"I left a message but he never got back to me."

"Figures."

"What property?"

"What?"

"What property were you going over there to get?"

"My guns."

"Your handguns? What are your handguns doing at Uncle Ed's house?"

"I know you been going through some rough times and I didn't want the guns around the house."

162

"You thought I was going to kill myself?"

"Yeah. I thought you might."

"If I was going to kill myself I wouldn't shoot myself. I'd take pills or something."

"Men and women is different...."

"So why did you need them back? What was so important that you had to break into his house?"

"I wanted them for protection. No. That's not true. I wanted them because I was going to kill Peter Vanderburg."

"Are you serious?"

"Yes."

"I guess it's a good thing you didn't get them."

"Yeah, I guess it a good thing."

She put her hand on my arm, and looked me straight in the eye. Her voice started to crack.

"Don't ever do that again."

"I won't."

"I don't want to lose you. You're the only thing that's been consistent for me throughout this whole thing."

"I haven't been consistent about anything. I've made a mess of it all. I've done everything so poorly."

"No. You haven't. You did the best you could. And that's always been enough."

"There is so much I should have done. Could have done. I have failed you in so many ways."

"How?"

"I should have protected you."

"If you really want to protect me, don't go after Peter Vanderburg. I don't want my father to go to prison. If you really want to protect me, just keep doing what you're doing. All right?"

"All right."

"You did the best you could."

Since we were doing all this truth telling stuff, there

was a little piece of business I had to get out on the table.

"Did you talk to Ricardo?"

"He sent me a text message, but I didn't see it until the audition was over. I didn't start checking my text messages until I noticed you were gone."

"He called to tell me about the audition. I was supposed to tell you because you weren't answering your text messages. But I didn't get a chance to because I was in jail."

Jill sighed. "Well. I probably wouldn't have gone to the audition anyway. And if I had, it wouldn't have worked out. I never would have got the job."

I made a sandwich for her and she went to her room to study. I went out to the couch and watched YouTube and commenced to drain that 12-pack. I thought a lot about how I blew her chance at that audition. Could I make it up to her now? No. Whatever I could do for Jill, whatever was possible before was now a million miles gone.

Chapter 15

The next day I went to work, naturally, it being Monday. We were pretty steady until about two o'clock, and then I took lunch. I decided to call Ricardo and leave a message on his phone. Not to say much, just "howdy." To my surprise, he picked up.

"Hey Mr. Hauck. What's going on?"

"Ricardo? Hey. I'm, um. Howdy."

Ricardo kind of caught me off guard. I wasn't actually wanting to talk to him, I just wanted to leave a message.

"What's up?" he said.

"Oh, nothing. Just calling to say 'hey.'"

"Jill never got back to me."

"Yeah... she kind of wasn't checking her phone, I reckon. Not sure why."

"Did you talk to her?"

"You know, I was kind of indisposed. Had to go out of town suddenly."

"Oh. That's too bad. They're having all kinds of casting problems."

"Really? How so?"

"Not enough dancers."

"Do you think they'd see Jill?"

"I don't know. They're not saying much to us about it. But that's the scuttlebutt."

"Hmm... so, uh, how's rehearsals going?"

"Rough. We've only been at it a couple days, but it's a real back breaker. Sir David is a great director, but he's a heck of a task master. Brutal, brutal man."

"Sir David?"

"Sir David Derrick. He's directing the show."

Suddenly, that name came swimming into my memory. David Derrick. Sir David Derrick. I know that guy. He was the guy I sat next to at *The Nutcracker* back in November. He called me Lynyrd Skynyrd! He likes me. He wanted to talk to me. He actually came out to the lobby to find me. He was laughing at everything I said. Maybe if they're short of dancers, maybe he can give Jill a chance! Maybe I *can* fix this!

"Ricardo. Where are you rehearsing? Downtown at the Convention Center?"

"No, we don't go into the theater for another month or so. We're at the Ballet Academy of South Texas, over here on Broadway and Hildebrand."

"How long are you there? Till when? Five?"

"We'll most likely go later. Hey listen, Mr. Hauck, I got to go. It was good talking to you. Tell Jill I said 'hi'." We said our goodbyes and hung up.

I know this guy will give Jill an audition. I know he will. He likes me. Ricardo said they don't have enough dancers. That means they haven't cast the show yet. Which means Jill has a chance, Jill has a chance to be in the show! I know he'll take her on! I know it!

All right. What do I got to do?

I told my crew I was stepping out for a few hours, got in my pickup and headed back to the house. Jill was at school still, and I wasn't about to tell her what I was doing or what I was about to do until I actually did it. I went inside and fished my Lynyrd Skynyrd t-shirt out of the dirty clothes basket and put it on. It was wrinkled but it didn't smell bad so I figured it was okay. Then I headed over to Broadway and Hildebrand.

I got stuck in traffic along the way. Laid on the horn a couple times at the cars which seemed to be stalled out in front of me. "Come on... come on... I got to go see a guy...."

I ran into the academy and said to the receptionist:

"Is David Derrick here?"

"He's in Studio A."

"Thanks."

"You can't go in there!"

"UPS!"

I ran in about three feet and stopped. There was a guy and a gal there, dancers, standing out in the middle of the floor. They was obviously playing Romeo and Juliet. They both looked to be half scared out of their wits. That's because Sir David was in a screaming match with who I come to find out is the artistic director of the San Antonio Ballet, a woman named Elaine Riche. I remembered her from earlier, from the night of *The Nutcracker*. She was the one with the black dress and the pearls who said something like, "I don't care what you think, Sir David."

Apparently, she still didn't care.

They were both screaming at each other, red in the face. She looked like a fire hydrant with teeth and eyebrows.

"You can*not* do this ballet in the round!"

"We can, and we will!"

"This is not what we agreed to!"

"How many times must I tell you this, you manky bag of anthrax? You have got to think differently!"

"The Nureyev Foundation is very specific!"

"It's specific about the steps! It's specific about the choreography! Nowhere does it state the ballet must be performed on a proscenium!"

"We hired you to direct the Nureyev version!"

"And that's exactly what I'm giving you! I'm giving you the Nureyev version in the round! Now leave us! We are in rehearsal! If you want to make yourself useful, go back out there and get me some boys!"

"We're finding the boys! I told you!"

"This show is going to be a disaster! We've started rehearsal and you're 'finding boys'? You're pathetic!"

Then his eyes fell on me. I suddenly felt terrified because I knew he was going to start shouting at me.

"Who are you?" His voice was hoarse, guttural, rage coming from deep in the lungs. I just looked at him.

"Well!?"

"Hey... Remember me?" I pointed to my t-shirt. "I'm Lynyrd Skynyrd. From *The Nutcracker*. Remember me? We sat next to each other at the show."

"So?"

"Um..."

"What do you *want?*"

"I, uh..."

"Do you think you can just walk in here and — What are you *doing* here?"

"I came... I-I came to talk to you."

"Why?"

"Uh... Because..."

"Get out."

"What?"

"*Get out!*"

I started to back out, mumbling apologies, when I saw something pass over Sir David's face. He looked at Ms. Riche, the artistic director, and then he looked at me.

"Stop!"

I did what I was ordered to do. I looked over at Romeo and Juliet, and they just looked down at the floor. I'm sure my face had that wide-eyed look an armadillo gets just before a car runs him over.

Sir David came over to me. He spoke quietly now, almost gently.

"I'm sorry I shouted at you. I get a bit carried away sometimes."

"I-It's okay."

"So what do you want?"

"I'd... I'd like you to audition m-m-my daughter."

I heard the artistic director snort and go, "Ah!" Sir David cut her off with a look, then turned back to me.

"Audition your daughter?"

"Yes sir."

"That's what you want?"

"Yes sir."

"Don't call me sir, please.

"Yes sir. I mean—"

"Lynyrd Skynyrd."

"That's me."

"I remember you."

"From *The Nutcracker.*"

"Right. Can I ask you a question, Mr. Skynyrd?"

"Yes."

I wasn't sure where this was going. For a second there I thought he might say something like, "What makes you think you can just walk in here and start asking favors from me? Who the hell do you think you are?" But he didn't. He didn't ask me about Jill either.

"Who's your favorite dancer?"

I looked at the artistic director. She just shook her head, like I was stupid. I took a deep breath.

"Daria Klimentova."

He smiled. "Interesting choice. Why is that?"

"Well... It's because... she... she was a journeyman ballerina all of her life... and she didn't become a big star until she was at the end of her career."

"And she's pretty."

"Her looks are okay."

"You don't think she's pretty?"

"No, she's pretty. But that's not why I like her. She's kind. She's a kind person. You can watch interviews with her and you can tell, she's nice. She's got a good heart."

"Well enough. Who's your favorite male dancer?"

"I don't know the male dancers that well."

"Well, of course you don't."

"But there's this one fella who's from up there in Canada I like a lot. I wish I could tell you his name. Something like Gil Kotte."

"Guillaume Côté."

"Yeah, that's the fella. It's hard to pronounce, you got to admit."

"And why do you like him?"

"Well, he's into a lot of different things. You know, you listen to a lot of dancers being interviewed, and all they know about is dance. That's all they can talk about. But he's different. He's a singer, he plays piano, he writes music. And he's got a wife and a kid. And he's really into being a dad. He seems pretty grounded."

"Do you watch a lot of dancers being interviewed?"

"Fair amount, I reckon."

"What do you do for a living, sir?"

"I run a repair shop. An auto repair shop."

Sir David turned out, and faced the artistic director and the dancers.

"Behold the man, Lynyrd Skynyrd. He owns a garage. He fixes autos for his daily bread. He gets dirt under his fingernails. Distinctly working class, wouldn't you say, sir?"

"And proud of it."

"And proud of it. Yet, I can ask him a question about the ballet, and he can answer that question. I can ask him for opinions, and he has them. He and I could probably commiserate about the ballet for hours, about what we like and what we don't like, what works, what doesn't work. Wouldn't that to be the case, Mr. Skynyrd?"

"I'm sure you know much more about it than I do, sir."

"My point is, this man thinks differently. He does not think as you would expect him to. What's the best ballet company in the world?"

"I guess it kind of depends on what you like."

"So what is your taste, sir?"

"I like the Royal Ballet. I've seen a bunch of their videos. I like Daria Klimentova, like I said, but I also like Graciella Nuñez."

"Marianela Nuñez."

"Marianela Nuñez, sorry. She's great. Nobody can bow like that Nuñez gal. She's a great dancer, but when she bows, she really looks like a dancer, like a prima ballerina."

"I know what you mean, exactly."

"I like ABT. That Misty Copeland's got gams like a racehorse."

"Yes, they're quite impressive."

"New York City Ballet has a lot of really good dancers but I don't care for Peter Martins much. You can tell he's really into himself."

"Yes, he's a complete prat."

"I like the Mariinsky a lot but I don't like the Bolshoi."

"Ah! The Bolshoi. I can't bear them."

"They're all crazy."

"Those people at the Bolshoi are quite nutters."

"Right. Crazier than a diabetic on Sugar Island."

"Well, I'm not sure about that, but I get your point."

He turned back the artistic director and the dancers.

"So you see? This man thinks differently. And so should you. Art isn't about copying. It's about creating. It's about taking something and looking at it in a different way. Yes, the Nureyev *Romeo and Juliet* is not done in the round. But great art involves risk. Picasso didn't paint cubes because everyone else was doing it. He did it because nobody else was doing it. Think differently. And we shall all rise."

Then he turned to me and tapped me on the chest.

"You."

"Yes?"

"Have your daughter down here in two hours in tights ready to audition."

The artistic director spoke up. "We don't need any more girls."

Sir David said calmly, "Why don't you let me decide who goes into the show, as our contract states? Now please. Go down to your office and get on that rolodex and start finding me some boys."

The artistic director stalked out. Sir David turned to me. I had to ask:

"How did you know I knew anything about the ballet?"

"I didn't. But I know you think differently because working men don't come by themselves to the ballet in their jeans and t-shirts."

"What if I couldn't answer any your questions?"

"Then I would have asked you about that night, about seeing *The Nutcracker.* I wasn't trying to humiliate you, I'm not an ogre. I was making a point to the artistic director and my dancers."

"Okay then."

He touched his wristwatch. "Tick tock tick tock. Ready to go in two hours. If you're late by one minute, no audition." He turned back to Romeo and Juliet.

"Thanks, David!" It was 2:40. I had to be back by 4:40.

172

I was just about at the door when he called out.

"Wait!"

I stopped. He motioned me over with his hand, like a man calls his golden retriever. I came padding up. He pulled a dollar out of his wallet and handed it to me.

"I need you to do one thing. Go over to the Starbucks across the street and order me a two shot latte with extra foam and two raw sugars. And be quick about it." Then he turned back to his dancers.

I thought about that time at my garage when that Korean kid Jimmy Song asked me to get him a latte and I yelled at him.

"Sure, I'll be right back."

I ran across the street and got the coffee, then I went back into Studio A and handed it to him. He did not thank me, or even look at me. I got back in my truck and peeled out of the parking lot. Twenty minutes had already passed.

Jockeying between cars, racing up Hildebrand. It was around 3:00, which is when classes end. But would she be at school? I could beat it there and try to catch her before she left, but what if I missed her? I didn't know where she was exactly, but I had to find her and I had to find her right away. I called of course, sent her a text message CALL ME RIGHT NOW EXTREMELY URGENT, but she didn't answer back.

Home. She'll head home.

I pulled in front of the house but she wasn't there. She usually gets back sometime after 3:00. If she gets here at, say, 3:20 that leaves us an hour and twenty minutes. I decided to wait for her. I turned the truck around and pointed it in the direction of Hildebrand.

Minutes passed. 3:30. Then 3:40. We had one hour left. 3:50. Dang it, where could she be!? Why wasn't she back yet? I went into the house and knocked on her door even, but got nothing. I decided to head to her school.

I burned up the road, did a 20 minutes drive in 10 minutes, got to Providence and pulled up to the front gate. Through the fence I saw her car in the parking lot. Hot dog! I started to drive through but was stopped by the security guard.

"You can't come in here."

"My daughter goes to school here!"

"It's okay, calm down."

"I need to see my daughter right away! It's an emergency!"

"I need to see some ID."

"Oh for crying out loud, man, I got to find my daughter and I got to find her quick!"

"I need to see some ID if you want to come in."

"I've been calling her! She won't pick up!"

"Kids these days."

I fumbled my wallet out of my pocket and pulled out my driver's license. He glanced back and forth between the picture and my face, leisurely and casual as you please, then tipped it back to me.

"Go on in."

"Do you know where I can find her?"

"How would I know where your daughter is? She's probably not in a classroom because they're all locked up after school's over. She may be in the gym. Or the library. They have different after-school activities at different places. Best go to the principal's office, they'd know."

I remembered where the principal's office was from when we registered. I gunned the truck and screeched to a halt in a parking space next to Jill's car, then ran towards the building.

Out of the corner of my eye, I saw the library. She wouldn't be in a club. She doesn't socialize much anymore. She has to be in the library. She has to be!

I made a pivot and ran up the library stairs and burst through the doors.

Inside it was quiet. My fat, sweaty, out-of-breath body couldn't take it no more; I had to put my hands on my knees and catch my breath. A few of the girls looked up at me, then went back to their reading. After a few moments of gulping air, I got it to where I was only half-panting and I started moving through the desks and bookshelves.

I found Jill in the back reading her physics textbook.

"Come on, we got to go!"

She was startled. She took off her glasses and looked me up and down.

"Why are you so out of breath? What are you doing here?"

"Come on. We got to go!"

"Shh! Go where?"

"I got you an audition with the San Antonio Ballet! It's for a part in *Romeo and Juliet!* But we have to be there by 4:40! You have to be warmed up and ready to go by 4:40!"

"That's forty minutes!"

"Let's git!"

Jill quickly picked up her books and followed me.

"How did you get me an audition with the San Antonio Ballet?"

"I know people."

We got out to the parking lot and Jill jumped into the passenger's seat. I shouted "Warm up in the back!" so she got out and plunked herself down in the pickup bed. I pulled into the traffic, headed back to the studio. Jill started stretching. We were on our way.

Only there was another problem. Jill knocked on the glass panel behind my head and I slid her open.

"Daddy!"

"What?"

"I don't have my ballet clothes! I don't have any tights! Or my pointe shoes! We have to stop by home!"

"Sweetie, if we stop by home we won't make it in time — hold on!"

I slammed on the brakes at a stoplight. I whipped out my smart phone and punched through my call log. I don't get that many calls, so it wasn't too hard to find Larisa Lakewood's number. I hit the call button, and Larisa came on after the second ring.

"Hello?"

"Howdy Larisa, this is Billy Jim Hauck."

"Hey handsome. What's up?"

"Are you at work?"

"Yes, but I can always make time for you. What's going on?"

"I'm having something of a ballet emergency."

"A ballet emergency?"

"My daughter is going to audition for the San Antonio Ballet, and we're heading to the audition, but she doesn't have any of her gear."

"What does she need?"

"Why don't I put her on?"

I handed the phone through the window, and Jill and Larisa chatted it up. It got very frenzied. I couldn't hear exactly what they were saying but it fast and furious. Jill handed the phone back to me.

Larisa said, "She needs tights and a leotard and her pointe shoes."

"I know!"

"I could bring you a pair."

"You could?"

"Sure. Isn't that why you called me? I could bring you a pair. I could swing by the dance shop and pick you up a pair of pointe shoes. Tights and a leotard too."

"Oh, you'd be a lifesaver. I really owe you for this."

"You owe me?"

"Yes. I owe you." This next bit I should have left out, but it just came out of my mouth before I could stop it. "Whatever you need, just ask."

"Okay. I want you to be in that recital we're doing at Blue Skies."

"What?"

"The old folks home. Remember? I asked you to be in the recital? I said I need a dancer for this short piece, just for the old folks. But you said no, that you weren't a performer, that it was Jill's thing, not yours."

"Uh... I remember..."

"Well, that's what I need. I need you to be in the piece I'm choreographing for the old folks. Can you do it?"

"Yes."

"Good. What's the address again?"

I told her and she hung up, laughing gleefully.

Deceit! Chicanery! Hornswoggling!

How in the name of heaven did I let this big-headed liberal vixen outsmart me? She ought to be in the rodeo, she's so good at roping and branding. She done roped me into this and she's fixing to brand me a fool. Now I have to dance the ballet in front of a bunch of old folks — me, dance the ballet! — and make a total fat ass out of myself! What the heck did I just agree to?

Maybe I'll tell her I've changed my mind. Maybe I'll just tell her I won't do it. That I refuse to do it. She took advantage of me. In our time of need, she should not be asking me to do this. It's unfair!

No. She's coming through. Whatever you can say about it, taking advantage of me or not, Larisa's coming through. Jill wouldn't be able to do the audition without her. You're lucky in life when you have folks that actually do what they say they're going to do. This is one of those times. Whatever Larisa is, she's somebody I can count on.

So I should just appreciate that and quit bellyaching.

Thirty minutes later, at exactly 4:35, we pulled into the academy parking lot. Jill was nowhere near ready, I could tell, but it'd have to do. She didn't have sheet music either. This was all about to blow up, I had a feeling. Larisa was nowhere to be seen.

We got into the building, and I walked up to the gal at the front desk again. I told her we was here to see David Derrick, and she kind of squinted at us and told me to have a seat. Which we did. It was almost 4:40.

But the receptionist gal didn't do nothing. She didn't call nobody. She didn't go into the studio. She just sat there. We sat there too. I got up after a moment and went back to the front desk.

"Listen, he's expecting us."

"What did you say your name was again?"

Just then Larisa came in through the front door. She had plastic sack with her, Jill's stuff. We said our hellos, then she said to the receptionist:

"Where's the dressing room?"

"Around the corner."

"Come on, honey."

She grabbed Jill and they disappeared down the hall-way. I turned back to the gal behind the desk.

"Listen, I know you're probably having a hard day, young lady, but there's such a thing as manners."

"I know."

"You should be nicer to people. It doesn't kill you."

"I know. But I was afraid that, if I interrupted him, he'd yell at me."

"Who?"

"Sir David."

"Did he yell at you before?"

"He yells at everybody."

"Don't worry about Sir David. He's a pussycat."

I walked to the outside of Studio A and waited. I could hear piano coming from inside but nothing else. Jill and Larisa came out of the dressing room directly. Jill was in her tights, leotard, and pointe shoes. She looked great.

"Don't be scared," I said.

"I'm not."

"Have fun with it. No reason to do it if you're not having fun."

We walked into the studio.

The piano player was tinkling the keys absently. David Derrick was sitting against the back wall mirror, in mid-conversation with a short bald man who looked to be about 35. They were going over some charts, what might have been plans for set pieces. There were a few dancers scattered throughout the room warming up.

The three of us walked up to David Derrick. I tried to sound as jolly as I could.

"Hey, we made it."

"You're three minutes late." He looked Jill up and down, then he got up and put his hand behind her head, and turned her head from side to side a couple times. Then he sat down again.

"What piece will you be auditioning with?"

"We didn't actually have time to—"

"Excuse me, sir. Are you going to speak for your daughter?"

"No, she can speak for herself."

"What will you be auditioning with?"

"I'd like to do 'The Sugar Plum Fairy' from *The Nutcracker*."

"Sam, do you have sheet music for *The Nutcracker?*"

The piano player shook his head.

"Play 'Dance of the Knights'." Sir David instructed. Then to Jill: "It's from the show."

The piano player looked dubious. "Umm ... you want

me to play 'Dance of the Knights'?"

"Yes."

"For her audition?"

"Play it, Sam."

Jill said, "I've heard it."

"Do the best you can, dearie."

The piano player started. The music was strange. It sounded military, like a march or something. Jill started dancing, and for something that she was basically making up as she was going along, I thought she was doing really well. And she looked like she was having fun. She was smiling anyway.

I looked over at David Derrick. He watched Jill for about ten seconds, and then turned to the short bald man and continued his conversation. The piano player kept playing, and Jill kept dancing, and Sir David continued to ignore her.

Pretty soon the artistic director came in. She watched at the door, a smile creeping across her face.

The piano player finished, and Sir David continued talking. Then he noticed the music had stopped and he said to Jill:

"Thank you. We're done." He came over to me.

"You didn't even watch her." I was livid.

"I did too."

"For about ten seconds."

"Are you angry?"

"Yes, I'm angry."

"Well, don't be. I can tell whether or not a dancer has chops in ten seconds. I don't need to watch the whole piece." He turned to Jill. "You did fine. Your name again?"

"Jill."

"Jill. You did fine. Have you ever done any sword work?"

"I've done some fencing at school. Not much, but

some. We learned it as part of a production of *Cyrano.*"

"Really? Hmm... How would you feel about playing a boy?"

From across the room, I heard the artistic director shout, "No!"

"Think differently," he said.

"I told you we're rounding up boys. We're not casting girls in the boys' roles. If we were, we'd cast a girl from our school, not bring in an outsider."

"Well, we're bringing in this outsider." He turned to Jill. "You'd have to cut your hair. Short."

"That's not a problem."

"And you're going to miss six weeks of school. Much of what you'll be rehearsing is stage combat. You'll be with the fellows."

"Okay."

"We're rehearsing in every studio here. Four studios, four rehearsals. We're short of boys — well, we say boys, but of course we really mean men — we're short of boys and we're having to do triple casting. You'll be in the corps de ballet, so you won't be doing any solos, but you'll be on stage every night."

"That sounds wonderful. Thank you. Thank you so much."

"We have one rule and this is it: If you make a mistake and I correct your mistake, and you make the same mistake again, you're fired. Do you understand that?"

"Yes."

"Good. Are you religious?"

"Yes sir. I'm a Christian."

"Okay. For the next six weeks, I am Jesus Christ. Now go into Studio C. We'll draw up your contract by the end of the week."

Jill nodded, said another thank you. We were almost out of the studio when the artistic director stopped her.

"Young lady."

"Yes."

"If you take this job, I can promise you, you will never work in San Antonio again."

David Derrick laughed. "Is that a threat? Surely you can do better than that. This girl wants to dance in New York City. She wants to dance in London, Monte Carlo, Berlin. You think she wants to stay in San Antonio all her life and do ballet for the sheepherders? That's not a threat. If you want to threaten her, you should tell her that if she takes the part you'll make sure she never leaves." Then he turned back to Jill. "Studio C. Let's go. Tick tock tick tock."

Jill walked us out to the truck. She said she'd get a ride home with Ricardo, and asked me if I could pick up her car. There was one thing I wondered.

"Do you have experience with swords?"

"No," she said. "I lied about that."

"Good."

Then she went back inside.

Chapter 16

I got back to the house and found this movie online called *Romeo + Juliet* that I watched because I wanted to get an idea of the story. Wouldn't you know, it had that same actor fella, that Leo Deprecia dude that's in *Titanic*. I can't seem to get away from that guy. Is he in everything? The movie was okay I guess, but I never figured out why he was so hot and bothered about this Juliet gal. She was not really my type since, as I said, I'm not into the skinny ones. That gal was so skinny she looked like a piece of dental floss with a blonde wig on top. I wanted to reach through the screen and give her a cheeseburger.

Jill came home the next night with her hair cut short, but not too short. I guess you could say she looked kind of like a boy. Almost.

Providence, her school, was very supportive and gave her time off without penalty. She met with her teachers and collected assignments for the next six weeks, and she did her reading and homework when she wasn't rehearsing. They were all very proud of her, as we all were, I think I can say.

As the days passed, Jill seemed to bloom like a winter

jasmine. She was having fun again, and it was good to see. She laughed a lot when she recounted things that happened during rehearsal. She liked training with the swords, working with the boys. She was excited by life again.

She even liked Sir David, if you can believe that. She said that he yelled at them constantly and insulted them all the time, but he was a great director and — this really surprised me — a great teacher. He encouraged his dancers to research their parts, to read up on medieval times and get to know their characters. Sir David was also into learning about different cultures himself. He told them he was planning on going to Mexico as a side trip when he could get a day off.

The show was going to be brilliant, she said. She and all the boys were constantly trying to please him. Whenever he gave them a compliment, they knew they were improving because he rarely said anything nice.

Jill also got the lowdown on what was happening over there at the San Antonio Ballet, mostly that it had bitten off more than it could chew. It was really a medium-sized company, but this artistic director gal had decided she wanted to go to the next level so she hired David Derrick and committed to a production she did not have the money for or the talent to pull off. And by talent, I mean boys. She had enough girls to do any production she wanted to that was female-heavy, but she chose Nureyev's *Romeo and Juliet*, which was originally a cast of seventy-seven, most of which was men. Why she chose to do that is anybody's guess. Prestige, maybe? Ego? It didn't hit her until rehearsals started how much it was going to cost — she didn't budget well — and how hard and expensive it was going to be to get male dancers. She had to go looking for fellas who could do swordplay, and in South Texas there just ain't that many, so she had to do it with less, a total of nineteen dancers, and Jill. Twenty "men" in all. She was also scrambling for grant money.

184

I think back to before Jill's audition, and Ms. Riche and David Derrick were having that shouting match about doing the show in the round. (For you fellas out there what don't know, a show "in the round" is where the audience surrounds the dancers. The audience is the donut, and the dancers is the hole.) There weren't really any reason to get upset about whether or not the show was in the round. She'd sold some tickets already, and she'd have to refund them or get the ticket buyers to exchange them for other seats, but she hadn't sold that many. I think the reason she got upset was because she saw the production slipping away from her, and she was losing control over it.

Folks do that when they lose power. I'm sure Ms. Riche had staked her career on the success of the San Antonio Ballet, and when the thing starts spinning out of control suddenly and she don't know where it's going to land, well, that can be pretty stressful. And sometimes you just want to be right, even when you're wrong and you *know* you're wrong.

The men principal dancers was having a particularly hard time of it. *Romeo and Juliet* was only going to run for eight shows, but because of the shortage of men there were four casts, which means the guy who played Romeo on the first night would play Tybalt on the second, Mercutio on the third, and Capulet on the fourth, then repeat that schedule the next week. Think about how many steps that'd be to learn. So confusing.

Jill didn't have to worry about that, thankfully. She was in the corps, as most of the cast was, so she did not have to learn other parts. The big problem that Jill had was her shoes. The costume designer made all the boys wear boots, and hers weren't a good fit and was rubbing holes in her feet. She'd come home every night and soak her feet in the bathtub. They was swollen and split and the skin was rubbing off in some places. It looked real painful.

Jill and Ricardo started kind of seeing each other, which I thought was pretty inevitable. At first, Jill drove her car to the rehearsal, but then after a few days she and Ricardo decided it would just be easier to carpool. Then about a week later I saw them having a serious talk on the front porch of our house. She had what you might describe as infatuated puppy dog love face. It was touching. She'd gone through so much.

I got a call from Detective Neary. She said that Peter Vanderburg had been arrested several weeks ago and charged with uploading naked pictures of underage girls to the internet. None of the pictures were of Jill, though the pictures were similar — half-dressed kids that looked to be comatose, or catatonic. Vanderburg had his plea hearing that afternoon and the judge scheduled his sentencing in three weeks. His lawyer had managed to cut a deal with the DA, three-to-five years in the state pen at Huntsville with the possibility of parole after two years, and on the sex offender registry for life. Neary asked me if I want to attend the sentencing and I said I did. Yeah I wanted to hear what he had to say for himself. You bet I did. Then I said "Goodbye, Julia," and thanked her for being such a good soul, and then hung up.

I thought later about what the detective said. She said *girls*, as in Vanderburg uploaded pictures of *girls*, as in more than one, to the internet. It wasn't Jill, so it must have been at least two *after* Jill. Which meant he went out and did again at least twice. Why would he do that? He was already a suspect. Why would he go out and do it again when he knew the cops was looking at him for rape?

Yeah. I really wanted to hear what that boy had to say.

Jill had a Sunday off so we went to The Hill to see my dad. This was about three weeks into rehearsal. I wasn't sure she would want to go. She was limping a lot on account of the foot sores she'd got from those dang boots, so I figured she'd want to stay off her feet, but she said no, she wanted to go, so away we went.

My dad wasn't doing so hot. He was pretty ornery, actually. He was mainly ornery because my brother Ed was there for a visit, and Ed talks all the time and that annoys heck out of Dad so that makes him a little ornery. My dad loves Ed, naturally, because he's his son, but as you know, Ed's really hard to take sometimes.

We walked in and Ed was in the process of re-telling my dad about our last meeting.

"Well lookee here, it's the jail bird. We was just talking about you. We was just talking about how I bailed your ass out of jail after you broke into my house."

"Don't say 'ass' boy. I don't like it."

"Yes sir."

"How are you, Dad?" I asked.

"Not bad. Well, hello, young lady."

"Hi Grandpa."

Ed went on, "So anyway, Dad, I pick him up—"

"Didn't you tell me this story already, son?"

"—and I'm taking him to the auto pound so's he can get his truck—"

"Billy Jim tells me you're in a ballet now."

"—and he's acting all mad, like it's my fault he broke into my house."

"Yes, I'm doing *Romeo and Juliet* down with the San Antonio Ballet."

"Well that's right good. Wish I could come see it."

"Dad, listen. Hey Dad? Don't that beat all. Tell them what you said, Billy Jim, about how those Stahlwille tools is yours, and about how dad give them to you. Oh, and he wants his guns back too. After he dang near tore down my house, now he wants his guns back."

Then my dad said, "I'm remembering back to a time..."

"Do you think I ought to give him those guns? 'Heck no' is my opinion."

"Shut up, Ed. What was you saying, Dad?"

"Don't tell me to shut up."

"Let him talk."

"All right. But don't tell me to shut up."

"Children!" My dad continued, "I'm remembering back to a time back when we lived on West Elsmere."

"I remember that house," I said. "We drove by there a time or two."

"I must have been about seven or eight," he said. "My brother, your Uncle Joe, must have been eleven or twelve. I don't know what prompted my brother to come up with this grand idea, but he decided I should shoot the ten-gauge shotgun."

"Boy, you really changing the subject, ain't you?"

"Ed?" I said.

"Okay."

Dad went on. "It belonged to the family, this shotgun did. It was my dad's. It was an old family gun. Been around for years. Well, this house we lived in, this whole house was built at street level, but to get into the kitchen you had to go up a long flight of stairs, probably, oh, fifteen or twenty feet in the air, something like that because it was built on a slope. So a long flight of stairs up the back way. And alongside the back fence were these trees. There was a whole battery of trees there, tall trees, you know, to get shade in the summertime.

"So my brother, he decided I should learn how to shoot the shotgun. So the stairs had a banister to keep you from falling over the side. Outside the kitchen door was a platform where you could bring your groceries up and set them down before you went inside. And around this platform was this banister. And so he decided that it would be a good place to rest the shotgun because it was really heavy for a seven- or eight-year-old kid. I wasn't nine yet because when I was nine we moved to Meredith, where you're living now, Billy Jim.

"So anyway, he lined me up there on the porch and put the barrel of that shotgun on this banister so that the shot would go up in the air and go through the trees and disperse before it hit the houses a block away. So he got the thing all loaded up and put me up against the gun, and he said, 'Here's the trigger, just pull it whenever you're ready.' Which you have to know about a ten-gauge shotgun: first, they don't even make them anymore they're so big. Everything is 12-gauge now. The biggest shotgun you can buy is 12-gauge."

"Tell me something I don't know," said Ed.

"I didn't know," said Jill.

"Shut up, Ed," I said.

"This was a ten," Dad said. "So it had a lot of kick. I didn't know kick from schmick. Anyway, he lined me up with this shotgun with the barrel over the banister and he said, 'Okay, whenever you're ready,' and I pulled the trigger on that thing and that thing knocked me clear through the screen door and halfway across the kitchen. I mean, it really had a kick. And of course, I probably weighed sixty or seventy pounds, something like that. The gun weighed almost as much as I did. Anyway, it blew a hole in those trees like you wouldn't believe. You could see the universe from the hole in that thing. It just blew all those leaves out and there wasn't anything left.

"I just picked myself up off the floor like, 'What happened?' Your Uncle Joe just stood there a-laughing. He knew what was going to happen, for sure. He was four years older, so he knew. It knocked me right on my butt, right through the door. And he thought that was real funny."

Ed said, "Great story, Dad. What made you think of that?"

My dad thought about it. I'm not sure if he really knew.

"My brother and I were never close when we got older," he said. "He moved to Baton Rouge after he got back from Vietnam and I only saw him six or seven times after that. You know what? I ought to call him. It's been so long."

"Dad," I said. "Don't you remember? Uncle Joe died five years ago."

"He did?"

"Yeah. He had a heart attack."

"Oh. Yeah. I remember that now." Things got quiet, then my dad said, "You're going to need to give those guns back, Ed. And those tools are his as well."

"Forget it," I said. "Keep the guns. Keep the tools too. But I want my hunting rifles."

Me and Jill stayed for another half hour or so. My dad had all kinds of questions about what she was doing. Then we left.

Later that night, I got up in the middle of the night and went out into the kitchen to get some water. It was late, after two.

While I was standing there at the sink, my ears perked up to a sound coming from somewhere in the house. I heard it... I heard... crying. I heard crying. It was Jill. She was in her room and the door was closed. I could hear the muffled sound coming from the other side.

I stayed in the kitchen for a few minutes, banging around the cabinets like I was looking for something because I figured if she heard me rooting around, maybe she'd come out and talk to me but she didn't. I didn't want to barge in on her suffering, whatever it was she was going through, so I went back to bed. The noise drifted down the hallway into my bedroom. The crying got less and less and then it stopped.

The next morning she was slow getting up, slow getting to the kitchen for breakfast. She moved like an old woman, deliberately, like her bones were creaky.

I'd fixed her some juice and toast. She slowly spread jam on the toast, and then put it on her plate. She didn't eat it. She just looked it, with her knife in her hand. Then she dropped the knife on the plate, and it clattered "BANG!" and made us both jump. She sucked in air, mumbled "excuse me," and went back into her room.

Ricardo came knocking on the front door not long after that. I let him in and he sat on the couch and waited. She came out a few minutes later and made her way to the front door without looking at anybody or saying anything. He followed her out and they got in his car and took off for Monday morning rehearsal.

I was home when she came back that night. She seemed like her old self, like this ghost of my daughter had never actually made an appearance at breakfast. She was smiling and excited and talked all about what they did that day, and told this story of how one of the young dancers had been bragging about his credits to the others, so Sir David demoted him to being a flag carrier in one of the major dances. She was really tickled about that.

I laughed along with her, but inside I was not really amused. I didn't know who this person was I'd seen in morning. Or when I'd see her again.

Chapter 17

It was a Tuesday night. I'd been working all day at the garage. I'd just finished my adult ballet class, which was being substitute-taught by Inez Garza. I was tired. Last thing I wanted to do was rehearse this piece we was supposed to be doing at the old folks home but a deal's a deal. We'd agreed to rehearse twice a week Tuesdays and Thursdays after class. Our "performance," if you want to call it that, at Blue Skies was scheduled three weeks after Jill's show closed, seven weeks out.

Larisa Lakewood came in, dressed in sweats. She hugged Inez Garza and the two had a little chitchat, laughing like schoolgirls, about what I got no idea, and Inez handed over the keys to the studio and told her to lock up after we were done. The other adult ballet students were milling around, packing up and leaving.

Larisa don't take ballet on Tuesday night. She come when the class was over. She was surprised to see me.

"You already warmed up?"

"I take class on Tuesday night," I said.

Arched eyebrow, electric grin. "You do?"

"Thursday and Saturday too."

"I know, I'm in your class on Thursday, doofus."

"Yeah, I recall."

"Taking ballet Tuesday, Thursday and Saturday. Why, you're just a little balletomane, aren't you?

"What's that?"

"That's a person who really loves the ballet."

"Uh, I don't know about that."

She brushed my forearm with her fingertips. "I bet you are. Well, let's get started!"

She set up a CD player, and by the time she got her memory stick plugged in and her song cued up, everybody else had left. Now it was just her and me.

"First of all," she said, "thank you for agreeing to do this."

"It's okay."

"I want you to know though that if you really don't feel like it, if you really don't want to, you don't have to. I won't hold it against you if you want to back out."

I'd thought about that. I really *didn't* want to. I'm not a dancer. This is just a hobby, and probably one I won't have once I figure out why I'm doing it in the first place. I look ridiculous dancing. I look like a big bear. People are going to look at me and laugh. I'm going to be a big joke, a big *fat* joke. I'm going to embarrass myself. Everybody is going to laugh at me.

Only... Only...

Only I really want Larisa Lakewood to be my girl-friend. I can't help it. I mean, I'm *really* lonely. I got nothing in my life except my daughter, and she'll be leaving soon. And here comes this bright, beautiful woman who for some reason seems to be attracted to me. She seems to be. I don't really know that she is. If she is, I don't know why she is.

What do I know is that I want her. Yes, she's a liberal, but if we stay off politics, we'll get along okay, I reckon.

I'm doing this dance at the old folk's home because I want to be with her. I want to be with her. I want to fall in love with her. But I can't tell her that. That sounds so stupid!

I want to have sex with her, of course, but that's about fourth of fifth on the list. The most important thing is, I just want somebody to care about me. I want somebody to care about what I do, who I am. I want somebody to be interested in me. I want somebody to say, "How was your day?" and they really want to know. I want somebody to look me in the eyes and say "I love you," and mean it.

I'm turning into my dad. My dad lost his wife and his life went downhill and he never recovered. Now I've lost my wife and my life is going downhill and I'm looking at the same thing. I'm looking at being in an old folks home by myself watching Fox News and waiting for family to come and visit me once a week and being angry and spitting at everything. I don't want that. I don't want it!

"So do you still want to do it?" she said. "The dancing?"

"Oh, I reckon I can. Just don't expect too much."

"Fine, fine. You're going to be great, Billy Jim."

"I, uh... you're going to choreograph, right?"

"Yes siree."

"And you're going to dance too?"

"That's right."

"So you're going to choreograph and dance at the same time?"

"Whoa, you got this logic thing down."

"That's just surprising to me."

"Why?"

"Well, I figured you'd want to choreograph, or you'd want to dance. I didn't know you'd want to do both. Or could do both."

"I've always wanted to try it. And anyway, if I brought

in another dancer then I'd have to share you, and then I wouldn't get you all to myself."

"Ah. So, um, what are we doing?"

"We're doing a section of the grand pas de deux from *Don Q.*"

"*Don Q?*"

"*Don Quixote.*"

"Oh." Playing dumb of course. I know what *Don Q* is.

"We're going to adapt the choreography by Marius Petipa. You know who he is?"

"No." Lying.

"He's this Frenchman who choreographed all the great Russian ballets. Look him up sometime. He's pretty amazing."

"Okay." I been watching stuff about Petipa and other famous classical choreographers for months. YouTube's got all that.

"And we're going to use the original score by Ludwig Minkus. But our little show is going to be a tad different."

"How so?"

"Well, Billy Jim, look at us. We can't do it like the pros because we're not pros. And we can't do it like the young folks because we're not young. So we're going to have to figure out what's best for us and go and do it that way."

She hit the "play" button and a twist song from the 1960s came up and she started dancing. I just stood there.

"Come on, Billy Jim!"

"What's that? Is this the music we're using?"

"Does that sound like Ludwig Minkus? Come on, now. Show me what you got!"

Eventually, I start moving too. I thought, I really need a drink for this. Yes, this would go way better with two or three beers.

We listened to some old songs, the music we grew up with,

and the Minkus pas de deux we'd be dancing to. We talked about what we wanted to do. I told her, honestly, that I didn't really want to do much. A man's position in the ballet is to make the female dancer look good, and that's what I wanted to do. I did not want to do a solo, I did not want to do a jeté or any of that. I wanted to stay in the background while she danced. Larisa pointed out that what a man does *is* dance, and whatever movement I did while I was onstage, it would be dancing.

There's basically four things that happen on a pas de deux, all of which we've studied in adult ballet class: you got your jumps, your turns, your promenades, and your lifts. There's lots more stuff in a pas de deux, naturally, but that's the basic stuff.

First is the simple side jumps. The guy dancer lifts the ballerina into the air, lifts her higher while she jumps. If you really want to get crazy, the guy dancer can throw her high in the air and catch her when she comes down.

Next is the turns, which look easy enough for me. The ballerina does a pirouette, meaning she spins around and around, and the guy dancer stands behind her with his hands on her waist, stabilizing her while she's doing it. Cake.

Then you got your promenade. So the ballerina gets on pointe, meaning she gets on one tipee-toe, and the guy dancer takes her by the hand and once she's steady he walks around her in a circle, turning her as she goes.

Then finally there's the lift. This is where the ballerina is lifted high in the air, where the guy dancer basically picks her up and holds her up over his head, and she stays in that position until he brings her back to earth again. Sometimes this ends in this thing called a "fish," where the guy dancer basically drops her, and then catches her at a downward angle right before her chin hits the floor. Then they hold that position for the audience, like they having their picture took. Folks sometimes say a lift looks sexy because the guy has the girl sitting on his shoulder, or she's arcing over his head, but brother, I'm here to tell you, it sure don't feel that way. You lift some girl in the air and you're just thinking about too many things, like "Is this on time with the music?" or "Is she balanced?" or "Is she at the right angle for the audience?" or "Am I going to drop her?"

Larisa wanted to follow the Petipa choreography as close as we could, changing it here and there when we need to. I just nodded my head. It all sounded okay to me. Then we got on YouTube and watched some videos of *Don Q* being done by the pros.

Looking at the way the pros did it, I thought there's just no way in tarnation we were going to be able pull this off. For one thing, the shortest bit that we could do was four minutes long, and just checking off the steps, it looked like this: promenade, turn, promenade, turn, jump, turn, jump, turn, lift, turn, jump, turn, turn, turn, lift, fish. That comes to two promenades, nine turns, three jumps, two lifts, and one fish. In four minutes, with actually a whole bunch of other stuff thrown in too.

Larisa asked me how I felt about it. I said fine. I could torpedo this by being a Negative Ned, but I decided to go along with it. She was going to have to do most of the work anyway.

The first thing we did was the promenade, following the Petipa. That really went pretty well. It's easy for me. All I have to do is walk in a circle. Larisa was also giving pretty solid direction. "Try to keep my hand in front of my solar plexis. And look me in the face. You can tell if I'm balanced by looking at my face."

Then we went into the first turn. This is when the girl spins around and around and the guy stands behind her and steadies her torso. "Start with your left hand. You have to put your left hand in first. If you don't, I'll lose the momentum and you'll have to physically turn me. Try to focus on what we're working on right this second. Don't get ahead of me."

She did three turns and stopped. The back of her head was in front of my nose. She didn't see me do this, but I closed my eyes and took a big sniff of her hair. It was strong and feminine, like cherry blossoms. That's really some shampoo. I opened my eyes, and I noticed that she was looking at me in the mirror. She smiled. I didn't say nothing.

"Well," she said. "That's the first bit."

"That took all of twenty seconds."

"Let's get to it."

And we did. We cut one of the lifts so now there was only one, at the end of the piece. Also, one of the things we started doing was calling the steps. So the music would start and we would both call "promenade" and then go into a promenade, and count the beats, ("Promenade and one-two-three-four-five-six-seven-eight") the next stop was a turn, so we both would call "turn" and she'd go into a turn. This was her idea. She said she was going to call the steps at first, but she changed her mind and wanted me to call them with her because she figured I'd get to know what was coming if I called them too. So that's what we did.

We worked about two hours and got the first minute and a half done. It wasn't pretty, let me tell you. What Larisa did was good, but I certainly didn't look like no dancer.

Larisa is cheerful most of the time and she has a great attitude, very positive, but I felt like I was only getting to know one side of her, the smiling side she wanted me to see.

Then one Tuesday afternoon I met her at work. We were going to get in a quick rehearsal because it was her mom's birthday, and she and her brothers were going to throw her a surprise party so she couldn't meet that night. I told her I'd pick her up on my lunch hour, which I did, and we'd go off to the studio together. So I was sitting in her real estate office waiting for her to get off the phone, and I heard her yelling at her brother, who had decided he wanted to go bowling instead of going to their mom's surprise party. Larisa was chewing him up like gristle on a T-bone. She was so mad the vein on her forehead was standing up like a lawn weed.

"You want to go bowling!? No, you're coming and you're coming at seven! And if you're late, or if you don't show, I'm going to track you down and I'm going to smack you so hard your toupee is going to be the only thing left of your head! No... No... *No!* Now tell me you're coming, or I'm going to come over there — over to your work! — and I'm going to drop you out a window! I swear to god I am going to open the window and I'm going to throw you out of it! Now say it! Say, 'Yes, Larisa, I'm coming. I'll see you at 7:00'... Good. And don't be late!"

She hung up, sat back in her chair and steamed. I must have been smiling a little because she said, "What's so funny?"

"Yeah, I don't' think I've ever seen you lit up."

"My brother's a moron."

Later, on Saturday, Larisa called me after class and asked me to have dinner with her. She said it was just a spur-of-the-moment invite, that she didn't have anything planned, but if I was free, I should come over. So I did.

There weren't nothing in the fridge, so we ordered a large pepperoni from Pizza Hut. While we were waiting for it, I started doing what Ricardo was doing when he was over at my house, looking around at all the pictures on the wall and making comments. "That there's your daughter? Well, she's real pretty. What grade's she in?"

I noticed that one of the family photos had a boy with Down's Syndrome, who looked to be about twelve or so.

"That's Rupert," she said, handing me a glass of red.

"Who's he?"

"He's my younger brother's son. He's very sweet."

"Huh..."

"That's why I took a little umbrage when you used the word 'libtard.'"

"It's just a word."

"It's a cruel word. And if you had kin that was mentally handicapped you'd think it was cruel too."

"It's just an expression. I didn't mean nothing by it." I was starting to get a little annoyed by the lecturing. "And anyway, you call your brother a moron."

"That's because he is a moron."

"Okay, I won't say 'libtard.' How about if I say 'lib-moron'?"

"Perfect."

We sat on the couch and commenced to drink wine. Before too long, Larisa was feeling no pain. At least she was a happy drunk.

"You know what I like about you, Billy Jim?" she said, putting her foot in my lap.

"What's that?"

"Nothing."

We talked for about an hour. She told me all about how her marriage ended when her husband the car dealer traded her in for a younger model. She told me about her son Christian, who was off to college at Texas A&M, and her daughter Abby, who may look pretty in the picture on the wall but was going through a phase where she hated everyone and everything, except Jesus and this band I'd never heard of called Cackling Hags and her best friend named Cindy.

Larisa got up to get another bottle of wine and I was

sitting on the couch just relaxing, kind of feeling cozy and at home. I started thinking, "Is this how it starts? Should I lean in to kiss her? Will she make the first move? She *is* liberal, after all. Is this what she wants? She's flirting with me, right?" Then I heard keys clicking in the front door lock and Larisa's daughter Abby stepped in.

This girl was about seventeen, dressed in torn-up jeans and a t-shirt that said "Just Do Me." She had piercings all over her cheeks and spikes in her ears. No, she didn't look nothing like her picture in the living room.

"Who are you?" She was kind of mad.

"I'm a friend of your mom's. The name's Billy Jim Hauck."

"Where is she?"

"In the kitchen."

"Mom!" she called out.

Larisa appeared in the doorway with a bottle of wine in her hand. She looked kind of shocked and — what was it, guilty? — to see her daughter.

"Wh-what are you doing home? I thought your band was playing tonight and then you were going to stay at Cindy's."

"We broke up."

"The band broke up?"

"No, not the *band*," she practically spit out. "Me and Cindy."

She sat on the couch and snatched some pizza out of the box, started chomping on it. "Is this all we got for dinner?" Then she grabbed the remote and turned on the TV.

"*Titanic?*" she said. "That movie blows!"

Chapter 18

The day of Peter Vanderburg's sentencing came, and I headed down to the courthouse.

They brought him into court about thirty minutes late, dressed in an orange jump suit with the words "Bexar County Jail" in black letters on the back. There, right in front of me, was the boy I almost killed.

The thing that struck me most about him was his age. He was just a kid, a handsome kid too. I could see why Jill might have a crush on him, if only for his looks. But so young. He looked like he'd lost his baby teeth just a couple years ago. That didn't make me feel sorry for him. But it made me wonder how he got here. He ought to be out tossing the football with his friends or riding bikes, camping with his family or hanging out with his girlfriend. But here he was, about to be shipped off to that House of Horrors known as Huntsville State Prison.

There was a woman and a man sitting behind him, obviously his mother, crying, and his dad next to her, emptied, haggard. What an unbelievable state of affairs to be in, to find your son, your flesh and blood, about to get sent to the penitentiary for sex crimes. I wondered if they knew the full extent of what he did. They had to, right? They had to know their boy was a rapist, a serial rapist actually, and he'd done this to innocent girls like Jill. His victims weren't in the courtroom for the sentencing because there weren't any kids in the courtroom. Just me, the Vanderburgs, and two other couples. I assumed these folks were the fathers and mothers of his other victims.

The judge was already sitting when they brought him in and the bailiff sat him next to his lawyer. The judge shuffled through some papers, and then said very curtly, "Peter Wayne Vanderburg, please rise." He did. "In the matter of the *State of Texas vs. Peter Wayne Vanderburg,* how do you plead?"

"Guilty, your honor."

Then the judge asked him a lot of questions like, "Do you understand the charges against you?" "Do you know the consequence of the plea?" "Do you know that by pleading guilty you lose the right to a jury trial?" "Did anyone force you to accept this settlement?" and he answered as he'd been directed. Then the judge said, "Are you in fact pleading guilty to the distribution of child pornography?" "Yes." Then the judge said, "Do you have anything to say before I impose sentence?"

"Yes, your honor."

"You may proceed."

"First of all, I... how can I... I'd like to apologize to the people I've hurt... I know, uh, that, uh... I wish there were some way to excuse, uh, explain myself but there just isn't, your honor.

"I don't know why I did what I did. Meaning I don't blame anybody, your honor. It isn't my parents fault. I was never physically or sexually abused as a kid. I was never really in need of anything. My mom loves me, and my dad too and I always knew they did. But I've always — how can I say this, your honor? — I've always hurt folks without knowing why. I've gone to counseling to try and figure it out. Sometimes I think there is a snake living inside me, your honor, and he comes out from time to time to choke the living hell out of people and then he goes back inside me and he sleeps. I want to kill this thing. And I think I can. No. I will. But I got to figure out what it is. And why.

"I know what I did was wrong and I lie awake at night feeling really guilty about all the suffering I've caused. What I did goes against my upbringing and against my Christian values. I think deep down I wanted to get caught. That's why I left a trail. I could have erased the pictures or made it harder to trace, but I didn't.

"I know that I got to pay a debt to society, and I'm willing to. I wish there was some way I could, but I don't think there is. I don't think I can pay it."

Then Peter Vanderburg looked at the families in the courtroom.

"I am deeply sorry and ashamed for what I've done to you and your kids, but I don't expect you to forgive me so I won't ask. If I get killed in prison, that'll take care of it. And, you know, maybe that's okay. Maybe that's God's plan."

Then he turned back around and stood quietly. The judge let it sit there a moment.

"Are you finished?"

"Yes, your honor."

"I accept the plea bargain agreed to by the district attorney and your defense council. Peter Wayne Vanderburg, you are hereby sentenced to three-to-five years in the state prison at Huntsville, minus time served. You will be eligible for parole after two years. You will be placed on the federal sex offender registry for the rest of your natural life. Do you understand the sentence?"

"Yes sir."

The judge nodded to the bailiff.

The sentence was too light. The judge should have ignored the plea bargain and handed down more years. If he serves his full term he'll be out when he's twenty-two, and I got to tell you, I got a hard time believing he's going to come back reformed. And if he gets parole, he'll be out at nineteen.

If Jill had agreed to testify, or the others had agreed, and we'd won, he'd be looking at walking out of prison as a man nearing fifty, which makes him much less of a threat. Lord knows what kind of person he's going to be when he gets out now. That snake living inside him is just going to get bigger, I reckon.

The bailiff came over to the defendant's table. Vanderburg stood up and shook his lawyer's hand and smiled.

"It worked," he said. "Thank you."

The lawyer did not smile back, or even nod. Vanderburg was handcuffed and taken away. He did not look at his parents, but stared straight ahead as he was led out. The judge hadn't heard or seen this exchange. He was shuffling through papers.

It was all very clear to me from that little comment that everything Peter Vanderburg had said — about being sorry, about wanting forgiveness, about having this evil inside him that he didn't understand — all of it had been a lie.

I still hadn't got the answer I was looking for so I went out to the hallway and waited for his lawyer. He came out about five minutes later. I'm guessing he was waiting until the other parents had left.

This guy was in his early thirties. Camelhair sport coat, brown corduroys, slicked-back hair. His face was pretty non-descript. I wish I could tell you he was rat-faced, but he wasn't. Nothing distinguishing at all about this loser.

"Why did he do it?" I said. He jumped a little. I'd startled him.

"Who are you?"

"Let's just say I'm a concerned parent. The detective who worked his case called me and told me his sentencing was today, and I'd get to hear him speak to the court."

"What's your interest in this case?"

"I think you probably know. Or you can figure it out. You coached him, didn't you?"

"He's my client."

"He didn't really believe any of that stuff he said, did he?"

"Why would he say it then?"

"I heard what he said to you. 'It worked.' I heard it."

"We prepared his statement to the court to serve the defendant's needs."

"So why did he do it? Why did he rape those gals?"

"He never admitted to that."

"He didn't have to because he got a plea bargain. Look, all I want to know is the why. Why did he do it? Does he even know?"

"We never talked about rape."

"Well, why do you think?"

"Why do I think?" The lawyer sighed. He started to say something, and stopped. Then, if you can believe this, he told me the truth. Or at least what he thought was the truth.

"Why did he do it? That's a really good question. Maybe it's because he grew up in a house that gave him everything he wanted and told him he was special and never told him he was wrong. But he's not special. And not only is he wrong, he is criminally sociopathic. But there is more to it than that. I do not believe it's because he's young and stupid, or it's simply because he hates women. He lives in a culture of brutality that celebrates violence and money and fame and not much else, where children can watch porn on their smartphones all hours of the day and night, and see all kinds of abuse and degradation of women and girls, and 'oh look, all girls are promiscuous and all women are whores who will have sex with you because you have money' or 'they're all nymphomaniacs who just can't get enough.' A guy like Peter Vanderburg, he buys into all that. He thinks if a girl shows interest in him, it's not because she has a schoolgirl crush, it's because she's a whore and she wants his dick and it's his prerogative to rape her and take pictures of her to humiliate her and put them on the internet for the whole world to see. And he'll tag her, so the picture will follow her for the rest of her life, so when her children google her name thirty years from now that's what they'll see, a permanent record of their mother's humiliation. And you know what? Guys like Peter Vanderburg think that's really funny. Because it's what those whores want and it's what they deserve."

"And you defended him."

"That's right, I did. And I'd do it again. And you know why?"

"I don't care."

"Because even the vilest defendant is entitled to an attorney who will fight for his interests. That's part of living in a free society."

"But it's not fair."

"It *is* fair, and it's the way the system works. But I certainly don't expect you to like it."

The attorney turned and walked away and my dealings with Peter Vanderburg were done. At least for now.

Chapter 19

It was Saturday night and Jill called me from rehearsal. I was at work cleaning up, about ready to go home.

"Daddy?"

"Hey, Jill."

"Sir David wants to—."

The phone when through a muffled change of hands and Sir David came on the line.

"Lynyrd Skynyrd?"

"Yes?"

"Jill tells me you're a hunter."

"That's right."

"I want you to take me hunting. The dancers have a day off tomorrow so I have free time. Why don't you pop by the Starbucks on Broadway and Grandview and pick me up at, say, around seven in the morning? I have an apartment close to there and I'll be having my breakfast tea. Cheers!"

He gave the phone back to Jill. I heard her say, "Daddy, I—" and then the line went dead.

It's kind of funny, the way folks act sometimes. David Derrick is one of these fellas who snaps his fingers and everyone falls into line. I guess he figures that will happen everywhere he goes and with everybody he talks to, which ain't nothing but bald arrogance if you ask me. If I was in a different state of mind, I would have snorted and hung up. But I kind of like David. The man's got a spine, if nothing else. So I decided to take him hunting.

Trouble was, it wasn't a good time of the year. Deer season was done. We was in April already so hunting seasons for most wild game was over. I got on the Texas Parks and Wildlife website to see what we actually could hunt, and where. And there weren't much.

I didn't have any guns. I hadn't gone back to Ed's to collect my rifles so after work I stopped by his house and got them, plus a couple of .22 rifles we'd need for tomorrow. I had to leave a check with him as a deposit, of all things, because Ed thought I might decide to keep his stuff.

Later, when Jill got home from rehearsal, she told me what happened:

"See, Daddy, we were in break, and I was sitting there with Ricardo and the guys, and Ricardo mentions that we have this buck mounted on our living room wall, so that means you're a good shot and he had to be careful how he treats me or you'll come after him, and everybody thought that was funny, and everybody starts laughing, ha ha ha. Then Sir David walks in. He sees everybody's laughing, and he goes, 'What's so funny?' and I go, 'Ricardo told this joke about my dad being a hunter' and he goes, 'Your dad's a hunter?' and I go, 'Are you kidding? He's been hunting all his life,' and he goes, 'You're Lynyrd Skynyrd's daughter, aren't you?' and I go, 'Huh?' and he goes, 'You *are* Lynyrd Skynyrd's daughter. Your father is going to take me hunting tomorrow. Call him right now.' And I did."

So I picked up Sir David the next morning at the Starbucks. He was dressed in a long-sleeve shirt and jeans with a light coat, which is fine, but no hat, so I let him use one of my orange gimme caps, and gave him an orange vest to wear, like mine. Then we got in the truck and drove to the site.

In the truck he said, "You are going to have to teach me how to shoot. I have never actually handled a gun before."

"Yeah, I reckoned that was the case. Don't worry. When we get out there, I'll learn you how."

"I have a question."

"Okay."

"When hunting, where do we aim? Do we aim for the torso? I really know nothing about it, I'm a complete novice."

"Aim? Well... let's say we're talking about deer," I said. "When I first started hunting deer, I was taught to aim for the heart, which is just behind the shoulder. I did this for a couple of hunts, and that shot was okay, but if I was two or three inches off, then the deer didn't die quick, even took a few futile steps afore dropping. It's the shot most people take because it's a sure kill if you ain't too far off the area of the heart, but I personally never liked it because the deer might live half a minute or a little more. So not long after I started hunting I changed to aiming for the head — particularly for the area where the neck joins the skull. If executed properly and the weather, especially the wind, doesn't alter the flight path of the bullet it's an instant kill and the critter never knows what hit him. He's dead before he hits the ground.

"Also, and very importantly, none of the meat is affected in the least. It's really a clean kill that many hunters don't have the patience for. It's also a real small area, about the size of a silver dollar, but well worth the effort to do it right. If you shoot and miss, the deer lives another day. I just wouldn't shoot it running away — not a clean kill and the intestines would most likely become involved. Not a pleasant thing when cleaning up."

"What happens if it's just wounded? What do you do then?"

"Well, if for some reason I can't imagine I was to shoot and hit one and it didn't go down, I would feel obligated to track it down and finish it off. That's the best thing about a head shot — either it's a kill or an escape. The rifle and scope have to be in perfect condition to pull this off successfully, but then mine is kept that way and checked on a firing range before going on a hunt. Don't got no scopes on these guns though."

Then it was my turn. "Now David, if you don't mind me asking..."

"Yes?"

"Why do you want to go hunting all the sudden? Jill said you wanted to go to Mexico."

"I did. But do you have any idea how big this state is? It would take me a day just to drive there and back, and I can't spare the time."

"So hunting's just a spur of the moment thing or..."

"Do I not seem the type?"

"I wouldn't say that."

"There are two reasons, actually. Firstly, I'm an experience junkie. I like doing new things because anything one does in life can be used in art. I wanted to take a brief sojourn to Mexico, but since I can't, tracking game in the wilds of Texas, shotgun at ready, is an excellent alternative, potentially affording both adventure and excitement. Secondly, well, how do I explain this? There is a character in the story of *Romeo and Juliet* named Tybalt — do you know the story?"

"I heard of it."

"Juliet's cousin is this hot-tempered swashbuckler named Tybalt, and at one point he fights and kills Romeo's friend Mercutio. Then the fiery Tybalt and the enraged Romeo stalk each other on stage like primal brutes before Romeo dexterously and passionately slaughters him. I want to feel what that's like. If I can tell my dancers what it feels like to stalk and kill prey, then I can relate what the characters do as they circle each other, and bring out this dance of the killer."

"Whoa. Maybe we should have brought the guy playing Tybalt with us."

"That sissy? He wouldn't come. So what are we hunting today? Wild boar? Horned Stags? Don't say bear. I'd wet myself if I saw a bear."

"Rabbit."

"*Rabbit?*"

"Yeah."

"You're joking. Look, if this is some attempt to try and humiliate me—"

"You're here at the wrong time of the year! This is April. The only critter that's on season all year round is rabbit."

"No deer?"

"No deer. No javelin. No turkey. Alligators are in season, but we don't got none around these parts."

"So it's rabbit then?"

"So it's rabbit then. But look on the bright side. You'll get your experience. And you'll still be stalking your prey."

"Yes, a little furry bunny rabbit. Some prey."

We drove out to a site northwest of 1604. There's a designated wildlife management area on Spettle Road in Lakehills that only costs $20 for a daily permit. We got there plenty early, around 7:30, but even then there was only two permits left, which we snagged. There is a firing range by the entrance, so I showed David how to shoot a rifle. He wasn't a half bad-shot either, much to my sense of "huh...?" Then we headed off onto the land.

We walked along not saying much. The hunting area sits on a 260-acre ranch in the Texas Hill Country. Lot of trees, rocks, weeds, wildflowers, sage brush, sticker burrs, and dead brown grass. Hills and more hills. It was a Sunday morning in April, a little on the cool side. It was nice.

"What do we do in the event we shoot a rabbit?" he asked. "Eat it?"

"Yeah, we'll eat it."

"I wasn't serious."

"I am. If we kill a rabbit, we'll cook her up and eat it."

"Right, then…" Sir David did not sound too enthused.

We walked along in silence. After about a half hour, we were in a thicket of trees that came upon a lake. I had to smile.

"What do you find so amusing?" he said.

"My dad brought us up here when we were kids. I guess I'd forgot it was up this way."

It was Lake Medina. Where my dad caught the bass with the perch in its mouth. I should bring him up here someday. He'd like that. Wheelchair and all. But maybe he wouldn't. He can't do the things he used to do and I think that frustrates him most of the time.

"Feeling nostalgic," said Sir David.

"Reckon so."

We sat on some boulders. There's granite boulders all over the Hill Country, especially up near Marble Falls in Burnett County, but plenty of them here too. I had a thermos and some flat paper cups in my vest, so I pulled them out and poured us a couple cups of coffee, and we sat there drinking them. I handed David a piece of jerky.

"What's this?"

"Jerky. It's deer. I have it processed at a place in Orange over by the Louisiana border. Go on, try it."

He did, and we sat there and chewed our jerky and stared off at the blue water all quiet like.

"It's lovely out here," he said. "Peaceful."

"Yeah. I ain't been out here in a long time."

There was something I wanted to talk to David about. Something I needed to ask him. Now was as good a time as any, being that his guard was down and he wasn't barking orders at folks.

"Since I got a captive audience..."

"Yes?"

"Do you mind if I ask you a question?"

"Go right ahead."

"I want you to tell me about my daughter."

"All right."

"And don't sugarcoat it."

"Do I strike you as the type of chap who would sugarcoat?"

"No."

"Ask away. But as I warn people who preface this way, do not ask if ye cannot receive."

"Okay." I didn't really like hearing that, but as you can probably tell by now, I don't like fiddling around with niceties all that much myself.

"Do you think Jill is talented enough to be a professional dancer?"

"Meaning do I think she can do it for a living?"

"Yes."

"No, I don't."

"Oh."

"But hold on. Don't look so crestfallen. You asked me if she is talented enough to be a professional dancer, and the answer is no, but she's only 16. She cannot be a professional right now. She needs to keep with her professional training, and if she does that, and she doesn't quit or get injured, I think there is a very good chance that Jill can do it professionally."

"Really?"

"Yes. I could tell when she first auditioned that she was quite good. And I've been watching her during the rehearsal process and I've seen what she can do. She has turnout, flexibility, strength, turns, jumps. But she's not just a technician. She's quite a performer, and she has wonderful musicality. Physically she's got brilliant legs, hips, knees, back. Her feet, she's having a problem with her feet, but it's because of those cursed boots. We've replaced them, but she's got terrible sores."

"I know."

"She needs to be attentive to weight loss. Meaning she shouldn't be too thin. Bone density problems are a result of getting too few calories in the dancer's standard intake. Eating scarcely also predisposes one to injury."

"She likes chocolate."

"So does Jill have the talent? Yes, she does indeed. She has everything she needs. She's extremely well-equipped. Will she be a ballet dancer? It's hard to say. A career in dance is difficult to realize. If she were really, really lucky, she might get invited to join a company and be relegated to the back row of the corps de ballet for her entire career. If she were very fortunate."

"I spect Jill was hoping for something a little more."

"Being in the corps is what every dancer should hope for. She shouldn't dream of being a prima ballerina, or even a soloist. The competition is just too fierce, and there just aren't that many spots. If she found a good company and she made it into the corps and were able to dance for ten years, that would be enough. The dancers in the corps are often astonishing. They are just a slight tick lower than the ones who become stars. And even that's subjective."

"Okay. Well, that answered my question."

"What are Jill's plans?"

"She don't got none right now, I don't reckon. She was supposed to go to YAGP but she missed it this year."

"She could apply to the Joffrey in New York City. They're still taking applications for their ballet trainee program, I think, but she needs to hurry because they start in September and she would have to audition soon. I could make a call on her behalf. That would help. She'd have to write an essay to get in."

"That would be great."

"Consider it done." He stood up. "Shall we continue our hunt for wild beasts?"

We picked up and walked along a narrow trail that went around the lake. I let him take the lead because the last thing I wanted was an inexperienced Hemingway wannabe walking behind me with a loaded gun. The morning was still cool, but you could tell it was fixing to warm up. The wind was kicking up out of the south, a little warmer, and you could see what looked like a thousand yellow fingers shimmering off the water. It was early, so there weren't any jet skis or drunk college kids out yet.

We walked for a time, then came to a clearing and sat down on a concrete sea wall someone had built some time ago, presumably to keep the water from eating up the shoreline. Didn't have to worry too much about that now. The lake was down because of the drought, and three foot of rocks and sand and driftwood swept out before our dangling feet. This wall used to hold the water back. Now it was just a hard bench.

I looked out across the water. The bare gray trees and the evergreens stood thick and at attention on the hill across the way. They stretched into the sky, branches reaching tall and strong for puffy white clouds that floated lazily along, miles overhead. It was one of those mornings when you feel the sun soaking into your skin, your pores opening up like a sunflower and taking it all in.

A perch jumped out of the water and hung there in the air for a split second, then plopped back in.

David said, "Why would a fish do that?"

"Reckon he was looking for something to eat. He probably saw something hovering over the water that looked tasty and he figured he'd make a grab for it."

"Speaking of something to eat, do we have comestibles?"

"You got chicken salad sandwiches in your vest pocket. Case we don't bag that rabbit."

"Oh, we're still on the rabbit, are we?"

We headed off into the woods again, onto a path that was wide enough for two. The trees were still pretty dense, and the tops of the tree branches tangled and crisscrossed against each other, blocking out patches of the sky. We stopped and looked out at an open field dotted with cactus, rocks, dirt, and brown grass.

David casually adjusted his rifle against his shoulder, and when he did the barrel pointed right at my face. I backed out of the way.

"Oh, sorry," he said. "That was quite the faux pas."

"Okay," I said. "If you want to go hunting, there's rules you got to follow to make sure everything is safe. I should have gone over these with you when we were at the firing range but I didn't."

"Let's do it now," he said.

"First, muzzle control. Always hold your gun like you're doing right now, pointed to the side, when you're walking with somebody. You can do a cradle carry so's not to tire out your arm — that's where you put the barrel in the crook of your arm while holding the butt with your right hand, like this — but never walk next to somebody doing a cradle carry if the muzzle's pointing in that direction. You can do what's called a trail carry, that's pretty comfortable, where you just basically hold the rifle to the side with your hand on the balance point, like carrying a suitcase, but never hold it like that when you're walking behind a fella."

"Right."

"Always make sure the safety is on. I did that before we left the range, so yours is set."

"Check. Safety on."

"And never put your finger on the trigger until you intend to shoot. Always keep your fingers outside the trigger guard."

"Outside the trigger guard, yes."

"When you're walking, always keep your eyes on the horizon in front of you, but at the same time, watch where you're putting your feet so's you don't trip. There's all kinds of holes and uneven ground out here."

I demonstrated this next part, and made him follow me. "Now when you see one of these critters, stop. Click off the safety, and scan the horizon to make sure nobody is in front of you, no other hunters or some guy with a walking stick. Raise your rifle to your eye," I did this, and David followed my lead. "Real quiet like or you're going to scare him. Aim for the critter's head. And squeeze the trigger." I did not squeeze the trigger. Neither did David. "Try to control your breathing, like we did at the range. Breathe out as you pull the trigger and you'll get a much cleaner shot." We lowered our rifles and started walking again.

"Right," he said after a few minutes. "Who are you?"

"What do you mean?"

"I mean who are you? You don't seem like anybody I've ever even heard of. You defy all stereotypes."

"How's that?"

"The hunter / vehicle mechanic / working class Texan. A Republican, I presume?"

"A right-wing Republican."

"Hunter / mechanic / right-wing-Republican / Texas *man* who mysteriously enjoys the ballet, and can actually have a conversation about it. Has actually watched enough ballet to make a distinction between dancers and companies. You read about the ballet too, don't you?"

"Yeah. But I haven't really seen a lot of ballet. I only went that one time. I watch a lot of it on YouTube, but it ain't the same thing, really."

"Where did this come from?"

"Yeah, it seems kind of funny, don't it?"

"Is it because of Jill?"

"I don't know. I thought maybe it was a way for me to get closer to Jill, but I'm not sure that's it. If that was the case I would have gone to the ballet that one time, the one where we met, and then I would have got home and forgot about it." It was actually because of the rape, and Jill's sickness and refusing to leave her room or talk to me. That's what pulled me in. But I wasn't going to tell him that.

"What is it then?"

"I'm a little crazy. Or I'm going through a thing. Whatever it is, it don't seem all that strange to me now. See, ballet is something guys can be into, but for different reasons than women, you know?"

"Illuminate, please."

"I don't really know how to explain it. I'm not too good with words. Men and women think of ballet differently."

"I suppose that is indeed the case. I've never really considered it."

"Women are into the actual dance more than guys are, or at least this guy. I watch the dances on YouTube — and watching a recording on the internet is not the same as watching a live performance, I get that — but watching recordings of ballet aren't all that interesting to me. I'm more interested in who these folks are, and what they did in their lives. What they had to fight against."

"Whom do you mean?"

"Well, take this George Balanchine fella, for one. There's all kinds of videos online about this dude, and most of them are about what a great dance guy he was, and how he created New York City Ballet, but that's not all that interesting to me. Finding out where he came from though? Now you're talking. He was from Russia, right? And during World War I, when he was just thirteen years old, he was so underfed he had boils on his skin from malnutrition. And he killed and skinned alley cats because there weren't nothing else to eat. Talk about stalking your food. And he was offered this big job when he was just a young buck, I mean just twenty-two or so, the first of his career, and he couldn't do it because he came down with TB. And later in life he only had one working lung. That's interesting to me. The dancing is interesting too, but the 'this thing' is not as interesting as the 'what's behind this thing?' You get it?"

"I understand completely."

"Or take this dude Petipa."

"PET-ee-pa."

"What?"

"You said, 'pet-EE-pa.' It's 'PET-ee-pa.'"

"Okay, so take this dude PET-ee-pa. Here was this fella who worked all his life, had a forty-year career as a choreographer — am I pronouncing that right? Thanks — and at the age of seventy, he starts doing his best work."

"*Swan Lake*. Right. And *Raymonda* and *The Nutcracker*. Well, parts of it."

"That's right. But he was seventy! At the age of seventy, he *starts* doing his best work. The stuff that he's remembered for, he was an old man when he did it! And I look at what he did, and I think, I want to do what he did."

David smiled. "Does that mean you want to be a ballet master when you're seventy?"

"No," I said. "It means I want to get better and not worse."

We moved back on the dirt path. Our shoes crunched

the sand and rock bits. Sparrows squeaked and peeped in the branches overhead.

"Transformation," he said.

"Not sure about that."

"Transformation. Remaking. Reawakening. That's what ballet has always been about. It's about rebirth in tragedy. Taking something damaged and making it extraordinary and mystical and sublime."

"If you say so. I don't really understand all that."

"Are you going through some kind of transformation?"

"No." I've had to deal with a lot since Thanksgiving but I didn't tell him that, of course. The crime against my daughter. Me almost shooting a kid. Getting arrested and spending three days in jail. Starting ballet class. I hadn't watched Fox News in nearly a month. My drinking had tapered off considerably. I actually might be dating a gal. I was rehearsing for a performance at an old folks home. But a transformation? That would mean changing into something else, and I was still the same idjit.

We stopped and looked out at the horizon, at a low southern plain that you could imagine rolling out into sand and then into the Mexican desert. Ashe juniper trees dotted the landscape, and thinned out until there was nothing but dead brown brush and yellow-thorned cacti. It wasn't hot, but it *looked* hot.

To our right, about two o'clock, I spotted a rabbit. We'd been out here for about four hours and this was the first shootable critter we saw.

I touched David on the shoulder and pointed it out to him, then I put my finger to my lips to shoosh him so he wouldn't talk and scare it away. David raised his rifle slowly, took a deep breath, exhaled, and squeezed the trigger.

Pop! A puff of dirt bloomed about two feet in front of the rabbit. Old long ears knew he was in serious then and these fellas with the wooden sticks that made fire out the end were up to no good, so he started running like a halfback to the underbrush about fifty yards away. I raised my rifle, got a bead on him and shot him in the head. Looks like we'd be eating rabbit after all.

The look on David's face was something akin to awe. "That was — phenomenal!"

I just shrugged. "I been doing this all my life practically."

We started out to fetch the rabbit. "You know who's a good shot?" I said. "My dad. I've seen him make shots that I wouldn't believe possible. Once we were at Lake LBJ fishing, and we saw this water moccasin swimming in the water, but he was doing this serpentine thing, you know, zigzagging back and forth, and my dad went to his truck and got his .22 Ruger — that's a pistol — and shot that snake right in the middle of the head from about fifty feet out. I never saw anything like it. It seemed like an impossible shot, like a trick shot. But he done it."

"But that's what you did just now."

"No it ain't."

"Yes it is. You just did the same thing. This rabbit was zigzagging too, just like the snake you describe and you hit it right in the head."

"Yeah, I guess, but—"

"No, no buts. You're just like your father."

"Maybe so."

"Remarkable. I've never seen anything like it."

I put the rabbit in the zipper pocket in the back of my vest, and we walked around the hunting ground and talked about a lot of stuff. David is an interesting guy. I asked him why he treats everybody so mean, and he said, "I don't. Who said that?" but he was smiling, so he knew it was true. I told him I saw the way he acted towards Elaine Riche, the artistic director, and he said, "Oh, that silly cow.

I acted that way because I need her to be professional and fulfill her contractual obligations. Her way of getting things done is to have shrill fits and say 'no.' I don't work like that. I don't pamper incompetents. So in order to get what I want, I must behave in a certain manner at times, and it can be rather bristling, but it works."

We stayed out another hour or so and then drove back to the house on Meredith. I fired up the grill, skinned the rabbit (we only got the one) and we ate that sucker with Fritos and chased it down with a couple of cold ones. Sir David balked at eating the rabbit at first, saying he wasn't "feeling the least bit peckish at the moment," but after explaining exactly what the term "wuss" meant, he finally said yes. And you know something? That old English boy really loves the jackrabbit.

It was getting time for him to get back. He said he had some work to do that night on the show. He was just about to leave when Jill came out to join us. She'd been home all day with her feet propped up. They were bandaged now and she had on flip flops. She looked really surprised to see Sir David. She shouldn't have been. She knew we was hunting.

David took a look at her, and then looked down at her feet. "Sit!" he commanded. She did. He started to unwrap her bandages and winced at what he saw.

"Daddy," she said. "Uncle Ed called. He wants you to call him back."

I looked on my smart phone, and sure enough, Ed had called in the middle of the afternoon. I had it on airplane mode so it wouldn't go off while we were out hunting. I suppose he wanted to know about when I was bringing his guns back. I dialed him and he picked up.

"Son of a gun!" he said. "I hear you're taking ballet!"

"Uh..." This was not good. This was a disaster. No way out. "Yeah. That's right."

"Jill tells me you're going to be doing a show at an old folks home!"

I looked at Jill. She could hear what we were talking about. She said sheepishlike, "It slipped out."

"Yeah," I said to Ed. "What about it?"

"I want to come. And bring Dad!"

"No, you can't come. It's a private thing."

"No it ain't. They have shows at old folks homes all the time. I went with Dad once at The Hills. Some magician. He only did tricks for about ten minutes. It was free."

"Well, I'm not going to tell you where it is."

"It's at Blue Skies of Texas on Highway 90 south of 1604. I can't wait! See you then, you old walrus gut!"

"Do what you want then." I was p.o.'ed but I'd be durned if I was going to show it. Now Ed's going to come to Blue Skies and bring Dad. Great. I hung up and got back to the business of Jill's feet.

I've never noticed this before, but Jill has the ugliest feet I ever seen. They look like Quasimodo feet, like bumpy, knotty, deformed things. Her feet were covered with large bandaids, which David tore off. The tops and bottoms of her feet were spotted with sores, the toes were covered in bloody blisters.

"You need to let these breathe," he said.

"I have been. I just put those on."

"Give them air overnight. Put fresh ones on in the morning."

"I have a suggestion," I said.

"What?"

"I got some slices of venison in the freezer. She could put that on her feet. Might ease the pain."

"Daddy, that sounds gross."

"Your father may be on to something," said David. "The Tartars of the Golden Horde used to put meat under their horses' saddles to heal blisters and sores. Ballet

224

dancers have been doing that for years. Where did you hear about that?"

"YouTube."

"Well, we don't need to do that, I think. Antibiotic ointments and toe pads will suffice for the 21st Century. Do you have any lamb's wool or toe pads?"

"We have bacitracin, but we don't have any toe pads. I used the last of them this morning."

David looked at me. "Bring on the steaks."

We decided that if we were going to do this, we'd need to bring her back inside and let her get comfortable, so Jill put on her flip flops and limped into the living room and sat on the couch.

I went into the freezer and brought out the venison I'd cleaned about six months ago. It was still edible for another couple of months as deer meat in the freezer is good for about nine months, but of course we wasn't going to eat this. I'm just telling you this because I want you to know it hadn't gone bad. After a quick stop by the microwave to thaw it some, I sliced it into thin little strips, took it out to the living room on a plate, and David and me attached them to her wounds. "Hmm... It actually feels pretty good," she said. Then we put on Band-Aids real loose so the meat wouldn't slip off. He told her to keep the meat on for an hour or so, then take it off and let her feet breathe overnight.

When we were done, I drove David back to his apartment. He asked me how ballet could get more working joes like me to come to the shows, and I told him he'd have to lower ticket prices. Folks like me think ballet is strictly for the elites because it takes some serious gators to get in the door. It ain't for the elites, I come to find out, but when you price things the way they do, it sure looks that way. If a guy with a job wants to take his wife and two kids to the ballet, and they want to sit in the good seats, a night out is going to cost pretty near $500, and that's just too dang much.

I pulled into David's apartment driveway under the green canopy and shut off the truck.

He said, "Well, thank you, kind sir, for taking time out of your busy schedule and bringing me on the hunt. I learned so much."

"Not at all, friend, anytime. Come back next year when deer's in season and maybe we can get us a fine buck."

"Yes, that would be excellent. Well..." he hesitated. "Do you want to come up for a drink? I think I have your brand of beer in my refrigerator."

"No, that's okay. I think I probably ought to get back."

"Well. Good night then."

He leaned over and gave me a hug, which was odd, and I gave him a hug back, and to tell you the truth, I was feeling mighty awkward about it. And then you know what he did? He tried to *kiss* me! He leaned in with his mouth open and his eyes closed, and I pulled back.

"Whoa, what are you doing?"

"It's all right..."

"No, it's fine... It just..."

"It's all right..."

"No, it's fine..."

"I should probably get back to my apartment. I have a lot to do."

"Yeah, and I have to get ready for work. I have to go to work tomorrow early."

He got out of the truck, and leaned on the side door. He looked for once to be at a loss for words.

"I'm coming opening night." I said. "I'll see you then."

"Let's sit together. I'll reserve a comp for you. Then Jill can give her comp to one of her friends."

"Okay. See you Thursday." And then I drove away.

I was kind of hoping to take Larisa to the opening. I knew she wanted to go and I hadn't got around to asking her yet. It was supposed to be our first real date. But I just agreed to go with Sir David, so going with Larisa was out now. David trying to kiss me was a little weird, but it wasn't the worst thing in the world. And brother, I know you're going to think this is funny, but after all I been through, it's nice to feel appreciated.

Chapter 20

I met Larisa on Tuesday night for rehearsal. We worked the routine, but mainly the lift and the fish. The lift was not that hard because Larisa is pretty light, but the fish is another story. The fish is pretty much dropping her and catching her just as she's about to smack the floor with her chin. It looks good but it looks dangerous too, like we're doing a circus routine.

During our break, Larisa brought out a tape measure and a notebook.

"So," she said, "we've got to get this costume fitting out of the way. Don't mind me, I've got to take some measurements."

"Whoa, nobody said anything about a costume."

"Well you can't do the thing in your underpants."
Stretch, she measures my pant leg, writes it down in her book.

"I'm not going to wear costume."

"Yes you are." *Stretch,* she measures my gut.

"What kind of costume are we talking about?"

"Pants. Vest. Puffy shirt." *Stretch.* She measures my chest.

"You want me to wear a puffy shirt ... with *frills* on it?"

"Something like that." *Stretch,* she measures my waist. "No way!"

"Look, it's a period piece. Lift your arm." *Stretch,* she measures shoulder to cuff. "You can't do it in a track suit. They didn't have sweatpants when Don Quixote and Sancho Panza were chasing down windmills."

"I'm not wearing it." *Stretch,* she measures my neck. "You can drop your arms now."

"I'm not," I said. She scribbled numbers down in her book, ignoring me. "Seriously, I am not wearing a costume." She continued writing. "Did you hear what I said?" Then she put her pencil to her chin, looked me up and down.

"The brown will look nice on you," she said. "It's a nice earth tone. And the shirt is eggshell."

"I'm not kidding. I'm not wearing a costume. Under no condition. No, no, no, and that's final."

"Would you stop?"

"It'll looks feminine! I'll look like a girl!"

"When John Wayne made movies, he dressed up as a cowboy, in a cowboy costume. When Mad Max was kicking ass and taking names in the Outback, he had on that leather suit and shoulder pad. Did he look like a girl?"

"No, but—"

"No. You could wear a pink bridesmaid's dress with matching bouquet and hair ribbons and you wouldn't look like a girl."

"I don't want to wear a costume."

Larisa sighed. "I tell you what. Don't think of it as a costume. Think of it as a uniform."

"A uniform?"

"You know something, Billy Jim? Sometimes you just got to trust people, you know?"

"I trust you."

"I'm not trying to make you look foolish."

"I know, but——."

"You got trust issues. I'm not your ex-wife."

"She don't got nothing to do with it."

"I'm wearing a brown skirt and an eggshell blouse that I'm hand-sewing. What I'm wearing matches what you'll be wearing. Should I wear a sweat suit? How would that look?"

"I'm not saying that you should."

"Then wear the costu — the uniform," she said. "You're going to look great."

I didn't want to, but arguing about it was a lost cause.

"Okay, I'll wear the dang uniform."

Women. Sometimes it's just better to just shut up and not start arguing in the first place.

Chapter 21

Thursday come, and it was Jill's opening finally. I'd been looking forward to this ballet for the past six weeks. Her feet were a lot better. She'd been rehearsing every day from morning until night, but she'd been taking care of them preciously like they was a couple of mewing kittens, taking off her shoes whenever she wasn't working, giving them air, padding them, putting ointment on them, pampering them. They weren't pretty, but they weren't going to wreck her show or keep her off the stage.

It was 7:30 in the morning and I knocked on her door. I expected she'd be up and dressed. Ricardo was coming by to pick her up, and I wanted to tell her goodbye and I'd see her after. But she didn't answer. I knocked again. Still no answer. I called her name. Then I pushed open her door and went inside.

Jill was in bed. She was staring at the wall, her head poked out from under the covers. She had that look. That drowned, gray, mourning.

I said, "Jill?" but she said nothing.

"Are you okay?" Nothing. "Are you sick?" No answer. "Do you want me to call Amy (Amy Landreau, from that time in the ER, was her counselor)?" No answer. She just looked at the wall. Then she said:

"Go away."

"What's the matter?" No answer. "Hey..."

"Leave me alone."

"Come on out and have some breakfast."

"I don't want anything to eat. I don't want to do anything. Please, just... leave me alone."

"Sweetie, you got rehearsal in thirty minutes."

"I'm not going to rehearsal."

"Tonight's your opening."

"I can't go."

"After all the work you put in, you're not going to do the show?"

"No. I just sent a text to Ricardo and told him not to pick me up. Will you call Sir David and tell him I'm sick? They have an understudy. The understudy can go on for me."

"Are you sick?" No answer. "I'll call him if you want me to, but..."

"I'm sorry."

"It's all right."

"Thank you for not making me do it."

"I couldn't make you do it anyhow."

She had fallen into that dark place again, like the one she was in that night I heard her crying, like the one she was in when she wouldn't come out of her bedroom for weeks on end.

"I understand how you feel. I been in your shoes before."

"No you haven't."

"Yeah, not like what you got. But I've been blindsided by life before. Caught up in sadness when I didn't expect it."

"Yeah... well..."

"Your mom leaving."

There. I said it. It was something we never talked about. It was something I didn't want to talk about with Jill *ever*. I hate showing weakness.

"I know it was hard for you," she said.

"How would you know that? I'm pretty good at keeping things in. Like you."

"The screaming."

"The what?"

"The screaming."

"What are you talking about?"

"You used to... Never mind."

"No, tell me. What?"

"You used to get drunk and lie on the floor and scream. You did it, sometimes, for hours."

"I don't remember that at all."

"Why do you think I wanted to move out?"

"Because you wanted to live with your momma?"

"It was because you were acting like a maniac. I was already depressed and these screaming jags made me feel like I was going crazy."

"I know.... I know..."

It was time to cut the lies. Once and for all.

"Okay. Really. The truth is, Jill, I remember the screaming."

"You do?"

"It was at a very bad time. Your momma left and I had come to this point in my life where everything I believed in was falling away. It was all breaking down. I failed completely. And I felt that sense of loss that I think you're feeling now. And near constant regret."

"You used to roll up into a ball and scream," she said. "The TV was turned up real loud, and it was turned to Fox and those guys were shouting at each other and you were screaming and there were beer cans everywhere and the whole house smelled like stale beer. And you wouldn't stop. And then you eventually went to sleep. Only it would start again the next night."

"But things changed," I said.

I thought of something, and I didn't know if this would backfire on me or not, if Jill would think I was some sicko or she would think I was into children. But it was all part of the puzzle, a piece of darkness or light that fit together to make up this time.

I sat down on her bed, took out my wallet, and pulled out that picture I'd ordered from Walgreens. I handed it to her.

"This is a gal I knew in eighth grade. Her name is Dee Dee Arnold. I was sweet on her for a time, for a whole year. But her parents moved out of state and I never heard from her again. I was wondering about her a few months back and I googled her name and this picture came up. It was taken that year, when we were both going to Wood-lawn Hills. So I saw this picture and I had it printed up. I don't know why. I could have just downloaded it on my computer and looked at it whenever I wanted to, but I didn't. I wanted to have a picture of her because I wanted something to hold in my hand. So that's what I did."

"Why?"

"I don't know why. I've thought about that a lot. I..."

"Do you miss her?"

"Jill, that was forty years ago. No, I don't miss her."

"Then why do it?"

"I'm guessing... I miss times that were simple. When love was simple and it was innocent. Seems awful foolish to me now. You can't go backward, even if you wanted to. What's past is past."

"You *are* better now though. Better than you have been in a long time."

"Because I keep myself occupied. You know, I started taking adult beginner classes on Saturdays, then adult ballet on Tuesdays and Thursdays. You know why I did that?"

"You're a freak?"

"Ha ha. No, it's because it keeps me busy. When I'm in class I don't have time to think about nothing else. I don't have time to think about your mom leaving, I don't have time to think about my dad or my brother or Peter Vanderburg, who I still want to kill. I got to focus. I got to put one foot in front of the other. I got to keep up."

I stood up and looked at the clock on her nightstand.

"And that's what you need to do. You need to focus your energies. Put one foot in front of the other. Fight this. Get out of bed, get dressed, and get to work. When you're working on something, when you're making something, like a dance or a ballet piece, it changes who you are. It makes you better. I know that sounds awful funny coming from a redneck like me. But it's true. Now will you get up?"

"I can't."

"Come on, Jill, get up. Get up!"

She didn't move. She wouldn't move. I failed. I failed again.

"I'm going to go out in the kitchen and make your lunch. While I'm doing that I want you to get ready. I'll take you down to the Convention Center, if you can go. We'll leave in a half hour, okay? If you're ready, we'll go down there."

"I can't."

"You don't have to do it but—"

"I can't do it, Daddy. I *can't!*"

I backed out of the room and went into the kitchen. I cut up an apple, then got out a bag of lettuce and some tuna and eggs and made a tuna salad, then I dumped it all in a plastic container. I had some ranch dressing, but I knew that was too fattening and she wouldn't eat it, so I rooted around in the fridge and found some packets of oil and vinegar. Then I pulled out one of her diet Dr. Peppers. I put it all in a paper sack, then went into the living room and waited.

And waited. Thirty minutes passed. Then forty. She wasn't coming out. It was over. Peter Vanderburg wins again. The devil, this darkness, keeps taking and taking and taking.

What now? Should I call her therapist? Should I just leave her alone? I had to call David and tell him she wasn't coming in. What was I supposed to do? I called out, "Jill?"

Then miracle of miracles, she walked out of her bedroom with her bag across her shoulder. She did not look like she was ready to take on the world. She looked frightened, and she trembled slightly. "Let's go," she said. Her voice was a little choked, shaky. She took a deep breath.

Courage, I thought. My girl's got some courage.

I didn't know this until later, but Jill was suffering from PTSD, Post Traumatic Stress Disorder. This affects people who have had violence inflicted on them, like Jill had. Soldiers get it, of course, but all kinds of other folks get it too. People who have survived war, folks who see violence, experience it, folks in serious accidents, folks who are attacked or beaten, or severely bullied. About ten years ago I had a friend named Able Dishner whose son James was bullied on a playground when he was in middle school, and the bullies tackled him and pinned him to the ground and force fed him dog feces. Well, James was never the same after that. He got hooked on heroin a few years later and died of an overdose in Austin, Texas, where he was living at the time. Poor James was just like so many other folks that have terrible things happen to them. He didn't know how to cope with the PTSD, with the pain, so he started self-medicating and it killed him.

And what happened to those kids that did that to him?

Nothing. They took a life and was never punished. They probably never even knew.

PTSD is terrible. Folks who are suffering from it have depression, panic attacks, fits of anger, flashbacks. And now because of Peter Vanderburg, Jill had it too. She couldn't get out of bed the morning of her big ballet opening. One of the biggest days of her young life, and she was shackled to her bed by depression.

She somehow found the strength to rise up, to get out of bed and face her fear, to face this thing that was scaring the bejabbers out of her. And I am so grateful for that. But I don't think she'll be able to do that every time. Some days she's going to lose her battle with this thing that's haunting her, and some days she'll win. Thankfully, she won today.

We walked out to my truck, I fired her up, and twenty minutes later we were sitting out in front of the Convention Center. Jill got out of the truck, not saying a word. She looked up at that huge white stone building, with its jutting steel beams and enormous glass windows, and she sighed. Then she slowly went in.

I quit work about four o'clock and drove home to get ready. I didn't want to look like an extra on *Hee Haw*, so I scrubbed my hands and my body till it was red in places, shaved my face, trimmed my mustache and nose hairs, and put on my Sunday-go-to-meeting clothes. I looked at myself in the mirror. I was ready.

I had one thing to do before going downtown. I had to see Larisa Lakewood. I drove by her real estate office and walked in unannounced. She was surprised to see me.

"Who are you? You look like somebody I know, but…" she said. A reference to the suit, no doubt.

"I'm going to the ballet tonight. Jill's show. Down at the Convention Center."

"Have a great time."

"I wanted to ask you to come with me but I couldn't."

"Why don't you have a seat?"

"Okay."

I sat down across from her, and for some reason, I started fidgeting, cleaning my cuticles with my thumb. I didn't look at her much, I was busy clicking my fingernails.

"So I wanted to ask you to come with me but I couldn't."

"That's okay."

"See, the director of Jill's show asked me to come to the opening with him, and he's been really nice to her, so I couldn't say no. But I wanted to go with you."

"Next time."

"How about next week?"

"Billy Jim, are you asking me out on a date?"

"Uh... Yeah..." I thought, gosh, I'm thirsty.

"When do you want to go?"

"How about her last show? That'll be next Sunday."

"It's a date."

"Okay, well. I'll see you then."

"You'll see me before then. We're rehearsing on Saturday."

"Right."

I got up to leave but stopped. There was something I needed to know.

"Larisa..."

"Yeah?"

"You like me, don't you?"

"Well, of course I do."

"I mean, you're interested in me."

"Yes."

"Why?"

"You mean, why am I interested in you?"

"Yes."

"Well, you seem like a nice person. The more I get to know you, the more it seems to me like you got a good heart. And you're open-minded. You say you're a right-wing conservative, and I don't doubt that for a second, but you're the most open-minded right-wing conservative I've ever met. In fact, if you weren't so adamant about being such a right-wing conservative, I'd almost think you were a dadgum lib-moron."

"Well, you know I ain't that."

"So that's basically it. You're a good person and open-minded. And you have a job. It's amazing to me how many guys out there just don't want to work. But they want *me* to work. And give them money."

"Well, I didn't think it was because of my looks."

"Looks? I'm fifty years old, bud. Anybody my age who puts a lot of stock in a fella's looks ain't got the sense God gave a rusty nail. And anyway, you're a handsome guy, Billy Jim, so you're not short in that department. You could lose a little weight. But couldn't we all?"

She batted her eyes at me real sweet-like. Gosh, she sure is charming.

"You're really funny," I said.

"Thank you," she said. "But there is one thing you might do..."

"What's that?"

"Shave off the mustache. That mustache looks like it escaped from a 70's cop show. And it makes you look older."

"I can't."

"Why not?"

"Because..."

"Because why?"

"Because of... the fishing accident."

"The fishing accident?"

I nodded. She said, "Oh. Okay," and nodded too.

It was time to head out. I said goodbye and drove down to the Convention Center.

I was early, *way* early, by two hours. It was six o'clock and the ballet started at eight. Funny thing is, I wasn't the only one there. There were about five cars in the parking lot, I reckon parents of some kids in the ballet. We should've had a tailgate party.

I just sat out in my truck and listened to classic country and thought about things. Two rows of Indian paintbrush and lemonmint flowers, in full bloom, lined the walkway to the entrance. They were so round and full they looked to be bursting. It was real pretty, friend.

Around 7:30 I headed in, got my ticket at the box office, and sat in the lobby. I still had another thirty minutes to kill.

After a few minutes of watching folks come in, I went into the bathroom and washed my hands, basically because I didn't have nothing else to do, then came back out. I was just standing there, wiping my wet hands on my pants, when who should walk by but Beth and John Lancey. I couldn't believe it. Of course my ex-wife is going to come to her daughter's opening. And bring her boyfriend. I wanted to look away, but it was too late, they saw me.

"Beth. John Lancey," I said.

Beth said, "Hello, Billy Jim," in a voice that said she was surprised to see me. "Fancy meeting you here."

"Well, you know. Jill's opening."

"Yeah. Yeah, it's Jill's opening. You're wearing a suit."

"Yeah, yeah. It's my churchgoing suit. Yeah. I didn't come by myself. I'm meeting a friend."

"Oh. That's nice."

"I got a friend who's meeting me here. David Derrick."

"David Derrick? Sir David Derrick? The director?"

She knew the name. This didn't really surprise me

none, she being into all that culture stuff.

"Sure. We go hunting together."

"You do not." She laughed a little.

"You're right. I'm just kidding."

"Sometimes you say the strangest things. How's Jill?"

"She's great, she's great. She misses you."

"Yes. We miss her too."

Beth looked at me and just for a second her eyes showed a recognition. Then something like pain. She bit her lip and turned toward the theater.

"Well," she said, "we're going in."

"Yeah. See you around."

And they slipped off into the theater.

Actually, theater might not be the right term. Since David decided he wanted to do the show in the round, the San Antonio Ballet couldn't use the theater space in the Convention Center because the stage was basically nailed to the back wall and it had a sloping floor and couldn't be rearranged, so David scuttled the plans for the theater and put the whole thing up in one of the adjoining ballrooms. The ballroom he chose, Ballroom A, was big like Carlsbad Caverns, and he had to bring in a lot of chairs, bleachers, lighting equipment, and set pieces and cram it all in there and make it all fit. The set was built into the ballroom and weaved in and out of the seats. I had no idea how this was going to work, but you know I don't know much about that stuff anyway. After the show started, I come to find out a lot of the set was on wheels, so it went on and off very quickly. The ballroom has a wooden floor that was made for dancing, so it was perfect for the cast.

I went down and sat in my seat, which was up two rows on the aisle. The lights went down and the ballet started. David must be somewhere in the house, but I wasn't sure where.

It was thrilling to see Jill on stage after this long,

long winter. She had a lot to do. There's a sword fight right at the start between the Montagues and the Capulets (Jill was a Capulet), and she was slashing away and jumping and tumbling with the rest of them. She gets killed in the opening fight, along with eight or nine other guys, but she's in the corps de ballet, so she's back onstage as another character in the next big crowd scene. When she was on stage I didn't watch nobody else because seriously, there ain't nobody on that stage near half as interesting as Jill.

In one scene she was a soldier, in another she played some funny looking stringed instrument things that looked kinda like a gourd, in another she and these three other guys had a dance with the guy who played Romeo. She was onstage probably 60% of the time, and she was constantly moving.

I recognized the dancers who played Romeo and Juliet from when me and Jill went to the Academy to audition. These two are some dancers too, let me tell you what. This dude had jumps that would make a kangaroo jealous, and that gal had legs so trim and sharp they could double as hedge clippers. This Juliet was super hot too, and full of energy and spirit. You could see how Romeo could fall for her, not like that gal in the Leonard Decapricorn movie.

About five minutes after the ballet started, David Derrick sat down next to me. He did not acknowledge me or say hello. He took out a legal pad and furiously scribbled notes. Then he started sputtering "Terrible. So terrible" and "What dreck" and "I can't watch."

After a couple minutes of this I turned to him and whispered: "David!"

"What?!"

"You're making too much noise! We're trying to watch the ballet!"

"Is that what this is? I thought it was the horse show.

Nobody in this part of the country knows the difference between a ballerina and a bob-tailed nag."

"Shh!"

"Don't shush me!"

"Shh!"

He was quiet after that, at least until intermission, when he started complaining again. I just listened.

After about five minutes, Elaine Riche, the artistic director, came down the aisle. She was beaming. She found David.

"The *New York Times* is here!"

"Of course the *New York Times* is here," he said. "They appreciate genius."

"You said they were coming, but I... I never imagined they..."

"Yes, yes."

"Oh, thank you, thank you, Sir David! It's such a great show!"

"Madam, leave me," and he waved her away, like a king would dismiss an annoying and unfunny jester. She didn't seem to mind though. She went back up the stairs giggling. David turned to me and continued telling me about what he hated about the show.

The lights went down and Act Two started and he began scribbling notes again, mumbling quietly.

So we watch the ballet all the way up to the end, to the last scene, and you know what? It really gets to me. Mainly because it's so senseless. Juliet is young, right? And she's lying in the grave, and this dude named Paris is at her side and he's mourning. For those of you guys who don't know, Paris is this dude that was supposed to marry her. Her family had set this all up, it was an arranged marriage, but she fell in love with Romeo so she wouldn't do it. So here she is, this kid, this little girl, lying in this crypt at night, and this Paris fella is there with her. Now you got to think, he probably really loves her, or why would he be in this here crypt in the dark all by himself? So Paris is there feeling all sad about Juliet when Romeo comes in and sees her, and then sees this Paris dude, and Romeo kills him — kills the guy! I mean, Paris really didn't do nothing. He was just kind of at the wrong place at the wrong time and suddenly he gets a knife in the gut. Then Romeo goes over to Juliet and he gets all crazy and desperate and he tries to bring her back to life but of course she's dead, and he drags her all around and throws her and tries to kiss her to wake up but that don't work, naturally, because she's dead as a dinosaur. Then he drinks poison and dies, and then Juliet wakes up because she wasn't really dead, and she sees Romeo and she gets all crazy and then she stabs herself and *she* dies.

And as I was watching this, I was feeling sorry for all three of them, you know? And then something happened. Sometimes in life you get these things, these realizations about life, and you just understand something. I got it sometimes watching baseball, back when I was a Rangers fan. You're really focused on the game, but your mind goes off somewhere else, and then something clicks, and you know something you didn't know before.

And this is what I thought about when I was watching that there final scene. *Romeo and Juliet* ain't a tragedy because a couple of young folks killed themselves. Oh no. That's bad enough, but that ain't why it's sad. It's sad because it had to be that way. The feud between their folks, the Montagues and the Capulets, this thing had been going on forever, and violence was all what they knew. So when Romeo come into the crypt, he didn't have any qualm or second thought about killing Paris, and when he thought Juliet was dead, the only way he saw of dealing with it was to be dead too, to commit a violent act on himself. Because that's what his family does. If he'd decided to live, Juliet would have woke up and they could have had a happy ending, and had a passel of babies and all that, but that never would have happened with these two. The only ending they saw for themselves was dying because they was tied so closely to their family ways. They could have lived, but living was never a choice or even possible these two. And that's a tragedy.

Now you know me, I'm not one for navel gazing, but I sat there thinking, "Am I like that? Am I tied to the past? Will I always be Romeo in the crypt, drinking poison because it's the only thing I know?"

The show ended and folks started applauding like a bunch of crazy people. There was lots of bows and roses. Then it was over. The house lights went up, and David turned to me.

"I'm flying out on the red eye tonight for New York City. I am directing a production of *Giselle* at New York City Ballet starting Monday. I wanted to give you this before I left. Don't open it." He handed me an envelope. It was sealed and had his signature written across the back. "It is a letter of recommendation to the Joffrey Ballet trainee program. Jill will also need to write a letter of introduction for herself when she makes the application. It should be about 250 words. Have her FedEx it on Monday as the deadline is this week. Don't bother to thank me. There is no way you could adequately repay me for the kindness I have bestowed upon your family."

"Well, thanks anyway, David. You're a heck of a guy."

"Yes, that was adequate. Maybe next time I'm in town — which will never be, I'm certain — you and I can hunt something other than the dreaded lepus. Goodbye, Lynyrd Skynyrd."

"Goodbye, David Derrick."

I stuck out my hand, but he brushed it aside and hugged me, which probably made my cheeks turn red. Then, with his mouth right by my ear, he whispered, "I love you."

Then he got up, stepped over my knees, walked up the aisle and disappeared into the crowd.

I went out into the lobby and waited for Jill. Beth and John Lancey were there too, but we didn't talk, we just waited out there with a bunch of other folks. After about ten minutes, Jill came out with Ricardo. He split off and went over to his parents, a Mexican-American couple in their 40s. His mom and dad were practically glowing they was so proud. Jill said hello to a couple of friends standing there waiting. Whether these gals were from Providence or City Ballet I don't know. After a minute she came over to us and hugged her mother. Beth said:

"What a wonderful show, dear."

"Did you like it?"

"It was fabulous. And in the ballroom too! I bet nobody has ever staged a ballet in that ballroom. What a fabulous idea."

"It was David's. He has a lot of great ideas."

"Apparently so."

"You were great, kid," said John Lancey.

"Thanks, John. It's a lot of fun."

"You were wonderful, Jill," I said. "I really liked the dance you guys did with Romeo. That battlement en rond was something else. You guys must got abs of steel."

Beth smiled slightly. "Where did you get those words? Your father's suddenly a ballet expert."

"He knows a lot about it, actually," she said. "What did you think of the show, Daddy?"

Jill was looking at me. Everybody else was too. I didn't know what to say, so I just started talking.

"Well, I liked it quite a lot, you know. That dude that was playing Romeo had to pretty much climb a dang mountain because he's doing the Nur-yev version - sorry, Nur-RAY-yev - and it's just hard to match the moves of somebody who's considered the best of all time. The height of his jumps wasn't anywhere near what Nureyev could pull off, like when he did his butterflies. His technique was dang near perfect, but he just doesn't have the rockets to lift him up in the air. I liked his acting though. He was believable as the character, and he's the right age, and he's a great athlete. I really like the gal who played Juliet too. People think Margot Fonteyn did a great Juliet, but I don't care for her all that much, mainly because she was so old. She was in her forties when she did that part, you know, and it's just hard for me to believe she's fourteen. This gal who played it tonight, this Russian gal, I'm guessing she's in her early twenties, so if I squint, I can actually believe she's close to Jill's age. She was great. She had so much power and oomph in her grande jeté. And I liked the fact that it's Juliet that cries over Tybalt when he's killed. That was a nice touch. I guess that was probably Nureyev's thing."

Beth and John Lancey stared, their mouths open like venus fly traps.

"Yeah, he knows something about the ballet," Jill said, bless her heart, but then she said, "He's been taking lessons too."

Then I felt really stupid. But they didn't say nothing. Probably didn't believe it.

We all went our separate ways after that. Jill went off with Ricardo to grab a post-show salad, and when she came home that night I told her about the letter of recommendation. She was really busy that weekend because she had to rehearse and perform for the next three days, but she had to finish the letter of introduction so we could send it along with the application on Monday. She told me she would work on it.

I did a little research about the Joffrey trainee program. It starts in September, and it is a four-year program of year-round training, with summers off. It is extremely

247

competitive. If she got an audition, we'd have to fly to New York to do it. If she got accepted, she'd have to move there. And there would be no guarantee of being invited back the following year, or getting a job once the training was done.

On Sunday night, after she got home from the ballet, she handed me her notebook with a scribbled, handwritten letter of introduction. I read it.

To Whom It May Concern:

Six months ago I was raped by a boy who I went to high school with. He put a drug in my drink and had sex with my unconscious body. It was ugly, dirty, and disgusting but because I was comatose, I don't remember any of it. He is an evil person and it's hard to believe that anybody could do that. He has since been sentenced to prison for uploading pictures of his victims on the internet. My picture was not one of them and I am fortunate in that regard. In the time since it happened, I have felt a lot of different things, but mostly self-hatred, anger, and fear, which have brought on panic attacks and depression. My therapist says I have to practice exposure, which means I have to approach things I have steered clear of since the event. One of the things I've been avoiding is crowds, because it happened at a crowded party. But you can't be a dancer and not deal with crowds because they are constantly looking at you and what you can do. Right now I'm in the middle of this production of Romeo and Juliet with the San Antonio Ballet, and it's great fun and I haven't felt panic attacks yet. I hope I don't, but if I do, I'm just going to have to soldier on. Which I hate because I don't know if I can. I know that my recovery won't be something that happens in an hour or a day. Recovery takes time, unfortunately, and it's just something I have to deal with. But it sucks.

The one thing I want to do, above all else, is to forgive the boy who raped me. But before that can happen, he has to realize that there is something he needs to be forgiven for, and I don't know if he knows that yet. I pray for him a lot, and I ask Jesus to show him and make him realize that what he did to us was evil, but he is a human being who is capable of being redeemed and worthy of forgiveness. The Book of Job says 'Man is born unto trouble as the sparks fly upward.' All of us now, he and I and his victims and all of our families, are caught up in the sparks.

"Well," she said. "What do you think?"

"You didn't put anything in about dancing."

"Do I need to?"

"Well, if I was running a dance school, and you were going to stay the whole year there, I'd like to know something about your commitment to dancing."

She scratched her cheek, thinking, then took back her notebook and went into her room. About thirty minutes later she came out and handed it to me. "How's this? I'll tack it on to what I've already got." This is what it said:

> *I'm sorry this letter isn't more about dancing. I should probably tell you that dancing is my life, but the truth is, life is like the body, and it has many parts. Dance is one of those parts. I like to think it's my heart, but I don't know if that's true. I think I could live without dancing but I obviously could not live without my heart. Maybe it's that part of the heart that feels love, and intense pain, and joy. My dancing, like my heart, is what keeps me going. If there is one thing I've learned from my experience doing this ballet, it's that art heals. Dancing acts as a spiritual connection to that part of God that heals. I'm not well, by any stretch of the imagination, but through art, through creation, I know I will be whole again.*
>
> *Thank you,*
> *Jill Hauck*

"Do you like it?" she said

"Yeah, Jill. I like it a lot."

We filled out the application online, printed it up, and I wrote a check for the application fee. On Monday morning I FedExed all that plus the recommendation and the letter of introduction. Now the waiting. Jill would hear something one way or another about an audition within two months.

I took Larisa to the last show of *Romeo and Juliet*. The thing I remember most is the blood that was spotting the toes of Jill's shoe when they were taking their final bow.

Chapter 22

Three weeks passed, and D-Day came. Time for our performance at Blue Skies of Texas.

Me and Larisa had practiced a lot and got to the point where we knew the dance pretty much without thinking about it. Calling the steps helped tremendously (turn and one-two-three-four-five-six, aaaaaaand jump) but we couldn't do that when the show started though because it'd look goofy.

The show was going to be in the home's dining room. They had a stage all set up and about 300 chairs. I say "stage" but it wasn't that, it was just a piece of the linoleum floor with the chairs in front of it. A wood floor would have been much better for Larisa's feet, but dancing on linoleum is not so uncommon, I'm told, for these kinds of occasions.

There was us and three other gals performing that day, and they were doing solo pieces. We rehearsed it in order a couple of times. Me and Larisa were last. The whole show was around twenty minutes from start to finish.

I know this was not supposed to be any big thing, it

was just a show in a retirement home for crying out loud, and the audience was supposed to be receptive, you know, because the show is free, and you know, they can't really see very well or hear very well anyway. But I was still nervous. In fact, I was *really* nervous. I never did anything in front of folks before like this and now here I was. I kind of hated Larisa for getting me into this.

Strange thing about this old folks home. I assumed it was going to be full of gray-haired grannies and grampies with canes and wheelchairs and walkers, wearing shawls and listening on tin horns saying "What? What?" That's what my dad's retirement home is kind of like. But some of these folks weren't too much older than me. And a lot of the men were in much better shape. Flat stomachs, thin faces. I saw one guy and his wife that, I swear, looked to be about sixty. That's five years older than I am! In fact, the minimum age to get into this place is fifty-five. My age! I'm dang near a senior citizen! I hate that!

Ricardo and Jill set up the lights and the sound board. Ricardo worked them both at the same time as there weren't many cues. There weren't many lights to speak of neither, maybe six or eight, so we'd never be mistaken for a Sir David Derrick extravaganza, but the music sounded pretty good coming out of the PA. While we were running through the dance, you could hear dishes clattering in the kitchen. I wondered if Nijinsky started this way.

Jill watched us while we were practicing and I tried not to look at her. I was nervous enough as it was.

Time was getting tight. The show was starting at 3:00 and it was 2.30. Some of the old folks started making their way to the chairs, so we had to go "backstage," which means we had to go into the kitchen and wait until it was time to start.

The nervous I was feeling was not good nervous energy. It was plumb terror. I didn't tell nobody, that wouldn't do no good nohow, but I couldn't wait till this thing was done so I could relax and get myself a tasty beer.

So I was backstage fretting and wishing it was over, kind of wishing the power would go out so we'd have to cancel, or maybe the roof would cave in, but not on the old folks heads for gosh sakes, I didn't want anybody to get hurt, I just wanted to have an excuse to not go on, when Ed comes in pushing my dad in a wheelchair! And there was Jill, walking in behind them.

"Hey bro. Nice costume! I thought you'd be wearing a tutu."

Did I mention the costume? I was wearing the costume Larisa made for me. Puffy shirt and all.

"Thanks," I said. "I think it looks kind of cool."

"Yeah, you would. You look like you're ready for the gay pride parade."

That went completely over my dad's head. "It's good to get out of The Hill," he said.

I introduced Larisa to Ed and my dad. She sized up Ed, unimpressed, you could tell. He had no idea.

"Dad," I said. "You excited? You're going to see a show."

"Yeah. We're going to watch a show. We're going to watch Jill in the ballet."

"It's not me, Grandpa," said Jill. "It's Daddy. My dad's in the show today."

"What? Your dad?"

"I did the show three weeks ago."

"Oh. Well. Too bad. I was hoping it was you."

"Sorry."

"Billy Jim, are you a dancer?"

"Yes sir," I said. "Dad, if you wanted to come to Jill's ballet, you should have told me. I thought you didn't want to go."

"I didn't want to be a burden."

"He couldn't go anyway," Ed said. "He'd have been asleep five minutes after it started and he snores like a chainsaw. They would have had to take him out."

"That's true," Dad said.

"That's why we came today," Ed continued. "Because Dad wanted to see Jill."

"But Jill's not dancing."

"I know. But I couldn't get him to come if I told him it was just you. If I told him a big chocolate drop with legs was dancing he would have said no."

"So you told Dad Jill was dancing?"

"Yeah, that's why he come."

"Well, we ought to be getting our seats, I reckon," my dad said, motioning to the exit. "See you after the show."

"Promise me you'll make us all laugh. Please don't disappoint." Ed wheeled my dad out into the dining room.

"Why do you take that from him?" Jill said.

"Habit?"

Larisa was leaning against the coffee maker. She was chewing on a plastic stir straw, her eyes touching on me, then Jill. Then she came over and stood next to us.

"Here," she said. "I need to talk to the two of you."

"It looks bad," I said.

"Jill, your father is very proud of you. Of your skill, your dedication, and your effort. He admires your work ethic so much, that you work so tirelessly to perfect your craft without complaining."

"Oh, I complain."

"He was so happy to watch you in *Romeo and Juliet*, he looked just like a piece of sunshine. He is proud of you because you're so good, excellent even. And all the work you've put in. Isn't that right, Billy Jim?"

"Well, sure."

"Now Jill, you're going away soon. I don't know if you're going into this program in New York City or not, but at some point, you are going away, and your dad is going to be here by himself, to start a life on his own."

"Okay…"

"Now, the two of you have never danced together. Chances are, the two of you will not dance together until your wedding day, which is a long, long ways off. Well, I've been thinking about it, and I think that you should dance in my place, Jill."

"Me? I don't know the steps!" The tone in her voice was saying *No, I can't do it* but the look on her face said *Really? Okay!* This is the girl who dances and the stars align, remember?

"I know. But you should do it anyway."

"How can she do it if she don't know the steps?" I said. "She won't know where to go. She's going to be dancing around and then I'm going to call 'promenade' and she's going to stop and come over to me we're going to promenade?"

"No, not like that. You're going to stand there. She's going to dance, and then *she's* going to call the steps."

"How?" Jill was a little perplexed.

"Do you know how to promenade, Jill?"

"I've done it in class lots."

"Do you know lifts? Do you know the fish?"

"I know it okay."

"Well, this is how we do it. You dance. On your own. Then when you want to go into a promenade, you call promenade. When you want to go into a jump, you call jump."

"And then I just do it? Support her?" I said.

"Right. We don't go on for another forty minutes. We can go over it. We can practice."

"You mean here? In the kitchen?"

"Yeah."

"It won't be *Don Quixote*."

255

"Yeah, it won't be *Don Quixote*, but who cares? Are you game?"

"But what about you?" I said. "We've been rehearsing this for a couple months now. You going to just give up?"

"We can do it any old time, Billy Jim. This might be the only time you and Jill will have a chance to do it in front of your dad."

"I reckon that's so."

"And won't it be a grand thing, to dance for your grandfather, Jill? He'll get to see you dance, and he may not get the chance again. We don't know what life holds."

"What about pointe shoes? She don't got no pointe shoes."

"I have an old pair in my car I was going to throw away," Jill said. "I've got a new pack of tights too, that I haven't opened yet."

"We don't need tights," said Larisa. "You'll wear this costume. A few safety pins, I can fix you right up."

Larisa started to take off her dress, and Jill rushed out to get her shoes.

"Why are you doing this?" This was a real sacrifice for her, and I knew that. I knew how much she wanted to do it, how hard both of us had worked and here she was, giving it up like it was nothing. "Why?" I asked again.

She didn't say anything. She put her arms around me and pulled me to her mouth, and then she kissed me.

Milly Forrest, the dancer before us, came back into the kitchen, dripping with sweat. She'd just finished "The Diamond Fairy" in *Sleeping Beauty*. We could hear the audience still clapping enthusiastically. These folks may be retirees, but they were full of spit and tarnation. "You're up," she said, panting.

Jill and I stood by the entrance. She suddenly had that flash of terror in her eyes.

"Breathe," I said. "Breathe. You can do this."

She nodded, and we walked out to the linoleum and stood next to each other. I saw Ricardo raise an eyebrow to Jill like "What's this?" but then he punched "play" and the music started. I called "promenade," and went into the turn. Jill followed. And it began.

The order of me and Larisa's pas de deux is promenade, turn, promenade, turn, jump, turn, jump, turn, jump, turn, turn, turn, lift, fish. That was out the window now.

Jill danced. I stood back and watched. The line of her body was perfect. Her muscles were taut, rippling. She was only sixteen, but all of her training had made her into a by-god physical specimen. Her technique was beautiful. Her arabesque was like an square-angle ruler. She did jumps, leaps, flips, all perfectly in time to the music. She stood in front of me and called "turn!" and I put my hands on her waist while she spun around. Then she shouted "jump!" and I grabbed her and thrust her in the air while she ran through a series of jumps. I let her go, and she danced again.

I looked out at the audience. It was if they was holding their breath, like nobody was breathing, like everyone was focused on Jill. I saw Larisa brushing her eyes. My dad was leaning forward, his hand on my brother's arm. He, like the rest of the audience, was taking it all in.

Jill called out "lift!" and I lifted her over my head and sat her on my shoulder. The timing was perfect. She sat up there like a princess on a throne.

In the seconds she was up there I thought about the past few months. It's every parents wish to catch their children and lift them up when they fall. And even though technically this weren't no fall — just a lift — I'd take it and be grateful.

She called "Fish!" and I thought, "Uh-oh, here she comes. Make it a good one." She swooped down and I caught her just before she hit the floor. Nailed it!

And then I come to think, in that five seconds we faced the audience, that this wasn't about me lifting her up. It was her lifting me up. And it wasn't me catching her before she fell. It was her catching me before I fell.

We stood next to each other again and the music ended. The crowd roared and stood on its feet. I was suddenly so nervous my knees were knocking together. My father was smiling, clapping wildly. He gave us the thumbs up. Ed looked glum.

"Great job, Daddy!"

"You, kid. It's all you."

Chapter 23

The San Antonio Ballet went broke after *Romeo and Juliet* and had to close. They overspent their budget and went into massive debt. They had a great show that got outstanding reviews in lots of newspapers and magazines across America, including the *New York Times, Chicago Tribune*, and *Time* magazine, and they were sold out every show, but that didn't save them. The grants they got from the state and corporations couldn't cover the money spent, so they had to fold.

It's a crying shame, and at some point this needs to open up to a bigger discussion about what it's all worth. Ballet has shaped what my little girl has become. She gets her resilience from her work, which comes from her love of ballet. If she didn't have ballet, who would she be, after all that has happened to her? Would she have slid into despair, never to recover? Would she have ended her life like Able Dishner's kid, dead in some strange city of an overdose of heroin? Because Jill ain't better than that young man was. She has a lot of strength and by-god character, but it could have gone either way. It still could. Jill's lucky that she has something she believes in, something she can do.

I've always thought that when a man has problems, it is up to him and him alone to pick himself up by his bootstraps and fix what's ailing him. I still believe that, but maybe in a different way than I used to. Truth is, a man can't fix his problem if he don't decide to get fixed, but even if he does, he can't do it alone. I used to think that all that I had, I made from my own sweat, without no help from nobody, but that just ain't so and I realize that now. A lot of folks helped me, especially my family. If my dad hadn't given me that money from my momma's accident settlement, I never would have had collateral and the bank never would have given me a loan, and if that hadn't happened, these days I'd be a mechanic working for some other stiff and not a business owner. And when I think about Jill, I feel pride about what she was able to do, because she actually did pull herself up by her bootstraps, but there ain't no way you could say she did it by herself. She was able to do it because folks stuck by her and helped her over the rough spots. Folks, meaning her family and friends and her counselor Amy Landreau, but also folks in the ballet, and yeah, even the ballet itself.

So do we, then, as taxpayers, fund the arts? Well, being the right-wing Republican I am, my answer to that would be heck no. I don't want my tax dollars going to pay for some goober in a beret spouting poetry in a coffee shop in Amarillo. But there has to be some way to support folks who want to do it because, you know, it's like Jill says: art heals. And if art is like medicine, then shouldn't it be supported? Not to the extent that medicine is, maybe, but in some way. Maybe tax cuts for businesses what fund the arts? I don't know. But I do know that losing the San Antonio Ballet is something that should not have happened. When we lose things like the ballet, what do we got left? If the best of culture can't rise up, then the worst of culture will take its place, which is what's been happening for years. American culture is so coarse now, so vulgar, nothing like what it used to be. It's all toilet jokes and violent rap, reality TV and boring songs you can't hum and can't remember. It seems like that's all we got now. American culture used to be the best in the world. What happened to it?

A couple months after we FedEx'd the application, Jill got a call from the Joffrey and was invited to audition, which was a big, huge deal, so we flew to New York City to do the thing, and two weeks later they called. I knew who it was by what she was saying to them, but she didn't sound happy at all, just very business-like. Then she hung up and told me she had been accepted into the ballet trainee program, and she was going to have to be in New York City at the beginning of September. I said something like, "Well, Jill, you don't seem all that excited." And she said, "I'm going to give this one more year. If it looks like I can get into a company, then I'll continue with it. If it doesn't, then I'm going to quit and go back to school and study physics." So we flew up there and she registered for the program and I put her in the dormitory and we said our teary goodbyes (well, I was teary, she was okay). Now she's up in New York City living the life. I'm afraid Jill is going to have bouts of PTSD, and that scares me because she wouldn't tell me about it if she was, that's just not her character. I hope she calls me when she needs somebody to talk to.

When I got back to San Antonio my mailbox was stuffed with fliers begging for money, naturally, but something else: a letter from the State of Texas that said my marriage to Beth was officially dissolved. I spent a couple of days drinking that one off, but then quit. I just couldn't work up being sad about it anymore.

There's lots of reasons for not wanting to get divorced. For me, it was simple. I made a vow to God in front of our friends and family that I would stick with Beth, come what may. Paralysis, poverty, disease. And she promised the same. I never would have made the promise if I thought it would be broken. Isn't that the point of marriage?

I didn't want a divorce. I never wanted it, and I still don't. But people change. Beth doesn't love me anymore, she loves John Lancey. If she'd stayed with me she would have been stuck in a life of misery, and anything she'd felt for me before would have turned to bitterness and anger, and then hatred. So I have to let her go. Damn it all.

If I ever get married again, which seems pretty unlikely, but if I ever do, I'm going to tell my fiancé before the wedding that I am never getting divorced. Under any circumstances.

I called Beth and set up a time when she was going to be at home, then I called up a moving company to come pack the rest of her stuff and take it to her. For the first time since we got married, Beth is finally and officially out of the house on Meredith Drive.

And now it's just me.

I have lots of time to think about what's ahead for me, and lately I been thinking about making a change. I know you're going to think this is strange, and don't laugh, but I've been thinking about opening up a ballet company. The San Antonio Ballet folded, which means the city needs one, a professional company. I've been dealing with figures most of my life, and I've run a successful business since I was twenty-nine years old. I know how to make stuff work. I know pros like David who could help out. We got schools in town and they could all funnel their students into the company. It wouldn't be easy, I know. I'd have a major learning curve, and I'd have to do fundraising and all that, and in the end it might go under just like the SA Ballet did. If it actually did work I would be really, really lucky. But it might be worth a try.

Life is extremely difficult at times. I've sat on my lonely old couch night after night after night for years and watched my life wash out on a wave of beer towards its end. I've failed in near everything I've ever attempted, except my job. I've been a bad father and a bad husband, and my failures haunt me.

In some ways my life is better now than it has ever been because I got people who love me. I know Jill does, and Larisa too. I know my dad loves me though he ain't the kind to show it much. Heck, even David Derrick loves me, which is kind of weird to me, but I'm not complaining.

But my life is worse too. What happened to Jill cannot be undone, and deep in my heart I know it's my fault. I can't help it. I may be chasing or running from that for the rest of my life. Folks probably wouldn't blame me for what happened to Jill, and if I told her this, she most likely would say I was crazy. But I know different. And you do too. Parents have a responsibility to take care of their kids. They just do. And when something happens to them, we can't help but feel somehow responsible. That's the price of raising children.

But I would have to check into Santa Rosa if all I had was this guilt. I've managed to accept it, live with it — and put it away. Because the love I've found has allowed me to conquer it, and has brought something like peace. I sleep better now than I have in years. I sleep the whole night through, no more waking up at 3am thinking about my troubles. And it's because I so appreciate those who love me, and I've dedicated what time I got left to doing something other than dying.

So maybe I will start that ballet company. Whether it's successful or not is kind of beside the point. Life shouldn't be about sitting around waiting for things to change.

Acknowledgements

There are some folks that need to be thanked. They are: Birgit Gruenberg, Joe Perez, Dena Mabry, David and Stacey Connelly, Jay Franke, Judith Gani, Forrest Smith, Tom and Sally Neary, Mara Casey Visconti, Anil Kumar, the guys who invented YouTube, and all the companies, dancers, and fans who've posted there. Above all, I would like to thank my father. Without him this book would not have been possible. And my mother, for her love and faith.